FRANÇOIS VILLON

IVA KENAZ

Identifiers:
ISBN: 9781799013105 (paperback)

Author: Iva Kenaz

Editor: Jenny Papworth

Cover Art: Ivana Axman

Cover Design: Gunnar Tryggvason

Poem Translations: Iva Kenaz

This novel is dedicated to those of you who also love François Villon.

CONTENTS

PART FOUR – Guillaume

PART FIVE – François

FOREWORD

I have been fascinated with François Villon and the story of his life since I was fifteen years old, as that's when I first read his biography written by the Czech author Jarmila Loukotková. From then on, I became obsessed with Villon's remarkable personality and wanted to learn more about his poetry. I was intrigued by the fact that he rebelled against the law yet always managed to outsmart it, which meant he must have been a very compelling, charismatic man. I also wanted to know how he managed to keep his zest for life and that delightfully crude sense of humour despite all his misfortunes. Ultimately, though, I was curious about why such a brilliant poet became a criminal. I sensed that the answer lay in one of his verses: *Necessity makes people vile just as hunger drives wolves from the wild.* However, Villon was not just a victim of the cruel times he was born into, on the contrary, he inspired people with his creative and emotional freedom in the crazy, harsh world that could have easily broken him.

I studied various translations of Villon's poems, researched everything that was known about him, and slowly developed my own opinion of the times in his life that remain shrouded in mystery. I also visited the places that Villon frequented, which helped me absorb the special, medieval atmosphere that is still there despite the fact that the places have changed significantly over time. I can't remember how many versions of this story I wrote until I finally felt ready to complete it.

In the end, I decided to split the book into five parts. One is told from Villon's point of view, but the others from the perspectives of the people whose lives he touched the most. Although Villon remains the key character throughout the novel and Paris the silent witness to his convoluted journeys, each of the other characters reveals a different side of the poet's soul. I chose this approach because I have always found the people around Villon intriguing and I think that sometimes, especially in the case of such complicated personalities, we see the hero best through the eyes of others.

I know well that I'm a sinner
Yet God decided to spare me
From the shackles and quiver
And let me repent my deeds
For while my sins may be dead
The divine mercy is endless
So if I dare to face my conscience
God shall forgive my performance.

But because I'm feeling weak
And poor in resources as in health
I shall use the last of my wits
Such I received without stealth
And never borrowed from anyone else
To write this final Testament
And the will it shall present
With my earnest, irrevocable intent:

Firstly, I offer my wretched soul
To the blessed, holy trinity
And pray to our Lady in the heavens
The chamber of divinity
To grant me her charity
I also pray to the nine celestial homes
To let me carry my gift with security
All the way to the sacred throne

I leave and bequeath my body
To earth, our great mother
But since hunger strived it
Worms should find another
Let it be delivered to her, don't let it burn
From earth it came, to earth it shall return
All things to one tend to seek
The place of their origins.

Extract from *The Testament* (1461-1462, François Villon)

PART ONE:

REGNIER

Item: I leave two hounds or three
To the noble Regnier de Montigny…

Extract from *The Legacy* (1455, François Villon)

Chapter 1

Disgrace

Paris, May 1451

How little did we appreciate our school years at the
Sorbonne! While we lived them, we wanted
nothing more than to break free, but once we found
ourselves out in the wider world, we longed to
return to the university's safe nest. We were the
lucky ones who were allowed to study as opposed
to labouring in the shadows of our beloved Paris.
Not that those days were easy, they were difficult,
even tragic at times, but I decided to hold on to the
cheerful memories. Student pranks were our
biggest passion, mainly because it made us laugh
and the city guards sweat. Our greatest

achievements were immortalised by none other than the art student François Montcorbier, alias Villon, a man who was as earnestly loved as he was hated. This was due to his crude sense of humour and sharp tongue, which mercilessly delivered whatever entered his busy mind. As for me, I have always been proud to call him my best friend.

Never had I met a man with such fresh and contagiously dangerous ideas. He was the brain behind most of our mischiefs, but he wasn't the only one who hatched them. The budding cleric Colin de Cayaux and I, Regnier de Montigny, made up the infamous trinity. Although the authorities dreaded us, our classmates applauded us, and as for girls, they were on the constant lookout for rogues, especially those who pretended only to care for the prim gentlemen types.

One spring afternoon, we set off for the bustling streets of the Latin Quarter right after school, killing time before we attended the birthday party of my cousin Katherine de Vaucelles. We ended up on Madame Bruyer's lawn. Villon had had it in for the widow ever since she spread a nasty rumour about his mother, Madame Montcorbier, and Father Guillaume. Losing his father when he was only three years old had left François and Madame Montcorbier in despair, constantly moving from one relative to another until they had ended up in the Latin Quarter where François fell ill. Father Guillaume Villon took them in and saved his life.

During the days that followed, he developed a fatherly affection for François and grew very fond of Madame Montcorbier as well. Bruyer supposed that just because she fooled around with the holy fathers herself, so would Madame Montcorbier, but little did she know how chaste that woman was. She was more interested in the Bible than men. Also, unlike some, Father Guillaume took his Christian mission seriously. I was quite certain that even if he had ever developed a romantic affection towards Madame Montcorbier he never expressed it. Nevertheless, he had become François' guardian and raised him as his own son.

For some reason, Bruyer had decorated her lawn with two erect stones that were ridiculed mainly because of their obvious phallic shapes. The taller one had a plaque that read *Devil's Fart*. I bet you can imagine why to us students, the stones were a daily source of fun. With a jar of ale in our bellies, we became more inspired than ever. While Villon prepared to recite his new poem to the widow, Cayaux acted out a silly scene, moaning like a lustful woman as he pretended to ride the taller stone. I didn't care much for the childish act. As opposed to the fool Cayaux, I was well mannered.

Despite being an impoverished orphan, my noble genes made me a man of honour, pride and occasional gallantry. My mother succumbed to a dreadful disease and my father died in the service of the King. Life's lessons had taught me how to blend in with all social classes, but the stuck-up bourgeoisie society was a true challenge. I was accepted to the Sorbonne thanks to my cousins who were both canons at Saint Benoit Church like Guillaume Villon. I had never become used to being a commoner, though; I couldn't ignore the blue blood that pumped through my veins.

The city of Paris, the greatest love of my life, eventually robbed me of my status. The only things that kept me looking like a nobleman during my early twenties were my fancy red boots and my greyhound. Had he not had a limp, any gentleman would have been happy to have him. His defect made some think he was not worth it, but I could relate to him, being a fallen noble breed myself. I named him Estienne de Montigny II, after my grandfather, and although people made fun of this, he was too smart to take it seriously.

The smaller erect stone on Bruyer's lawn was a good spot to sit and polish my red boots. Estienne de Montigny II often licked my boots clean, especially if there was a piece of lard to hand which could be used as a polish. Villon loved to make fun of me as he considered the shiny, luxurious boots a comic contradiction to my shabby clothing. In fact, he found most things about me amusing. He said it was mainly my proud posture and serious nature. I had never liked being made fun of, but for some reason, I didn't mind being his well of entertainment. The truth was that Villon was the only friend who really understood what I was about, and the only friend who always managed to lighten my mood. Therefore, I let him mock me all he liked as the bastard never meant any harm.

Bruyer was also fond of Villon, as were most Parisian women. I understood why, but not in that way, of course, as I myself had always been a desperate admirer of the feminine. However, nobody could overlook Villon's magnetic presence, wittiness, honesty and most of all his unique way with words. I suppose the dark, pensive eyes and unruly hair helped in that regard as well. Unlike me, he never banged his head on doorframes, and he had a better physique. When I looked in the mirror, I saw an elegant, bearded parsnip; my lush, brown curls making up for the melancholic eyes. Charming as I was, girls always looked at Villon before me. I still had it better than "Cayaux the Scarecrow", though, as he naturally repelled women, mostly due to his immature behaviour.

That sunny day, Villon greatly disappointed one of his admirers. Even though Bruyer's eyes gleamed at the sight of him, nothing could prepare her for the poem he had written about her love affair with Father Laurens who lived next door to him. Casual as always, Villon began to recite the verses:

I peeked through the keyhole to find
A bed by the fireplace, wide and fine
A plump canon sprawled on the pillows
Beside him, Madame Bruyer's skirts billowed
As her smooth and soft body let go of her dress
Flesh to flesh for greater pleasure they pressed
I watched them mess around and learned quite easily
That for alleviating sorrow it's best to live in luxury!

As usual, Villon managed to put a smile on my face, however, Bruyer didn't share my enthusiasm and threatened Villon from her window.

"You nasty imp! How dare you disrespect a man of God!"

Her high-pitched yell made the birds fly off her roof.

"I'm sorry if I've offended you, Madame," bowed Villon, and it looked like he was going to apologise before he added, "but I'm not the one who disrespects the priest. I go to confessionals to confess not to undress."

"Oh! How dare you! Be on your way or you'll regret it!" she threatened.

Villon bowed to her and waved at Cayaux and me. Although we were about to leave, Estienne de Montigny II had suddenly decided to top our offences off by marking the taller stone. That made Bruyer even more furious. She rushed inside her room and was back before we had managed to recover, hurling the contents of her chamber pot at us. Villon and Cayaux's reactions were faster than mine and so I received the full force of her excreta. Bruyer, Villon and Cayaux had a blast, but my faithful Estienne de Montigny II began sympathetically licking me clean. My garments didn't matter to me, they were just old rags, however, my shoes were a different story. When someone dared to touch the only thing I had left of my father, all of the usually suppressed anger broke loose. I swore revenge on Bruyer as I strode off to clean myself at the well, followed by the rumbustious laughter of my companions.

"Stop laughing, Villon! What will people think of us when we get to the party smelling like a pair of old goats? I don't have enough time to change not to mention anything to actually change into. I might as well not go…"

"No way!" protested Villon. "You have to go – stinking or not!"

"People will think I pissed myself," I muttered.

"You can always blame it on Sermoise, I'm sure he'll be there."

Phillipe Sermoise was a young priest who was often the victim of our shenanigans, simply because he was so gullible.

"What do you mean? Should I say that he pissed on me?"

"I suppose a more believable lie would be that he pissed himself. Just keep close to him and comment on the awful smell."

I grinned but shook my head. "I don't know, Villon... I don't even have a present for Katherine..."

"Why don't you take her some wine?" suggested Villon.

"Ha! If I buy wine, I'll have to fast for the rest of the week!"

"You mainly eat at my house anyway," pointed out Villon and we all knew that he was right. If it wasn't for the generous hospitality of Father Guillaume and Madame Montcorbier, neither I nor Estienne de Montigny II would have a bone to chew on.

"Come on, if you don't have enough, I'll chip in," he offered.

"I can't keep taking advantage of your hospitality, Villon."

"I don't mind, as long as I have enough, my money is yours. Friends should help each other, right?"

Cayaux nodded. "Of course, you can count on me too, Montigny."

The well water washed away some of the stench, but not all of it. I couldn't risk a fever, so left the well before I began to feel too cold.

"I should start working on Estienne de Montigny II's hunting skills, then I'd never have to worry about food."

Villon laughed. "If only he wasn't such a city boy like us!"

"Maybe we should bring more dogs to our pack – what do you think, Estienne? You are old enough to pass on your wisdom to the youngsters."

"Then you'll have more mouths to feed," remarked Villon.

"Every nobleman should have at least three hounds as companions," I objected, upon which Villon patted my back and said, "Before we discuss your noble pack, I just thought of how to get that wine for Katherine for free."

He went on to explain his brilliantly simple plan and, as usual, I was all up for it.

✦

After we said goodbye to Cayaux, Villon and I borrowed two identical clay carafes from the Sorbonne. We filled one with water and left one empty, chuckling at the thought of Villon's clever idea. We then hurried to a tavern that was famous for its fine wines and pretended to be experts. Due to my unpleasant smell, Villon dealt with the innkeeper while I secretly held the clay carafe filled with water behind my back. He gave the man the empty carafe and ordered him to bring us his finest white wine. After the innkeeper brought it forth, Villon tasted it and spat it out, claiming that it was undrinkable. The innkeeper argued with him, so he let me have a taste too. I did, and agreed that it was simply disgusting. While the offended innkeeper was arguing with Villon, I exchanged the carafes and hid the one with wine behind my back again. That's when Villon resolutely grabbed the carafe with water and returned it to the innkeeper who, although upset, poured the contents back into the barrel.

On our way to the birthday celebration, Villon and I laughed our arses off at his gullibility. I was glad to have a gift for Katherine and hoped it would make up for my unpleasant smell. As usual, however, I became the object of ridicule before people even caught a whiff of me.

"Montigny! You look splendid today! Isn't that your grandfather's tunic? Such brilliant pieces never go out of fashion, huh?" laughed one stuck-up arsehole upon seeing me.

Villon gave me an empathetic smile and said, "Don't let envy get to you, my friend. Your genuine nobility shines through even the stinky rags."

We both knew that he was just being nice, yet I proudly thrust out my chest and braved it out. Had it not been for the delicious food and fine wines, I certainly wouldn't bother visiting this pretentious herd of marionettes. However, before we could treat ourselves, we had to congratulate the young lady who was celebrating her sixteenth birthday. It came as no surprise that we found her surrounded by a clutch of suitors, but on the lookout for an escape. Everybody knew that the black-haired doll with cute, freckled cheeks longed only for the one who kept evading her.

Katherine de Vaucelles and François Villon would make a curious couple. Both were used to standing out and being the source of gossip: he because of his poetry and she because of her numerous male friends. They liked to tease each other, but nothing more. It was a game they both knew well, and neither one overstepped its carefully defined boundaries. Katherine's father, my uncle, would never bless a union with a random arts student, and even if Villon found himself respectable work, he was not built for a conventional life.

A servant guided us to the line of guests waiting to congratulate Katherine. Some remarked on her beauty, especially the artist who had painted her portrait for the occasion, and the successful merchant, Noël Jolis, who gave her a necklace to complement her – in his words – ethereal grace. Approaching her after this slick gentleman felt a little awkward, because neither one of us could afford such an expensive gift. Katherine didn't seem that interested in what we had to offer, though. I supposed that seeing Villon was good enough.

"François! Regnier!" she exclaimed heartily, and since we were the last two guests to greet her, she took us aside to avoid the eyes of her suitors.

"Thank you for saving me from all that boring small talk," she whispered.

"It's our pleasure," said Villon. "We couldn't miss celebrating the birthday of the oldest maid in Paris."

"Splendid," she beamed, unaffected by his words. "Though I must disappoint you, François, my maidenhood has been compromised by several tempting offers tonight."

"Don't mind them," he threw out his hand. "It would be a sin for a lively spirit like yourself to espouse. Look at all the fine specimens of manhood you'd have to give up for just one match."

He smiled at the men watching us and his gaze lingered over the vigilant Noël Jolis.

"Shush, François," said Katherine with that pretended innocence which barely concealed the rebellious flame in her eyes.

While Noël Jolis and Villon carefully eyed each other up, Katherine addressed me. "It's nice to see you, Cousin Regnier." She moved a bit closer, then caught the whiff of my soiled clothes and stepped back again.

"Are you all right?" she asked, and her kind concern made me even more uncomfortable.

"Of course!" I proclaimed confidently. To avoid explaining myself, I handed her the hard-earned carafe of white wine and paid my respects.

"Thank you, Cousin Regnier." She drew a breath then looked at Villon, curious to see what he had brought.

I wondered that myself, as I hadn't even asked him. To our surprise, Villon just showed her his empty hands and said, "I bring nothing..."

Katherine tried to hide her disappointment, but before she could say anything, Villon tapped his right temple and finished, "...nothing but my humble rhymes." An excited smile spread across Katherine's face as he went on, "I have been memorising the poem since this morning and know it by heart now."

Katherine fondly squeezed his hands and addressed the rest of the company.

"Attention, dear guests! Monsieur Villon has written me a poem!"

Everybody except for Noël Jolis cheered along with Katherine. We all knew that Villon never disappointed when it came to his poetry. However, since he was not known for writing polished odes to female beauty, I suspected that the spark in Katherine's green eyes would soon fade away. I watched in apprehension as he cleared his throat and began.

"This poem came to me as I thought of time's unmerciful passing…

Where is she? Can anyone tell me?
Flora who blessed Rome with her beauty?
And where is Alkipas or Thais
Her first-born cousin?
Where's the Echo of their sweet voices?
Did it drown in ponds, rivers, and seas?
The inhuman beauty – whereto has it vanished?
Where are the snows of yesteryear?

Where is the wise goddess who went by the name
Heloise?
The castrator of monk Pierre Esbaillart of Saint
Denise?
Oh, the poor sinner had suffered his sentence
And where is Queen Marguerite, the seductress?
The one who beguiled so many men
Then dropped them into the river Seine?
Oh, where are the snows of yesteryear?"

A dramatic bow followed. Sometimes people didn't know whether to praise or condemn Villon. This time, Katherine had the first word, though, as the poem was meant for her. I could tell that Villon was growing uneasy at the sight of her stern face, but luckily for him, she finally clapped and inspired others to follow.

"François!" she laughed. "Had I known you thought so lowly of contemporary women, I would have worn my toga for this occasion."

I was surprised and impressed that she had the humour to laugh at herself at that moment.

"What I have forgotten to add," said Villon then, "is that the snows of yesteryear are nothing compared to today's blossom in your cheeks."

He bowed to her with that characteristic roguish grin. Sometimes I wondered whether he was aware of the effect he had on women who saw him as a sensitive poet instead of a scoundrel who marked his territory in all the Parisian brothels. Noël Jolis seemed to be very aware of Villon's dark side though, and wasn't going to let him off the hook.

"Don't you consider the poem a bit cold, Monsieur Villon? One would expect more from a man of your… how to put it… passion."

Katherine and Villon looked at each other, and although Katherine was curious as to how he would reply, I noticed that something was troubling her. Villon cheekily raised his eyebrow and answered, "Well, I keep my passions tamed, as opposed to some."

The angry grin on Jolis' face boded no good. Katherine smiled and attempted to end the quarrel.

"Please, gentlemen, wouldn't it be nicer to enjoy this splendid celebration rather than taint it with arguments? Look, Monsieur de Montigny has brought us some delicious white wine! Help yourself to a goblet and have a taste."

She placed my humble gift among the delicacies on the table and as voices filled the room again,

Villon leaned over to Katherine and remarked, "Monsieur Jolis is as pleasant as usual."

I caught a hint of jealousy in his tone. I knew my friend well and was aware that although he regarded Katherine as nothing more than his acquaintance, he still seemed more taken with her than with any other woman.

"Well, he's been spending a suspicious amount of time at our house recently," admitted Katherine. "Father is quite fond of him."

"And you?"

"I find him a bit too serious, but he's prosperous. I think he might propose soon."

I sensed a challenge in her tone, and her curious glance at Villon confirmed it.

"You would really marry someone like Noël Jolis?" sneered Villon.

"Who else should I marry then? You?"

"If I weren't married already, I'd definitely marry you," replied Villon with a courteous bow, and then, as if trying to escape, he promptly left to greet the provost Robert d'Estouteville and his wife Ambroise. The couple had grown fond of him after he had written a delightful poem for their wedding.

I stayed behind with Katherine who was clearly bewildered, so I explained, "We both decided to marry Paris. She's a fine wife who never disappoints and gives us enough freedom to roam her streets as much as we like."

Katherine smiled, but her face showed dejection. Before she went off to mingle, she squeezed my hand and said, "Thank you for coming over and for the lovely gift. I know it must have been a great sacrifice."

I bowed to her, my hand resting on my chest in gratitude, and moved over to the brimming tables. While stuffing myself, I observed Villon entertaining the influential couple and thought of how well he was doing in this affluent society considering his background.

✦

After the boring birthday party, we decided to fill our bellies with ale at Margot's Inn, a tavern with a brothel attached. As soon as we entered, the local madam greeted me with a slap. "How many times do I have to tell you to leave your beast outside, Montigny?"

"Have mercy on him, Margot, it's not safe out here!"

Margot glanced at the poor hound and melted a bit. "Can he behave?" she asked, hands on her hips.

"He behaves better than most of the apes who come here."

"Like yourself, eh?" she teased, but then nodded. "All right, go on then. Just make sure to make up for it with generous orders."

That I could not promise, so I kept quiet. I knew Margot would eventually let it be. Her tough exterior concealed a warm-hearted nature. We all admired Margot, not just for her curves, and were indebted to her for providing us with food, drinks, and girls at a special "student discount" as she liked to call it. Her beauty shone out of her cute, round face, golden curls and pair of dimples. She never shared her age with us but judging from the few wrinkles on her face, it was clear she was in her mid-thirties.

After Margot let us in, Villon, Estienne de Montigny II and I headed over to the table where Colin de Cayaux sat with our younger classmate Guy Tabary, a complete loser in my opinion.

"Oh, wonderful, the birdbrain is here," I couldn't help but mutter to Villon.

"Be nice to him, Montigny," he winked at me. "Remember that we used to be like him once, seeking the company of the older boys."

I knew that Villon had developed a kind of big brother relationship with the youngster and so I learned to tolerate his company. Together we approached the table. Guy Tabary was laughing with his open mouth full of bread and cheese, telling one of his tall tales. Beside him, Cayaux was pretending to listen although his attention was focused solely on the lively maidens who were luring customers to the chambers on the floors above. I hadn't been with one for quite some time as I had to watch my spending. However, that night, Cayaux pointed out the newcomer: a goddess with striking brown eyes, hazel hair and a contagious smile that seemed to be imprinted on her face. Her name was Isabeau and she was the loveliest girl I had ever seen. Judging by the laughs she exchanged with Margot, I could tell that they were friends.

Villon looked distracted and didn't even glance in her direction. I couldn't help but ask him if he was thinking about Katherine, but he patted my back with an earnest laugh and said, "If I ever become foolish enough to dream of a girl with such high expectations, hand me a noose straight away. I'd rather end it than end up in a jail called marriage."

"You could just be lovers," I argued. "She once told me that there's nothing worse than binding a free spirit."

"Then let's drink to her free spirit and pray that Noël Jolis will not break it!"

He lifted his goblet in the air and made a toast with Tabary and Cayaux. Just the sight of the pathetic duo made me lose interest in hanging around. I shifted my gaze back to Isabeau, admiring her gentle physique and graceful movements. She didn't fit in with the rest. She was like a fallen star filling our dim world with a bit of heaven. I began to wonder whether she was one of Margot's girls at all.

"I would definitely skip my meals tomorrow for that one," I whispered to Villon. "The girl has me completely hypnotised."

"It's a shame that she's rarely available," said Villon, throwing his feet up on the chair before us.

"What do you mean?"

"Margot told me that although she hasn't known her long, she is very fond of her, and will only leave her in trustworthy hands."

"Whose hands could be more trustworthy than mine?" I argued, almost offended by the remark.

Villon laughed and continued. "There's more. She let her go with Sermoise once, not expecting him to become completely obsessed with her. From then on, he's been here every night, paying a fortune just to make sure that Isabeau goes with no one but him."

"Then he's an even bigger idiot than I thought. I don't see him around right now though."

"I bet he's lurking in the shadows somewhere," grinned Villon. "You know how oddly he tends to behave."

"Let him lurk. I'm ready to take my chance."

I stood up, ran my fingers through my curls and quickly polished my red boots. They still stunk, but I hoped it wouldn't matter to the angelic beauty who had already trapped me in her sweet web.

"Gentlemen, this one is mine tonight!" I pronounced, though first I had to ask for Margot's blessing. She gave it, and so I set off to meet

Isabeau, whose eyes locked curiously on to mine, as if sensing I was about to claim her. I was not new to Margot's establishment, and was aware that we students were more appealing to the girls than some of the old drunks. Isabeau's smile widened when I neared her, which helped me regain the confidence I had lost at Katherine's birthday party.

Before I could say anything, though, someone crossed my path: Philippe Sermoise in all his pathetic glory. I sincerely doubted that he knew how unappealing he looked. I genuinely pitied the priest, though, as we often went too far in teasing him. I often went to his confessional pretending to have sinful thoughts about the sacred statues in his church. Villon's prank was much better, as he once confessed his undying love for the priest himself. He even wrote him some cheesy poems and left him presents at the church. Sermoise was uncomfortable with the situation but was determined to guide Villon's soul back to light. When the joke became boring, Villon told everyone about it, and Sermoise had hated him ever since. One would think he had suffered enough because of our jests, yet we simply could not leave the poor man alone.

"Father Sermoise! What are you doing up so late? Don't you have a Mass to celebrate tomorrow?" I asked, overshadowing him with my height.

"Excuse us, Montigny," he muttered nervously. "Isabeau and I have a long evening ahead of us."

"Lord de Montigny," I corrected him with a courteous bow to Isabeau who rewarded me with an impressed nod.

Sermoise jeered at me, though. "Ha! Lord? I doubt that you can afford Mademoiselle Isabeau. She isn't one of those street whores who go for a sou, she charges more than Margot herself."

Isabeau looked me up and down and softly fluttered her long eyelashes. "Margot told me that your group has special prices over here."

"I can afford a full price, my lady," I said firmly, in my mind already begging Villon to lend me the sum. Isabeau hesitated, so I reached for her hand and planted a kiss upon it. She smiled at me, but Sermoise flashed her a furious look as if he owned her.

With a defiant look his way, Isabeau accepted my lead and we proceeded to the stairs when suddenly she stopped and discreetly covered her nose. "What's that God-awful smell?"

I panicked and began stammering, "That would be excreta, but not mine, it belongs to a widow who..." I paused, realising how strange that must have sounded. Sometimes I wished for Villon's wits, as my own verbal skills were as bad as my social status.

"Who what?" she asked, the sweet smile fading from her face.

"It's not worth mentioning…"

Sensing that he still had a chance, Sermoise stepped in again. "I'm willing to pay an additional ten sous!"

Isabeau looked at me, wondering whether I could top him. Under normal circumstances I would have, for she was worth it, but I was discouraged by the foul smell and insults that had followed me that evening.

"I'm sorry, Lord de Montigny," she said affably. "Perhaps next time?"

Although disappointed, I bowed to her, and let her go with the clean sinner. I was used to being let down by girls, but never by a whore. That was a significant blow to my reputation. Margot's girls were the only ones, besides my friends, whose arms were always open to me.

As I watched Isabeau taking Sermoise upstairs to her chamber, the built-up tension within me finally exploded into a wild fury.

"It's all Bruyer's fault!" I exclaimed as I returned to the table where Villon and his two companions sat. "I swear that I'll seek my revenge on her!"

Villon poured me some ale and tried to console me. "Calm down, my friend. Look, Prickly Rose is free now. Why don't you go with her? I'll lend you some money again."

I threw up my hand. "I've been humiliated too many times today. I'm afraid I would not even be able to perform."

Tabary laughed, but I gave him a look that made him stop in his tracks.

"What kind of revenge are we talking about then?" asked Villon.

"A one-of-a-kind one," I said, sitting down beside him.

Tabary leaned closer to us and said, "I say excreta for excreta. We could urinate on the Devil's Fart!"

"That's stupid," I replied, brushing his idea off and turning to Villon whose secretive grin suggested that something was brewing in his mind. He remained quiet, though, so Cayaux said, "We should write her a nasty letter. Villon could compose it."

"That's no revenge," I argued.

"I know what we should do," said Villon finally. We all moved closer to him, eager to know what his inner genius was scheming. He let us wait for a moment, teasing us with an impish smile before he blurted out, "I say we steal the Devil's Fart!"

I liked the daring suggestion immediately, so I embraced him with glee. "Now that's a plan! I wish I had thought of it."

"Careful, Montigny," warned Margot who had just approached with another load of ale, bread, and cheese. "Don't squeeze the life out of him."

"Indeed, I'll need that," agreed Villon, "my lady likes to squeeze tight."

Margot stroked Villon's arm and winked at him. He was her favourite, and it wasn't just because of his good looks and charm. She secretly hoped he would write a poem for her one day, and she wasn't afraid of reminding him of it.

"I'll squeeze even tighter if you heat me up with those promised rhymes," she teased before she left our table. We all gazed after her, addicted to her generous and well-proportioned curves and the way she carried them.

"But how do we steal the Devil's Fart?" asked Cayaux once Margot had disappeared in the braying crowd. "You know how heavy those bloody things are."

"And we are strong men, aren't we?" challenged Villon, though he wavered a bit at the sight of Tabary.

"But where would we store it?" argued Cayaux again.

"We could hide it in your room at the Sorbonne," shrugged Villon. "Nobody would look for it there."

"Why my room? It's Montigny's revenge! I don't want to get into trouble. Bruyer will know we did it and the city guards will not be lenient with us," continued Cayaux.

That's when I stepped in. "Who cares? The provost likes Villon, so he won't make a big deal of it. Trust me, this is a brilliant plan."

I lifted my goblet in a toast and Tabary quickly joined in, promising his help. Only Cayaux still seemed sceptical.

"You three are probably too drunk for rational judgment. School pranks are okay with me, but a real robbery? That's going too far," he said, crossing his arms.

"I'm highly disappointed in you, Cayaux! I thought you of all people would be supportive of such an idea."

"What do you mean by that?"

"You're the locksmith's son!"

"What does that have to do with anything?"

"Your father surely taught you a trick or two."

"My father is no thief," he frowned.

"Locksmiths are bound to be thieves," I replied with conviction.

Cayaux shook his head. "That's such nonsense, Montigny."

"See the blushing?" I teased him. "I bet you and your father work those chamber locks whenever you get a chance!"

Whether it was true or not, Cayaux eventually chuckled. I could tell he would agree to help us in the end, so we began scheming our first grand theft.

CHAPTER 2

THE DEVIL'S FART

A few more friends from the Sorbonne agreed to help us with the Devil's Fart theft simply because they found the plan so funny. Therefore, the next day after school, we took hold of a few gardening tools and a rope and went on with our plan not minding that it was broad daylight. We waited until Bruyer had left the house, and began digging out the taller phallic shaped stone. Her neighbours and people who passed us by wondered what we were doing, but Villon confidently told them, "Madame Bruyer asked us to help her. She wants to have the bigger stone moved upstairs to her bedroom."

People probably thought that Bruyer had lost her mind, and just went about their own business.

A few street kids helped us with the digging in exchange for some food, and one elderly lady spat on the Devil's Fart as we dug it up, proclaiming, "Thank God that you are ridding our street of this devil's creation, boys!"

Once the stone was out of the ground, we carried it away with a victorious cheer, but as bad luck would have it, we met Bruyer on the way. When she saw us with her favourite garden ornament, she began shrieking. "You rascals! Put it down! How dare you?"

We wouldn't give it up, though. Villon grabbed Bruyer's hand and kissed it.

"Don't worry, madame, we'll just clean it up and polish it for you so that it may keep you satisfied night after night…"

Bruyer slapped Villon who just laughed at her and continued to help us carry it away. Just then, Bruyer must have noticed the city guards in the distance, as she yelled, "Sergeants! Over here! Help!"

We hurried on, eager to escape the law. Whether it was God or the devil himself, someone mighty must have been on our side that day, because we managed to bring the stone to the Sorbonne before the sergeants saw us. We then hid the Devil's Fart under a blanket in my college lodging and drank to our victory for the rest of the afternoon, filling up on the fine claret that Villon had brought.

After our little celebration, we went on with our lives as if nothing had happened. However, Bruyer would not let it go. She went to the authorities the next morning, identifying Cayaux, Villon and me as the main perpetrators of the robbery. While we were out, the sergeants searched the whole college and found the stone hidden in my room. Luckily for us, due to the provost's connection to Villon, they let it pass as an innocent student prank.

The sergeants must have been greatly disappointed as they usually seized any chance they could to throw students into the Grand Châtelet prison. The animosity between the Christian Church and the law was deeply rooted because both sides wanted to have complete power over the city. The sergeants knew well enough that we students were under the protection of our alma mater, the Church, and that's why they hated our guts. They resented the fact that they couldn't bully us like the common citizens who were powerless when it came to their ruthlessness. For some reason, most of the sergeants themselves were dangerous ex-convicts. We often wondered why this was but assumed that they needed someone tough in that position.

Although I should have been happy that nothing tragic came out of the theft, I simply couldn't help but feel disappointed. My revenge on Bruyer was not as satisfying as I had thought. On the contrary, I found it quite deflating. To cheer me up a bit, Villon took me to Margot's to drown my sorrows in some ale.

"Maybe you should just forget about this silly revenge of yours," he advised. "We should be happy that the provost saw the funny side."

"I still think we ought to get it back," I insisted, not ready to give up. However, even Villon seemed reluctant to do this.

"I don't know, Regnier... Had they not decided to take the stone at the Palace Royale for safekeeping, I might be up for it, but breaking in there would be too risky..."

Risky or not, I felt a strange urge to pursue it no matter what. In some ways, I didn't even recognise myself. It was as if something had changed within me. With that thought, I noticed Isabeau at the back of the room. She didn't see me and moved gracefully through the sordid tavern like a detached deity. The humiliation I had experienced in her company last time filled me with even more vigour. I shook my head and resolutely said, "I'm not giving up, Villon. I will get the stone back, with or without you."

"Don't be foolish," warned Villon. "Just go with that girl that you've got your eye on. She'll make you forget all about it."

As he said this, he received a punch in the back. It came from Margot who loomed over us like a goddess of revenge. "When will you pay your debts, Villon? How much will those promised verses cost me this time?"

I realised that Villon was probably receiving his pleasures free of charge again, which was a big honour from the brothel madam who went only with those she really liked.

"I work on them each time I lay my eyes on you, dear Margot," said Villon, "but a woman such as yourself, complicated in shape and character, deserves proper research."

"Well, it better be worth the wait," she warned, and was patting his head ominously when something stole her attention. We followed her gaze and noticed Sermoise threatening a man who had been talking to Isabeau. Margot's cute, chubby cheeks flushed with displeasure.

"You could use a pimp around here," noted Villon.

"I don't need any damn pimp! I'm my own pimp." She clamped her hands on her hips and roared, "I've had enough of that puppy love of his! I told him he could have Isabeau as often as he liked only if he lets her go with others as well. Now look! He is scaring away that wealthy customer." She shook her head in disbelief. "It's too much. I'm fetching my weapons." And with those words, she set off.

Villon and I looked at each other equally as worried as amused. We had had the pleasure of seeing Margot in action a few times already, so were painfully aware that she could get rid of a man quite easily, especially one of a rather feeble disposition such as Sermoise. She had never killed anyone but was quite good at mutilation. No matter how much we teased the silly priest, we never wished him any real harm. We decided to help him out.

Villon briskly caught up with Margot. I watched him reason with her from afar. Judging from the fiery spark in Villon's eyes and Margot's laugh, I could tell that he was proposing a better plan of how to chase Sermoise away.

Meanwhile, Sermoise was still arguing with the wealthy customer and Isabeau stood to one side with her arms crossed, waiting for the heated discussion to end. Once Villon had managed to persuade Margot of his plan, he hurried over to the musicians who had been playing a familiar tune. He explained something to them, and when they beamed up at him, I realised he was about to perform one of his songs.

He leaped up on the nearest table and resolutely stomped his foot, calling out to Sermoise over the noisy room. "Hey! Sermoise! This one's for you!"

His words sent a signal to Ithier Marchant, the main performer in the band, who nodded and gave his bandmates a sign to play a well-known melody. The newcomers fell silent in anticipation, but we habitués already knew what would follow. We began to clap along with the drums, and soon Villon started to sing his local hit:

Whether you play false dice
Whether you sell indulgence
Whether you play wrong or nice
Striving for quick abundance
Where will all your money go?
To the taverns and whores!

Hey! the crowd chimed in.

Rhyme, have fun, play and sing
Join brotherhoods of outcasts
Play a fool, do a theatre, try everything!
As long as your audience lasts
But hear where all your money should go –
To the taverns and whores!

Grab your doublets, shirts, boots, and coats
Until you stand only in your underclothes
And before things get even worse
Take them to the taverns and whores!

The whole pub sang along with him, *To the taverns and whores!* and Sermoise finally stopped bothering Isabeau and the wealthy customer. Once the song had ended and another well-known melody had begun, Villon jumped off the table and asked Isabeau for a dance. Sermoise's face flushed with anger, but before he could react, Margot and I grabbed him by each arm. Along with Estienne de Montigny II, who was growling at him from behind, we escorted Sermoise out of the tavern. Sermoise knew that we were in control, so he didn't dare to struggle much, though he kept turning after Isabeau.

At the door, Margot hissed at the priest, "Go and pray for your sinful soul, Father! And know that if you keep harassing my girls, I'll chop off that filthy worm you hide underneath your cassock!"

She pushed him out into the night and asked him to say a prayer for her on Sunday. Sermoise left, but turned around with a deep frown. The fool had no idea that Villon and I had actually just helped him out, as Margot's punishment would have been a lot tougher had we not intervened.

"I don't understand you." Margot shook her head as the priest disappeared in the shadows of the night. "You keep torturing the man yourself, but when it comes to the real thing, you protect him."

"Maybe we don't want to lose a good source of amusement," I shrugged, and patted Estienne de Montigny II, praising him for helping to scare the priest off. Margot gave him a good-humoured look and said, "You were right, Montigny. The beast is tolerable."

✦

While Villon and Isabeau danced, I was left sulking in the corner beside Estienne de Montigny II. I assumed her new interest in Villon was due to the eloquent way he had just saved her from the uncomfortable dispute, but also feared she had taken a liking to him. To save me from my jealousy, Villon took his leave of Isabeau and went over to greet Cayaux and Tabary who had just arrived. Isabeau's eyes kept flicking in his direction, so I walked over to her.

"Sermoise should leave you alone from now on," I said, letting her know that Villon was not the only saviour of the day.

"I hope so," she smiled then said, "I promised my services to the gentleman over there first, but I'm free later tonight if you like."

"All right, I don't mind waiting if it's worth it."

"Oh, it is," she confirmed and added, "Lord de Montigny."

The words soothed me like honey. I let her go with the wealthy man who had been leering at her, knowing she would be back soon.

While Isabeau worked on her customer upstairs, I worked on persuading my friends to help me reclaim the Devil's Fart. Tabary would do anything we asked him to, but Cayaux and Villon still wavered. I ordering more ale, hoping it would persuade them, however, I ended up drinking most of it myself. That's why, when Isabeau returned from her duties, I had no energy left in me to take her upstairs and give her my royal treatment. She seemed keen on my company nevertheless, as she agreed to drink some ale with me. I ended up telling her all about our theft of the Devil's Fart and my secret plan to retrieve it from the Palace Royale. Her reaction surprised me. She found it amusing and even suggested she might come along, which was all that was needed for Villon to finally agree, not wishing to appear a coward.

We told her that it might be dangerous, and that we may all end up in the Châtelet, but she was open to the idea, nonetheless. I sensed it was because of Villon as she kept eyeing him up, and so I drank to stop myself from thinking about it. I wasn't lucky in love, so when I realised that my interest in this girl was more than just physical attraction, I began to worry. I found myself even more intrigued by her when she suddenly took my palm in hers and started reading from it. She described my past better than I could ever manage myself and claimed that all good palmists should focus on the past before they foretold the future.

"Can you read my future now?" I asked, partly curious to know more, but mainly just relishing the fact that I had her full attention.

"I can. I have to warn you, though, I see only the most important parts of the grand plan, and some people are afraid to know them."

"Well, I'm not," I said, bravely. She focused back on my palm, studying the lines in the dim light of the tavern lanterns when suddenly, her expression changed. I could tell that something was troubling her.

"What is it?" I asked, anxious to know what she had seen. She let go of my hand, and it seemed as if she had changed her mind.

"Nothing, I just... I have a temporary blur. Perhaps it's not the right moment to do this. It's not safe to do palmistry in public anyway... People consider everything to be black magic these days."

I could tell that she was avoiding the truth, but I also knew that no matter what she saw in my palm, I couldn't control my fate so I reckoned I might as well forget about it.

✦

Despite being richly intoxicated by the blend of ale, wine and each other's company, we were all feeling spontaneous that night, and so we decided to go ahead with our second attempt to steal the Devil's Fart. I feared we would be incapable at first, but the crisp breeze helped us sober up a bit. After crossing the bridge to the Right Bank, we began to feel stronger and our minds were clearer as well. We stopped by the well to have a sip of water and firm up our plans.

Firstly, we had to figure out how to get past the guards. Isabeau suggested that she could seduce them while we got on with the robbery. We had no doubt that she could keep them busy, so we agreed. A part of me dreaded the idea, but the darker part was simply grateful for the help. I was still confused by why I was so attracted to her. Then again, I had grown to like the opposite of what I was born to be. Commoners tended not to be as pretentious and boring as the upper crust.

Villon came up with the plan of pretending to be Isabeau's pimp to keep her safe. I felt ashamed not to be the one to think of it first, but blamed this on the distress and emotional turmoil I had been experiencing that night. I left Estienne de Montigny II on the corner, ordering him to keep guard while Tabary, Cayaux and I hid behind the wall to watch the scene unfold.

Villon confidently strode over to the guards with Isabeau by his side. The guards appeared intrigued when he began offering the variously priced services and hesitated over whether to follow their duties or give in to lust. We didn't hear the conversation all that well, however, it was clear that Villon was bargaining with them until they struck a deal.

Then Villon took the money, whispered something to Isabeau and loudly warned the men to treat the girl well or else he would have to castrate them. He then joined us and reported back.

"I saw the stone, and there's only one gate to scale. Isabeau will lure the men far enough away so that we can sneak in."

"What about the keys?" wondered Tabary, confused, an inexperienced thief.

"We have Cayaux," I explained and nudged the unwilling student. He was still uncertain about whether he had done the right thing by joining us. Breaking into the Palace Royale was, after all, a real crime.

"Lord," he crossed himself nervously, "please don't let my father find out."

"Your father taught you the skills himself so if anything, he would be proud," I assured him, but Cayaux looked like he was about to vomit so I simply pushed him forward.

"Prepare yourself to witness some lock mastery, my friend," whispered Villon to Tabary whose eyes gleamed at the idea. Cayaux finally set off and we quietly followed him to the palace entrance.

As we reached the gate, my gaze fell upon the three figures in the shadow of the lanterns. The guards were already preoccupied with Isabeau's body. I didn't like it one bit, and suddenly felt the need to stop the action at once. If I were a more decent man, I would have pulled Isabeau away from them and rushed off with her, but I was a wretch.

In order not to change my mind, I focused on Cayaux working the locks instead, while Villon and

Tabary exchanged excited looks. Such pranks made us all feel alive. We loved the risk that came along with it, though that night was not just a rash student rebellion. It was the threshold between juvenile larking about and criminality, only we hadn't realised it yet.

Cayaux was soon done, probably because the fear of being caught made him work faster. Before we passed through the gate, I felt Isabeau's gaze on me and turned to check on her. The strange, regretful look in her eyes struck me like an arrow, straight in the heart. I realised it was not right of us to use her like this. She was trying to slow things down for our sake, but one of the guards had already mounted her and the other hungrily stood by, waiting for his turn. She looked away to avert suspicion and I took it as a signal to move on. I suppressed the bad feeling her gaze had left me with and joined my friends who had already snuck into the yard.

Without knowing how, we managed to carefully creep out with our trophy, carrying it out into the darkness of the sleeping town. Isabeau meanwhile continued pleasuring the two men, pressing their heads to her bosom to keep us safe. We had escaped before the guards realised that the stone was gone and soon we were by the bridge where we had promised to wait for Isabeau.

"One of us should have stayed and guarded her," I said nervously after a few too many long minutes had passed.

"Calm down, Montigny, she's just a whore," said Tabary, trying to sound tough. I grabbed him by the collar and said, "And you are just a wimpy little cretin who hangs around Villon just to seem more important!"

Villon pulled us apart. "Stop it, you two. We are supposed to be brothers in crime."

Without saying as much, Villon was like an older brother to us all, the one we always turned to and listened to in the end. I let go of Tabary's collar and was turning away when at last we saw Isabeau running towards us. Villon welcomed her with a grateful embrace, thanked her, and gave her the pimp's money he had kept for her.

"Thank you for putting up with those two stinky dogs," he said.

"They could never compare to dogs!" I argued and patted Estienne de Montigny II who had begun to walk ahead of us, probably offended by Villon's comment.

"You'll have to apologise, Villon, you know how sensitive he is."

They all laughed at me and when I noticed that Isabeau chuckled as well, I couldn't help but join them. I put my arms around Villon and cheered. "And now let's go and celebrate our victory!"

Everybody agreed, so we proudly lifted the stone and marched back towards the Sorbonne. As we passed Bruyer's house, Villon came up with an even more outrageous idea: to steal the other stone as well. Feeling invigorated and brave, we were all up for it. Since that stone was smaller and not as deeply buried, we managed to loosen it up and pull it out without any tools. To top it off, we all urinated on her doorstep except for Isabeau who just shook her head at us. Estienne de Montigny II completed our revenge by marking the spot as well. Then Villon and I took hold of the bigger stone and left the small one for Cayaux and Tabary. Isabeau strode ahead of us, encouraging us to fearlessly march on. We were slower that time as we had fewer helping hands, but the sight of the goddess leading the way certainly made us move faster.

Once both of the phallic-shaped stones were in my room, we realised that since there could be only one Devil's Fart, we should name the smaller stone as well. Villon came up with the title "Cushion Fart" and we found it so hilarious that we instantly christened it with some burgundy. We continued celebrating until dawn, drinking and chatting, mainly telling Isabeau about our previous pranks.

After Cayaux and Tabary fell asleep in each other's arms like lovebirds, Villon, Estienne de Montigny II and I decided to take Isabeau back to Margot's. We had already sobered up and had more energy than usual due to the adventure we had just had. As was common after our drinking sprees, we were preparing to go to bed just as everyone else was waking up, but that morning was different. I felt as though I could stay awake even longer with Isabeau by my side and hoped that I would. Villon sensed that I wanted to be alone with her, so he headed back to his home at Porte Rouge.

Once Isabeau and I were the only two thieves walking the early morning streets of Paris, we fell strangely quiet. She was probably tired, but I was mainly confused about the way she made me feel and awkward about what had happened earlier.

"I'm sorry about what we put you through," I said with a sincere look. "I wish we had gone with another plan."

"Why?" she asked. "You know that I earn my living this way."

She proudly patted her cleavage where her financial reward was tucked and added, "Although he's no Margot, Villon makes a good pimp."

"Still, the guards weren't very appealing."

She shrugged. "I'm used to it. They were better than Sermoise – the man has no shame. I wish the faithful sheep at his church could witness the despicable things he made me do."

I frowned at the idea. "Did he hurt you?"

Isabeau shook her head. "Margot would kill him if he laid a hand on me, but…" she hesitated and when she saw the bewilderment in my eyes, she just smiled and said, "He's just peculiar, that's all."

The idea of perverted Sermoise sickened me, and the sight of her fragile disposition made me feel painfully protective of her. She seemed so gentle and unfit for her craft, but I assumed it could have been because she was new to it.

"I thought he was obsessed with you because he's in love."

"Oh, he's not in love, he's in lust, but I genuinely don't think he knows the difference," she laughed.

"Well, don't worry, my lady," I said, attempting to be courteous. "I will make sure that he haunts you no more!"

Isabeau gave me a grateful, though slightly distrustful, look.

"I hope you don't mind me asking," I said after a moment's hesitation, "but I keep wondering why a graceful young woman such as yourself would turn to Margot for survival. You are clearly more sophisticated than the others."

Isabeau smiled at some distant memory and began to explain. "My family was well off, but they all passed away during the plague. I was the only survivor and since then, I have had nothing and no one to rely on. I came to Paris in search of my distant aunt. She was the one who taught me palmistry, which was useful to earn a few sous after she passed away... It was not enough, though. Paris can be cruel."

I nodded, sympathising with her, but remained quiet to let her speak.

"I began to grow hungry after a few months living on the streets. Margot found me at my lowest and took me in. She has been a wonderful friend to me since. She takes such good care of me. Sometimes the girls are jealous, but I try to be friends with all of them. Margot makes us feel as if we are part of one family. Maybe I was born to be a whore, who knows... Had I married for money I would be a whore as well, just a more hypocritical one. At least I have some freedom at Margot's.

"Margot always says, 'If a woman wants to be free, she can either be a rich widow, a whore or a witch, but a whore has less chance of ending up being tortured or burned at the stake.' I think she's right."

She checked my reaction. I felt even more enchanted by her having heard her backstory so I finally dared to say, "I have never met a woman like you, Isabeau, and I have a feeling that I never will."

She smiled, but I could tell that my confession made her feel slightly uncomfortable. Was it because of Villon? Did she like him better? Although it would not surprise me, I didn't want to be left disappointed, so I refrained from asking. I looked up to the sign above us and realised we were already outside Margot's.

"Thank you, Regnier de Montigny. You are a good man," said Isabeau.

Then she planted a quick kiss on my cheek and hurried inside the house, leaving us on the doorstep. *You are a good man.* I kept repeating her words in my mind. Never had I heard anyone say that to me before, especially the gentler sex. I was surprised how good it felt. At that moment, I wanted to believe that it was actually true.

CHAPTER 3

CRIMINAL MINDS

The next day, Villon dragged me to Sermoise's Mass. As Parisians gathered by the church, I took the chance to polish my red boots. Villon noted that I did it excessively, but the reason I cared for the two beauties so well was because they were all I had left of my inheritance. I also prepared Estienne de Montigny II to wait outside. He was used to it, and unlike me, he had no objections about dogs being excluded from the house of God.

As we made our way to the queue of people, we noticed that Katherine de Vaucelles and her father had arrived. Katherine's eyes gleamed at the sight of Villon and she headed for us straight away, while my uncle mingled with his own kind. Unlike Katherine and her mother, who had sadly died in childbirth sixteen years ago, he kept his distance from me. I suppose he felt ashamed for not taking me and my sister in after our parents passed away. I once told him that I held no grudges. My sister married into a wealthy family soon after and I was better off on my own anyway. Still, he had been awkward around me since.

"You two wouldn't miss Father Sermoise's Mass, would you?" smiled Katherine, well aware of how much we enjoyed teasing him. "What is it going to be this time? Tell me what is it going to be so I have something to look forward to."

"That would spoil the surprise," winked Villon.

"I don't like surprises," she complained. "I prefer to know where I stand." The words had a clear subtext, however, he pretended not to notice.

"Maybe we haven't planned anything," he said evasively.

Katherine rolled her eyes and sighed. "Always mystifying or lying…"

"Oh, I may mystify from time to time, but I never lie," said Villon looking her in the eye. I could tell it made her as nervous as me. I always felt like the odd one out in their presence, especially when they exchanged those puzzling, long stares. Luckily, my uncle had just approached and broke the tension.

"Good day to you, Regnier," he nodded to me, and quickly turned to Villon. "And to you,

François. How is Father Guillaume doing? We haven't seen him around for quite some time."

"He is well, thank you for asking, Monsieur de Vaucelles. My mother takes good care of him – in a completely innocent way, of course."

We all knew that Villon was hinting at the rumour spread by Widow Bruyer, who suggested that they shared more than just a household.

"And how is school?" he asked me, just to be polite, since it was obvious that he only came over to fetch his daughter. I didn't really care about his lack of concern, but it felt good to be worthy of a question or two sometimes.

"Good, thank you for asking, Uncle," I said. "We will be graduating this year, and I'm sure I don't speak only for myself when I say that the freedom it will bring is highly anticipated."

"But freedom is not free, Regnier," argued my uncle. "Being torn from the comfort and ease that you have become accustomed to will be quite difficult, you mark my words. If you ever find yourself in trouble, though, don't hesitate to stop by for advice."

Of course, just advice, I laughed bitterly to myself. Although my uncle may have not meant it in a bad way, it sounded like he didn't believe in me at all. He wasn't the first and he wouldn't be the last. My professors often suggested that I should enjoy my school years while I could, because if I chose not to be a cleric, I would find myself with nothing but a useless degree. *Master of Arts.* I recalled how fancy it had sounded to me a few years ago.

Villon paid no heed to my uncle's words. He was whispering something to Katherine, and she was giggling despite her father's reproachful looks. Probably because of that, Noël Jolis suddenly interrupted us. He greeted us all except for Villon. Katherine smiled apologetically at him, and so did my uncle. We quietly decided it would be better to go, and so bid them both a polite farewell.

There was no need to compete with Noël, as Villon already knew that he had Katherine's attention, and even more so at the end of Mass. Just as Sermoise was blessing the chalice and taking a ceremonial sip of holy blood, his face contorted into an unpleasant grimace. I was the only one who knew that Villon had secretly snuck into the church before Mass and replaced the red wine with some real blood that he had purchased from the butcher's beforehand. Sermoise seemed confused at first, so he took another small sip just to make sure his mind wasn't playing tricks on him. The shock of realising what he had just consumed made him spit it out again, staining both his vestments and the altar. The congregation gasped in shock and Villon and I had to suppress our laughter. Katherine discreetly turned our way and smiled, having the same difficulty containing herself.

On the way back to the Sorbonne, we were still laughing at Sermoise and the unforgettable expression on his face when he tasted the blood for the second time. The closer we got to our college, though, the more concerned I became about the issue that my uncle had brought up earlier. I asked Villon what he thought of it.

"He was right," he said. "I often find myself pondering this. Unless we become clerics, there is not much use for us out there. We don't have any practical knowledge or skill, and the only thing we are good at is philosophising and coming up with new schoolboy pranks. Better face up to it: we are good-for-nothing fellas."

"Not all of us," I objected. "You have always been good at studying and writing."

"But what's the use?" he said with a careless smile. "Just to impress my friends or the girls."

"Impressing people is a damn good quality to have, Villon. Look at the provost, for example. It was because of the impressive poem you wrote in his honour that we have been pardoned for offences that others would pay harshly for."

He shrugged, then threw his arm around my shoulders and pronounced cheerfully, "Let's make a promise to each other, Montigny. Even if we become utterly non-prosperous and insignificant after our alma mater kicks us out, let's at least enjoy our youth while we can!"

I understood his reckless approach but didn't share it. Unlike him, I had nowhere to go and no family to rely on. My sister was glad to be rid of me, my uncle offered only useless advice and my cousins couldn't give me more than the education I had already wasted. Villon, on the other hand, knew that if the worst came to the worst, Guillaume would be there to support him. Though he wasn't rich, he had some resources and loved him to death.

"I suppose I should take life as it comes," I said. "The world is full of surprises, so if we should ever feel unwelcome here, we can simply move on. There are more cities like Paris out there."

"I dare to disagree with that statement," objected Villon. "There is no place like Paris. I'll never set foot anywhere else unless my life depends on it."

✦

Paris. My relationship with the city was as affectionate as it was bitter. Sometimes it cradled me in its safe arms while other times it thrust me into its lowest pits. Villon loved the city unconditionally despite all the hardships we had witnessed there. It wasn't just due to the Hundred Years' War. Soon after Paris and its vicinity had been liberated, all neighbourhoods were plunged into the most dreadful winter. It snowed for forty days straight, and as a result, thousands of people froze and even more starved to death.

Just as we thought the worst was over, we suffered a terrible famine, windstorms and finally a fatal epidemic that killed tens of thousands including my poor mother. As if this wasn't enough, packs of starved wolves then attacked the outskirts of Paris, devouring the frailest citizens, and leaving only the strongest behind. As Guillaume once said, "God must had been angry with this country for a long time to sacrifice so many innocent souls."

The fact that Villon and his mother survived through all these tragedies in such poor conditions was a miracle of its own, but an even bigger one was that Father Guillaume had taken pity on them at their lowest moment. He said it was because he saw something unique in the young François. He called it a spark that should be handled carefully, not destroyed or burnt out. Villon laughed at that metaphor and said it must have been the infernal fire of his sinful soul that Guillaume had sensed. My friend had a tendency to make light of the darker times in his life. He buried all the misfortunes he had experienced deep inside and never dragged them out. However, he once wrote something that made me realise that it had had an effect on him nevertheless. It went like this:

Necessity makes people vile
Just as hunger drives wolves from the wild…

✦

When Villon and I entered the Sorbonne that afternoon we were speechless. The college was a complete mess; there were clothes lying around, books, broken jars, spilled ink and all kinds of household objects strewn about. Our classmates were busy cleaning up, and the professors stood around, overseeing the scene with worry etched on their faces.

Everyone looked up as we entered, and judging from the cold reception, it was clear that whatever had happened must had been connected to the two phallic-shaped stones. We also noticed that many of our fellow students, including the youngest ones, were badly bruised, and some were even limping.

We were both in shock at first, but Villon snapped out of it faster than me, and rushed to find out what was going on. The professors who had initially found the prank amusing were now disconcerted, as they hadn't expected such a response from the law. The city guards had finally got their chance to treat the university with disrespect, and had thoroughly enjoyed it. Only one of the professors was willing to talk to us about it.

"The sergeants came to claim the stones. Most of them were drunk and behaved like brutes. Cayaux and Tabary were taken to the Châtelet for further investigation and the rest of us were pushed around. They even stole some of our food and wine…"

"How dare they!" exclaimed Villon, fuming, while I hovered beside him, feeling ashamed.

"They dare to because they can," replied the professor with a reproachful look.

"But the theft was just a silly joke…"

"Silly or not, there is a line between a prank and a crime."

I wanted to say something, apologise, explain, but remained speechless.

"The Church and university can only go so far to protect you," warned the professor. "The law is a force of its own, especially when it comes to criminal records. You may be safe from prison or the noose while you are students here, and you can plead the Benefit of Clergy* even after you leave these walls, but you should be smarter than to give the city guards a reason to come after you."

His eyes became softer when he saw our abashed faces, so he went on to explain. "I was also young once. I can relate to the mischievous ideas that fill your heads, however, sometimes it's wiser to not execute them."

While we both silently searched the ground, the professor concluded his reproof with the strict command, "Help the other boys. That's the least you can do after the suffering and shame you have caused them."

The professor liked Villon. Most of them did, because he was one of the best students at the Sorbonne, even though he often lacked good sense and judgment. For that reason, they didn't punish us as they otherwise should have.

Villon and I looked at our younger friends with a great deal of embarrassment and regret. It was mortifying to know that they had to deal with the consequences of our actions. We insisted on cleaning the halls up by ourselves, and as we went on with our work, we realised how arrogant and foolish we had been to think that the theft, no matter how innocent and funny it seemed at the time, would go unpunished. Moreover, I felt as if we had just received a second warning about our inauspicious futures that day. We spent the rest of the afternoon tiding up and sulking, feeling especially bad for Cayaux and Tabary, as they had taken the blame for us in the most drastic way.

Luckily, the two unfortunates returned the following morning. Nothing had happened to them because of the Benefit of Clergy, but a night in prison and the horror they witnessed there was enough to scare them off. Although they both swore they would never do anything criminal again, I sensed they didn't really mean it. In fact, I feared that this was just the beginning of our inevitable life of crime. Despite the chaos that the sergeants had caused for us, their hands were tied when it came to more serious reprisals. More than ever before, I realised how powerful the Catholic Church was, and how lucky I was to have been taken under its wings. Church leaders clearly had the final word when it came to criminality, perhaps because many of them were criminals themselves.

I also began to feel a familiar outrage. The city guards' arrogance astonished me and my thirst for revenge was awakened once more. However, I no longer wanted to tease some nasty widow or the sergeants themselves, I was ready for a more powerful enemy.

✦

That night at Margot's, we lifted our goblets in unison to honour our university and then I began my impassioned speech.

"We can't let the city guards push us around as if we were their puppets!" I said. "What they did to you all is unforgivable. We stole and they came for justice, but when they stole from us, no justice came for them. That's why Villon will write a petition to the provost, an official complaint about the bad behaviour of his sergeants."

*Benefit of Clergy was an exemption of the clergy from the jurisdiction of the ordinary civil courts and punishments.

My classmates' cheers gave me the confidence to continue:

"They hate us because they can't touch us. The Benefit of Clergy is our biggest, if not only advantage, my friends. Only students can get away with the same shit as the holy men, just ask any graduate you can see around here…"

Before I could finish, I found myself distracted by the sight of Isabeau who was descending the staircase with a neatly dressed man. They kissed goodbye and she waved after him without even glancing in my direction. I promised myself to shake her from my mind. I needed to distract myself and another prank would be one way to do it, so I went on, "Let's not forget that many of the sergeants are ex-convicts themselves. Most of them were thugs or even murderers before they were employed by the law to do its dirty work.

"It's unfair! We can't let them turn an innocent joke into a crime. Don't we have the right to a bit of fun? We are young, we are their future, therefore we should show them what that future is about! It's not about rules and limitations, it's about freedom and laughter!"

"Exactly," joined in Villon, though he was a bit more composed than me. "We are protected by the holy, mighty, indestructible Catholic Church yet the law dares to treat our university with disrespect. It's blasphemous."

Those last words made everybody cheer again, and soon they all started to chant, "Blasphemy, blasphemy!"

Since most of our fellow students were on their way to becoming clerics themselves, we had finally touched on a core principle, which was the need to protect their faith. I noticed that familiar spark of rebellion in Villon's eyes and reacted to it like a hungry wolf. We were born to be crooks, no matter how much we liked to hide beneath the cloak of intellect. That part of us seemed to appeal to Isabeau as well, who had finally joined us.

"Hello boys, so what are we scheming today?"

Everybody turned to her in surprise. The fact that she was still invested in our mischief and even encouraging it simply astonished us. Nobody could disappoint that beautiful face, and so in no time, we began planning another brilliant escapade.

We decided to rearrange the tavern and shop signs around Paris so that they united in symbolic couples: The Golden Goose would marry Robert the Locksmith, the Stag, Louis the Tailor, the Silver Goblet, the Red Rose and so on. It was childish but seemed ingenious in our drunken state. What mattered most was that we had plenty of fun doing it.

Isabeau joined us like last time but didn't pay much attention to me. She hung around Villon instead, which made me finish off the wine jar that was meant to last for the whole evening. Estienne de Montigny II helped me regain my composure a few times, and it was mainly thanks to him that I was able to keep up with the group.

As if some wicked fortune had planned it, Sermoise emerged from the shadows of the narrow streets just as we were pairing the Dirty Goat with the Blacksmith Fournier. It seemed that he had been following us the whole time, because he wasn't at all shocked by what we were doing, and just stood there with a frown. Villon and I exchanged a troubled look. We both knew that he had plenty to seek vengeance for, so had to stop him before he reported us to the authorities. Villon, who was not as drunk as I was, called out to him.

"Come out of hiding, our virtuous friend! Come have a drink with us! We celebrate your institution tonight! God bless the Church!"

The others joined in as if it was one of Villon's songs. "God bless the Church!"

Although Villon's invitation was sincere, Sermoise probably assumed that we were all mocking him. I could only make out half of his face in the dimness of the narrow street, but the hatred in his eyes broke through it nevertheless.

"I'd rather die of thirst than share a drink with you," he replied, unable to suppress his hatred.

"Please," begged Villon with a friendly smile. "I would like to take this opportunity to apologise for everything… And I'm certain that Regnier feels the same way. We both realise that we often go too far.

Would you find it in your heart to forgive your brothers?"

Sermoise spat on the ground and hissed, "You are no brothers to me."

Then he fixed his gaze on Isabeau and said, "I thought you were better than this, Isabeau. There will come a day when you will regret the way you treated me."

With those cold words, he disappeared into the night. We all had a bad feeling about the brief encounter, for it felt like a clear warning. We guided Isabeau home and told Margot about Sermoise's threat. I was mainly concerned for her safety, however, I also couldn't help but wonder whether Sermoise had a deeper reason to warn Isabeau that night. Did he know something I didn't? After we parted from the two worried women, I gathered the courage to ask Villon about Isabeau.

"Don't worry, Montigny," he laughed. "I would never dare to touch your girl."

Though I was relieved to hear him say the words, I was too proud to admit it.

"She's not my girl. I was just curious, that's all."

"She could be," argued Villon, "if you stop drooling from a distance and take action."

I felt like a boy who had been caught stealing bread. How strange that theft caused me less shame than showing my emotions. That was why I hid my blossoming feelings for Isabeau behind the idea that she only appealed to my more carnal instincts.

"Who would want a whore to be his girl?" I asked Villon, but mainly myself.

"I suppose only an unfortunate like you, my friend," he said embracing me like a brother.

CHAPTER 4

DANCE OF THE DEAD

The plan seemed reasonable: Villon wrote the petition to the provost and decided to deliver it personally along with his classmates including me, Cayaux and Tabary. Thank God I left Estienne de Montigny II at my college room that day, as he may have not survived what followed…

On our way, we snickered at the merchants and publicans who were losing their temper over the rearranged signs. Most Parisians found it funny, but those affected by it were cursing the rapscallions responsible. The city guards, including the sergeants who had broken into the Sorbonne, had come to their aid. I couldn't help but glower at these lowlifes, which attracted their attention. Villon elbowed me, advising me to stop staring at them. Though I knew he was right to worry, I just couldn't help myself.

We stumbled upon the provost even before we reached the Grand Châtelet, which was also his place of residence.

"Monsieur François Villon!" he proclaimed rather warmly considering the situation. "Have you come for your punishment?" The reproachful tone hid the fact that he was still fond of him.

"Actually, Monsieur d'Estouteville," bowed Villon, "we come to you with an official complaint." He handed him the sealed letter. "My classmates, professors and I were shocked by the barbaric way our college was treated."

"All right, I promise to read your petition, but you must promise me something in return. Stop provoking us if you can't handle the repercussions. And go and help the shopkeepers. We know it was you who messed with the signs."

"I promise we will, sir," said Villon with another courteous bow. The provost nodded and flashed us all a warning look. We felt relieved and grateful for his lenience, and so we headed to the Left Bank. By the time we reached the Notre-Dame Bridge, Villon began to sense that we were being followed. He wanted to return to the Châtelet, but I argued with him, encouraging everybody to carry on, foolishly thinking that nothing could happen to us if the provost had treated us so well.

We crossed the Île de la Cité and stepped onto the Notre-Dame Bridge, flanked by rows of tightly packed wood-and-daub houses. However, when we neared the Left Bank, I grew uneasy as well. Something was up. I felt it in the stone structure below and in the thick air above. The sun seemed to hide behind the clouds and the birds began circling us, already sensing that blood would be shed.

Villon and I were the leaders and so we gestured to everybody to speed up. Suddenly, a group of sergeants blocked our path. Their solid bodies created a barrier at the bridge's end. They were armed to the teeth with various weapons and their eyes burned with rage.

Villon and I looked at each other, fear clutching us both in its chilly claws. We instinctively turned around and hurried our friends back towards the Île de la Cité only to be met with another line of sergeants guarding the other end of the bridge. We were trapped halfway between the two banks, surrounded by rows of quiet houses on each side. We turned back and forth in despair. We didn't stand a chance.

I reached for the dagger that I carried tucked in my shoe, always ready to fight and protect my life, honour, and friends. The others took it as a sign and drew out anything that could pass for a weapon, be it a pocketknife or just a book. We must have looked pathetic to them, and this was reflected in their sneers.

I pulled on the door of the nearest house. Even though the houses might have been open before, they were carefully locked now as the siege got underway. Faces appeared in the windows, looking out at the scene with the thrill of anticipation. It was the dawn of a street battle between unarmed students and bloodthirsty sergeants. The people made me sick for they could have helped at least a few of us yet had clearly decided not to. If someone were to die that day, they wouldn't be seen as accomplices, they would simply be able to walk away.

I had witnessed such ignorance many times before in my life, but that instance changed something within me. My whole being realised that we lived among herds who went along with whatever the authorities decided. Only a few rebelled against it, and I wanted nothing more at that moment than to be one of them.

As the sergeants slowly approached us, enjoying the idea of our imminent loss, I turned to Villon for help. If we had ever been in need of his clever ideas, it was then. I could tell that his mind was racing, but we didn't have enough time for an exchange. It all happened too fast. The bridge became a sea of struggling bodies, punching and kicking each other, pushing and roaring. I used my dagger without hesitation, slashing our enemies as they wickedly attacked the least armed of our friends. Whether I injured one or ten men, I did not care. I just kept checking on Villon and Cayaux. I lost sight of them after one of the sergeants attacked me, and I escaped his spear only by luck. I was frantically trying to locate my two best friends while struggling to help the others.

As blood splashed on my face, I noticed that one of the younger students had fallen to the ground with a scream of horror, blood gushing from his stomach. The sergeants trampled him until one of them mercilessly finished him off. I raged towards the brute, stabbing my dagger into his back, and receiving a dagger strike in return. I hardly felt the impact, and in the rush of fury, assumed it was just a scratch.

When my opponent collapsed on his knees with my dagger stuck in his back, I moved away, looking for a way out of the hell. I was still desperately trying to locate my friends amidst the splashing blood, screams and clashing metal. I once again caught sight of the gaping faces in the windows; some were terrified, some concerned, others struck by a bloodthirsty fascination. Only one emotion united them all – fear.

Then, by luck, I spotted Cayaux and Tabary crawling on top of a nearby house, successfully reaching the chimney. They ran across the rooftops towards the Left Bank. I was impressed by the clever idea but couldn't join them without Villon. I had to find him first, armed or not. With this in mind, I fell on my knees and proceeded to crawl through the fighting bodies. I saw one of my classmates on the ground with a fatal wound. As his eyes met mine, I could sense his life slowly fading away. Never had I seen a man in such pain before, never had I felt death's chilling breath so close to me. The most horrifying realisation struck me then: this was my fault. I had brought them all to this utter misery. If that boy had to die so should I – the root of the tragedy.

After his spirit finally left his poor body, I froze as if in some kind of daze. I became numb and everything around me slowed down. I saw my end mirrored in the blade that stuck out of his chest. I was ready to rise and dance the last round with Lady Death, but before I managed to put my red boots to use one last time, somebody pulled me up and pushed me inside one of the houses.

Did one of those cruel bystanders finally decide to take pity on us? With this puzzling thought, I looked around, expecting to see a merciful stranger, but instead, I faced Villon. He locked the door and turned to the person beside him. I was quite certain that I had seen the man before at Margot's, as one could hardly forget such a character.

He looked like the spectre of some ancient warrior. His head was bald, he had a long, braided beard and his face was covered with old scars. His deep wrinkles complimented the tough expression on his face. They belonged to him like bark on a tree. The contrast between his rough appearance and noble attire was uncanny and somehow appealing. In a way, he reminded me of myself. He looked like an impoverished nobleman trying to wear his defeat with pride. He introduced himself as Jean de Loup but said that he mainly goes by the name of Wolf.

Villon patted me on the back then immediately rushed over to the window.

"We must help the others too," he insisted.

"Have you lost your mind? It's enough we risked our lives for this one," said Wolf with a distrustful glance in my direction. "If those sergeants see us hiding here, we're dead. Heroism is useless when you are outnumbered. Unless you are a highly skilled fighter, which judging by what I have seen, you are not, you either escape or you lose your life."

"But they are suffering for our mistakes! We must help them! Is there a secret door or something?" asked Villon in despair, still trying to find a way to save at least a few more lives.

"I'm not risking my life for a third time. If you do something foolish, I'll have to take action."

They exchanged a strained look. I noticed Wolf easing the dagger out of his belt so I gave a slight shake of the head, warning my friend to stand back. Villon muttered something and turned away from us both. His eyes were crazed, and his limbs wouldn't stop shaking. He was consumed with guilt and anger. I understood his inner struggle so well. We had become the cruel bystanders, and I felt sickened by it. Wolf was unaffected, though. He must have been used to such horrors.

"I've seen you at our tavern a few times," he remarked. The expression "our tavern" baffled us both. Villon didn't respond, but Wolf kept on talking to him. "You're the poet Margot keeps talking about, right? I enjoyed your ditty the other day."

Someone's painful scream startled us all. Villon and I exchanged looks, united in helplessness and shame. We had been brothers in crime, now we were brothers in death.

"Try not to listen," advised Wolf. "It will ease your mind. It takes time to make peace with this, but the pain will cease sooner or later."

Suddenly, I began to feel weak, so I leaned on the wall for support. It was becoming difficult for me to focus, and the chamber seemed to be spinning. I felt as though I were trapped in a feverish nightmare that I couldn't wake up from.

"Are you all right?" asked Wolf at the sight of my limp body. I nodded, but my waist felt strangely moist to the touch. At first, I thought I had spilled red wine on myself, though the liquid was thicker than that. It was only when I noticed Villon's terrified expression that I realised I was wounded. The shock had probably blocked out the pain. As I touched the wound, however, I began to remember the sting of the blade. It all dawned on me then: I was injured in exactly the same spot as the boy that I had witnessed passing away moments before. With that dreadful memory, I succumbed to panic, and everything turned dark.

✦

The flickering of a candle woke me up. I remembered why I had blacked out and checked my injury straight away. It was carefully secured with a white cloth and to my relief, clear of blood.

"Don't touch it. It's clean and sewn," said Wolf.

"Where am I?" I asked in a daze.

"Still at my house," he replied and pushed a goblet to my lips. "Drink up, it will make you forget about the pain."

I obeyed and drank the bitter medicine, although I couldn't feel the wound anymore, at least not until I tried to sit up.

"The wound isn't deep, but you have lost a lot of blood, and you may feel weak and dizzy over the next few days."

"Where's Villon?" I asked, alarmed.

"Over there," Wolf nodded in the direction of the window. "Still feeling guilty and waiting for you to recover."

Only then did I notice Villon hunched by the wall with his head down. Wolf set the goblet down on the table and eased himself into the armchair opposite. The gloom around us distressed me.

"How long have I been out of it?" I asked.

"For some time," answered Villon. The dark tone in his voice surprised me. Never before had I seen him so dismal. It discouraged me from feeling grateful to be alive. Wolf poured me a better medicine then and encouraged me to have a taste. "Don't be like your friend and refuse such a quality wine."

We both looked in Villon's direction, but he wouldn't budge so Wolf continued speaking. "I keep telling him that although it may have been your fault that you were attacked today, it's not your fault that they died. How can you be blamed for that? From what I know, your only crime was a set of innocent practical jokes!"

"How come you know so much about us?" I asked.

"Have you never noticed me at my tavern?"

"You mean Margot's?"

Wolf laughed. "Since when do women own such establishments?"

"Well, Margot seems like she could handle it," I answered with honest admiration.

"True," he agreed. "I'm just the owner and protector. She keeps the place in order. That's why I call it Margot's Inn."

"Are you her husband?"

He shook his head resolutely. "I'm not the marrying type. Margot is my sister-in-law. After my brother passed away, I let her do whatever she wanted with the place. She thought that turning it into a tavern with a brothel attached would be good revenge for the abuse and heartache that he caused her."

"Why do you live here if you own that house? Are you that rich?"

He smiled and shook his head. "A river bailiff doesn't earn much..."

"But a Coquillard does," Villon finished for him and finally turned to face us.

"How do you know?" asked Wolf, confused.

"The symbol on your tunic," explained Villon. "Margot told me about you Coquillards."

I followed my friend's gaze and noticed the embroidery. It depicted a cockleshell.

"Who are the Coquillards?" I enquired, anxious to know what they were talking about.

"A gang of criminals who are paid to steal, rape and kill," said Villon with a disgusted glare at Wolf who responded with a grin.

"Some gratitude!"

"I know your help comes at a price," fired back Villon.

Wolf laughed at his daring and admitted, "It's true that I have had my eye on your group for quite some time, mainly because I have always found your antics quite clever, at least up until today…"

Villon's frown deepened into a scowl, but Wolf paid it no mind and continued, "We are a very private group, though, so a man has to earn our trust before he can be a part of the brotherhood."

Villon looked at him in distrust, but I became alert.

"Crime seems to follow us every step these days," I mused. "Could destiny be showing us the right path?"

"Go ahead and take that road," said Villon bitterly. "I'm done with all this."

His judgmental tone worried me.

"Do you think I don't regret what happened out there?" I couldn't help but raise my voice.

Villon firmly shook his head. "I know you do, and I also know that you can do better than spend your time scheming revenge. We are students, not criminals."

"Not criminals?" I laughed despite my physical and emotional pain. "How can we not be criminals if everyone around us is! Look at our professors and the mysterious gifts they receive. Look at all those priests selling indulgences and whoring around. And look out there at what the so-called justice and law did to us!"

Villon turned away from me. He didn't like arguments, especially between friends.

"The sergeants who attacked you will pay," said Wolf. "I know both sides – law and crime – and there is no way that the provost ordered them to do this. The law is not as powerful as you may think. It's the Church that should not be messed with."

He looked at me in all seriousness then. "Villon is right, there is a fine line between justice and revenge, but you are right as well, Montigny, there is corruption in all the institutions we are supposed to look up to, so one has to learn how to play along."

"Don't listen to him, he's just trying to recruit new members," warned Villon.

Wolf just laughed at him, though. "I don't need to recruit anybody. There are countless men out there who want to be a part of our gang. Like I said, I took a liking to your group, but the decision is up to you. What I did for you today comes with no strings attached. I am a man of my word, no matter how corrupt I may seem."

Villon looked at me as if wondering what I made of it all. I was too weary to think, though, and was certain about only one thing at that moment: whatever I ended up becoming I would never be on the side of the law again.

✦

For the three days that followed, our classmates' blood was slowly washed away, and when the rain stopped, we visited the Notre-Dame Bridge to pay our respects to them. We lit candles and lanterns, said prayers and promised to keep their memory alive. Passing strangers joined us, others just stood aside, watching the sad scene from a respectable distance. I recognised a few of the faces from the bridge among them. They obviously regretted not helping us while they had the chance. I made peace with them in my heart, though, as I ended up being one of them in the end. I realised they were afraid to risk their lives and those of their family members for some students they didn't even know. No one felt guiltier than me about what had happened. I was the one who needed to apologise to the victims, and so I did in my mind, pleading them to forgive me for my reckless actions.

Later on, our group of four – Villon, Cayaux, Tabary and I – proceeded to Margot's, ready to honour our deceased classmates with a few drinks. At one point, Villon stood up to share a new poem with us. Quite understandably, it was more solemn than usual which surprised the tavern regulars, but not those of us who had witnessed what he had. When Villon announced that he was going to read a poem, the band stopped playing, and the whole pub fell silent as he started to recite:

I know milk with drowning flies
I know how people dress and why
I know rainy days and sunshine
I know the tree by the apple
And its sap for that matter
I know the idleness that never changes
I know hard workers and the lazy
I know everything but myself.

I know even that which I would rather not
I know the ashen and the red-cheeked
I know death, which devours everything
I know everything but myself.

Even though everyone cheered and raised their goblets, the poem upset us all, especially those of us who knew what was going on in Villon's mind: the guilt and subsequent feeling of loss, the sense of losing one's safety and trust. It showed a confused spirit, idly hoping for guidance in a time of grief.

I caught a look of empathy on Isabeau's face. I bowed to her from afar and smiled at her before Margot blocked my view. With her hands on her hips she said, "You are too young to be so downhearted, boys! You should celebrate your friends, not mourn them. That's what we do around here and it's certainly what they would prefer. The first round is on me!"

She then gave Villon a cordial pat on the back and gestured at the band to start playing again. We listened to Margot and drank to the fullest, drowning sorrows and swimming through the sea of emotions.

"Wolf is here," noted Villon when Cayaux and Tabary took themselves off upstairs with a couple of girls. I turned and saw him sitting alone in the corner of the room. I waved at him and was about to greet him, but Villon stopped me.

"We thanked him already," he said with a worried expression.

"That doesn't mean we shouldn't become more acquainted," I reasoned with him. "He could become a powerful ally to us one day."

"Ally?" he mocked, shaking his head at my foolishness.

"Just think about it, Villon," I started, with that same old persuasiveness of mine. "Our classmates died at the hands of the law, the part of our society that is supposed to look after us. Their deaths showed us what we should fight for and against."

"See, that's where we differ, Montigny. What it showed me is how fragile life is and that I should therefore enjoy it while I can."

"You can't enjoy life if you are penniless, and once we leave the Sorbonne, we will be on our own, unprotected and in need of direction. So far, everything is pointing to the fact that we are either going to become clerics or criminals and we both have more experience with crime than celibacy. Wolf is an outlaw working for the law – isn't that a brilliant combination?"

"We have more choices than that, Montigny," insisted Villon, ever the optimist.

"Very well, if you can come up with a more suitable plan, let me know. Until then, I will explore my own options…"

While we discussed our differing opinions on the matter, Wolf took the first step and approached us.

"Montigny! Villon! Good to have you in my lair again."

I greeted Wolf with a polite bow and a smile, but Villon just nodded a greeting.

"Don't worry, I'm not here to recruit you," said Wolf with an amiable smile and added, "I just thought that you might like to join our celebration at Montfaucon tonight."

"Montfaucon? Tonight?" repeated Villon, confused. "Does your gang conduct business so late?"

I also wondered who would want to visit the largest and most terrifying gallows in Paris at night. Wolf laughed at Villon's comment and explained. "It's a custom. We honour and celebrate our brothers at the location of their passing. One of the Coquillards drew his last breath at Montfaucon today, so we will make him a proper farewell there. I thought we could celebrate your friends too, because even though they didn't die at the gibbet, they were killed by the same institution."

The idea of dancing and drinking under the swaying corpses was delightfully morbid. I had never heard of such a tradition before, probably because I was not used to the company of gangsters.

"We take girls with us too. It wouldn't be the same without them," he nodded towards his friends. About ten men were already waiting by the door with a few of Margot's girls including Isabeau. I was surprised by how attracted to trouble she was. It seemed that we had more in common than just our tragic childhoods.

"What do you say, gentlemen, are you interested?"

I couldn't refuse the invitation, mainly because I was worried about Isabeau's safety.

"It would be my pleasure to join you and your friends," I said with a respectful nod and began to polish my red boots. Villon still had his doubts, but I could tell he was as curious as I.

"I suppose I could come along," he said after a moment's hesitation. "Though Montfaucon sounds like an awful place for a celebration."

Wolf challenged him with one raised eyebrow. "Indeed, that's why you should prepare yourself for a wild night!"

✦

On our way to the Gibbet of Montfaucon, we had to pass through the foulest part of the city – the Holy Innocents' Cemetery. For three hundred years, thousands of deceased had found their final resting place there in the arms of their predecessors, without the luxury of having a sepulchre of their own. The roofs of the surrounding houses were clustered with bones and skulls, the oldest remains that had become decoration in order to free up space for the newcomers. That was not the main cause of the awful smell, though. The unbearable odour came from the mass graves from which rotting flesh was protruding. It would be impractical to keep burying bodies beneath the soil if they were constantly filled with more, so our senses had to become accustomed to it.

As we passed the charnel house, we found ourselves mesmerised by a mural of the Dance of the Dead. It was lit by lanterns even at night to constantly remind us of our inevitable destiny. Villon and I shared a fascination with the cheery skeletons joining the living in the exuberant street parade. The colourful images haunted us, yet we admired the portrayal of death as a celebration rather than a tragedy. Villon thought that it was meant to encourage us to embrace the afterlife as something splendid, but unlike him, I didn't like to philosophise about life after death. I had enough on my mind already.

After we had passed the stinking spectacle and we could all breathe again, Isabeau distanced herself from the Coquillards and fell into step with us.

"I'm sorry for your friends," she said. "I will light a candle for them tonight."

Villon just smiled at her and walked on, giving us space to talk.

I was ready to enquire about Isabeau's availability, but was feeling nervous about it as my feelings for her had deepened. I respected her and viewed her differently to the other girls I had been with. Instead, I simply offered her my overcoat because she was shivering. She thanked me and gave me one of those endearing smiles of hers.

"You seem to attract bad company," I noted, nodding towards the gang members ahead of us.

"I suppose," she said, "but I trust Wolf. He takes good care of Margot and us."

We exchanged a few casual thoughts about her experience with Wolf and his double life as a criminal and river bailiff, until I finally gathered up the courage to say, "I was hoping that tonight…" As soon as she met my eyes, the words trailed off, yet I braced myself and continued, "Well, I thought that tonight you might join me and Estienne de Montigny II at our humble lodging…"

She raised her eyebrow, amused by the suggestion, and I realised how it must have sounded, so I quickly clarified, "I meant join *me*, of course, Estienne de Montigny II would only admire you from afar. He's used to it."

I sounded like Cayaux, and the worst of it was that I couldn't help it. Isabeau touched my arm, her expression comforting yet distant. "I don't think it's a good idea, Regnier."

It was the first time she had called me by my first name, and I realised it either meant something very good or quite the opposite.

"I would like to," she added quickly, seeing the sad look in my eyes, "but I have this feeling about you…" Her words trailed off and I couldn't read her expression.

"A bad feeling," I guessed, already disappointed.

"No, not at all," she protested. "I consider you my friend now, Regnier de Montigny, and that is more important to me than earning a few sous. I don't want to compromise the lovely connection we have."

I looked at her with longing, my loins on fire and my mind in a daze. "I understand," I lied.

She happily kissed me on my cheek and said, "I'm glad. I've never had a friend like you and I can't wait to see what happens next."

At first, I felt like an utter failure, but the more I thought about her suggestion, the more appealing it seemed, for it promised more than a shag on a street corner. I only hoped she didn't want to be just friends because she had her eye on Villon.

Once we had passed through the gate of Saint Denise, we turned right and passed through the quiet Parisian suburbs until we reached the foot of the hill where the dreadful gallows loomed and a real-life Dance of the Dead lay before us. We saw a group of men and women who had already been boisterously celebrating beneath the giant structure from which the bodies of criminals were hung. The gibbet had three levels and forty-five windows, if you could call them that. It was these windows that offered the trembling victims their final view, the windows that nobody wished to look out of.

Wolf and his company joined up with the other Coquillards. Most of them were already intoxicated, and they had all begun to sing in honour of their friends who swayed along with the other corpses. Isabeau and I snuggled up closer to one another, both feeling insecure about the strange gathering. However, as I expected, one of the Coquillards eventually asked her to dance. I let her go, as I always had done, because I knew she would be back.

While our hosts drank, sang and danced to the sounds of drums and flutes, I stood to the side with my chest proudly lifted in honour of the hanged men above us. Some were half-decomposed, others still looked like us, and while most of their faces depicted horror and their final struggle for survival, there were also those who remained bravely serene. The terrifying sight appalled yet drew me in. I could not help but wonder how my body would look up there, whether I would break down during my last moments or keep my cool like a true nobleman. Some invisible power seemed to seize my throat at the thought, perhaps Lady Death herself coming to warn me. A cold shiver ran down my spine, making me shudder. I felt so alone suddenly, alone with my own mind, which felt just as filthy as my surroundings. A soft whine brought me back from my dark contemplation, and I turned to my eternally loyal four-legged friend. I patted him, knowing that no matter how I lived or died, he would always be by my side.

I jumped a little when someone's hand landed on my shoulder and turned around in fright. Upon seeing her angelic face, all gloom faded away. Isabeau gently pulled me closer to the odd company, inviting me to join the deathly dance. Just as the whirl of colours sucked me in, I caught Villon's eye in the distance. I could tell he was experiencing the same premonition, because the new world we were becoming a part of that night whispered *heaven* but screamed *hell*.

PART TWO:

KATHERINE

Item: To the woman I loved
Who used to chase after me
Then depleted me of all pleasure
And replaced it with misery
I leave my heart as a treasure
It's pale, pitiful, weary and finished
But despite all of the hardship
I pray that God pardons her sins.

The Testament (1461-1462, François Villon)

CHAPTER 5

THE SHADOWS OF CORPUS CHRISTI

Paris, May 1455

I was too young to realise why I was so captivated by him when we first met. It happened one sunny afternoon. My nanny and I were playing with a ball outside our house when I noticed Cousin Regnier with some friends in the distance. I was about ten years old then so they must have been fourteen or so. I was used to meeting boys, but had never shown much interest in their company until I saw François. I became trapped in the unique, magical web of his personality and I couldn't look away. I realised that his friends looked up to him as well, as they all grouped around him whenever he spoke. He was like a star on an empty canvas of deep blue.

I remember that I wanted to win his attention somehow, make him remember me, so I did the first and silliest thing that came to my mind: I threw my ball straight at him. It bounced off his right arm, and he managed to catch it before it fell. He then turned around and noticed me. I smiled at him, trying to hide my intention behind the polite, "Excuse me, I'm so clumsy."

He grinned back, probably reading me as well as his schoolbooks, and strode towards me with his eyes confidently fixed on mine. It made me blush, yet I held his gaze.

"You are not clumsy, little lady. I'd say you strike quite well."

My cheeks reddened even more as I extended my hand out for my toy, but he held on to the ball.

"Shouldn't you apologise first?" he said with a challenging smile.

My nanny quickly stepped in and said, "Give it back to her, you rude boy!"

Villon didn't even bother looking at her and kept staring at me. Although I was focused entirely on his beaming face, I sensed his friends in the background, curiously watching us.

"I think the lady should apologise to me first," he insisted once more. Our eyes were locked. Neither one of us was willing to back off. I frowned and smiled at the same time, unable to decide whether I truly liked him or not.

"As you please," he said with a shrug, then still holding on to the ball, he strode away. My nanny hurried after him, yelling, "Come back, you rascal!"

But he was faster and soon enough, he and his friends had disappeared from sight while my nanny looked around for help. "Sergeants! Sergeants! That lowlife stole our ball!"

I found the scene rather amusing. I knew that despite his inappropriate behaviour there was something unique about him, something I had never encountered before. I wasn't able to put it into words until my twentieth birthday celebration when my father asked him about his career intentions, having graduated three years previously.

"I suppose I'll keep writing my poetry," replied François. "That's the only thing I'm good at."

My father argued with him. "But will that be enough to make a living?"

François shrugged and said, "Royalty employs poets at their courts, and I'm hoping to be noticed by someone soon enough."

"You already were, remember?" noted Regnier and proudly told the rest of us, "His Majesty

Charles VII was very impressed with Villon during his visit to the Sorbonne."

"The King himself?" my father exclaimed in disbelief.

"Indeed," continued Regnier. "Villon was asked to construct a poem for His Majesty, and he performed exceptionally well, as always."

"That's quite an honour," marvelled my father. "And what was the poem about?"

"Saint Katherine," said François with a look at me. I narrowed my eyes, expecting a joke.

"It has nothing to do with you, Mademoiselle Katherine," he assured me, "you are many things, but I honestly hope not a saint…"

As opposed to me, my father did not find the comment funny, so François cleared his throat and continued, "It was an ode to Saint Katherine, the patroness of the Sorbonne."

"It was not just the poem that charmed the King, though," remarked Regnier. "He was quite taken with François himself and referred to him as *a man who would be remembered*."

The King's description of him made me realise what attracted most people including myself to François. He was a man with a vocation and a zest to walk his path no matter what. He was destined to become great and that characteristic had been written in his face since he was just a boy. Nevertheless, he was also a man who tormented my heart. Although we had always been friendly with each other and I felt that he enjoyed my company, he never showed any deeper interest in me. He was also the only man who never commented on my charms. I had never cared much for flattery especially from those who were trying to get something out of it, but I just wanted him to like me, at least a little bit.

I certainly knew that according to most I was just an ordinary girl who came from a wealthy family and wished for nothing more than a prosperous marriage and a boring, bourgeois life. Only François spoke to me as his equal, as a friend he could tease and tell his secrets to. Yet I wished he saw me as more than that. I wanted him to see me for everything I was and wished to be. I needed to make his soul burn for mine, because even though I knew that the flame would become uncontrollable, extinguishing it would be the biggest mistake of my life.

However, during that particular birthday party, François was not as friendly as usual, and so while my eyes hungrily sought out his, he focused on anybody and anything else but me. Regnier noticed me gazing in their direction, and awkwardly nodded to me. I could tell he sympathised with me, as I heard that he also loved a mysterious girl from afar.

As opposed to François, Noël Jolis was all smiles and sweetness. I suffered him by my side as he tried to impress me with his latest wares, including a modern set of perfumes. He was a good match, there was no doubt about that, but I didn't want to settle down with someone who made life seem ordinary and dull. I politely nodded and occasionally smiled just to please him, though my mind was occupied by trying to guess what François and Regnier were talking about. They kept to themselves and were very secretive, as if scheming some rebellion.

Noël must have noticed that the two young men interested me more than he did, but he was not the type to give up easily. On the contrary, he tried to distract me from them in any way he could, and since his salesman's patter hadn't worked, he started to compliment me on my attire, hairstyle and all manner of things. If he only knew that instead of the sleek style I was forced into, I would happily wear a loose tunic and have my raven black hair as unruly as nature intended.

Our housemaid, Denise, called me an unexpressed rebel, and described me as a busy-eyed, trapped cat who constantly schemed her escape into the wild. She was way out of line, of course, but I liked that about her. She came into our household when I was twelve years old and became my loyal confidante and friend. In a way, Denise replaced my dear nanny who had taken care of me since I can remember. My mother passed away while giving birth, and my father never re-married. He was loyal to her in his heart and mind, and focused solely on business. Although I knew he loved me greatly, he often left me in Denise's care and under the protection of our servant Sebastian. I didn't mind, as long as he returned from his trips safely.

But back to Noël. He didn't see the true me and didn't even try to. He focused on some deluded vision of me as a jewel that he could adorn his empty house with, a woman who would stand by his side, bear his children and listen to his endless prattle. Although François didn't offer anything, we shared the same passion for life, but unlike me, he dared to express it.

Having lost myself in his face once again, I didn't even realise that Noël had become quiet, and was looking in François' direction with a deep frown. Our silent stares made François turn to us in bafflement. "Wherefore do I have your attention, if you don't mind me asking, Mademoiselle Katherine, Noël?"

Noël took it as a chance to be as offensive and bitter as always when he talked to him, and so he replied, "We were just trying to guess at your prospects, Monsieur Villon."

I flashed Noël an irritated look, as I wasn't even aware of ever having discussed François with him.

"Really?" he asked merrily. "And what conclusion did you come to?"

Noël answered for us both. "That no matter what you do, it will be hard without the Church cossetting you."

François laughed, but I could tell he was stung by the sharp comment. "As you may have noticed after the clash with the sergeants four years ago, Monsieur Jolis, the Church does not always come to our rescue."

Everyone fell silent then, sensing that an argument was in the air. Only the priest, Philippe Sermoise, dared to speak, joining Noël in the word battle against their common enemy. "That's because we have more important things to focus on than some stupid student pranks."

"Indeed, Father Sermoise," agreed Villon with a smile. "Parisian brothels are in far greater need of your attention."

A few women gasped in shock, and Father Sermoise reddened with shame and fury. Whispers soon filled the room and my father tried to appease them.

"Gentlemen please, let's not make this lovely gathering uncomfortable."

Noël nodded obediently to my father and said, "Of course, this day belongs to your mesmerising daughter."

He then lifted his goblet to pay his respects to my father and then also to François and Father Sermoise. "Let's drink to her grace, shall we?"

I blushed, feeling utterly humiliated in front of François, but he just kept glaring at Father Sermoise. I thought of an eloquent way to change the subject, and since I was used to encouraging François to share his writing with us, I thought of doing just that.

"Perhaps you could amuse us with some new verses, Monsieur Villon?"

"Of course, Mademoiselle Katherine," he nodded gladly, "but if you don't mind, this poem may be a bit crude."

"Aren't all your poems so?" I replied with feigned innocence, which made him smile. Had I known what his poem was about to stir in me, I would have never suggested it, but my mind was as naïve as my heart back then, so I just nodded and waited for him to start:

In the name of the eternal Father,
And the Virgin-born son,
God the creator or rather
The One, the Holy Ghost
Who saved those that Adam lost
And whose Heaven welcomes even frauds
Few merit from the dreadful cost
But trust that once we die we rise as little gods.

For dead were we in our earthly names
Damned in perdition;
Body rots away, but spirit remains

Under any condition;
But I propose an exception:
Regarding the patriarchs and the prophets
Because, according to my conception,
These never really bust their arses.

We were all stunned by the poem, but the biggest impact was on Father Sermoise: the verses were a clear provocation. The hateful flare in the priest's eyes alarmed me. Heresy was the biggest crime, such that it was regarded even more seriously than murder. We all knew that François enjoyed teasing his superiors, but this time he had gone too far. I turned to my father for help, hoping he would come to the rescue like he always had, however, before he managed to say anything, Father Sermoise exploded.

"How dare you! You ungrateful villain! God provided you with such a fine nest at a priest's home, gave you the honour of becoming a part of his holy university and Church, and how do you repay him? By mocking it?"

Never had I seen a man become as upset as the priest that afternoon. He scared us all, except for François.

"In all due respect, Father Sermoise," he replied calmly, "I was presenting my ode to God in the way I perceive his glory. Don't you too believe that God is present equally in all souls?"

"Though shalt not take the name of the Lord in vain, you heretic!" shrieked Father Sermoise upon which Villon respectfully touched his chest and replied, "And thou shalt not bear false witness against your neighbour, Father Sermoise."

The priest stared furiously at François, and after a moment of tense silence, he hissed through his teeth, "Sinners shouldn't quote the holy book."

François fired back without hesitation. "Then why do you quote it every Sunday?"

At those words, the atmosphere became even tenser. Only Cousin Regnier couldn't choke back a chuckle. Father Sermoise turned to him in utter disbelief.

"You think your friend is funny, Montigny? I bet he will be even funnier with his tongue hanging out at the gallows! I wonder which one of you thugs will end up there first."

Cousin Regnier just shook his head and smiled at the priest. "Why can't you ever laugh at yourself, Sermoise?"

By leaving out the polite "Father" he had topped François' insult, which made our guests even more uncomfortable and, for us who cared for him, scared for what would ensue.

"I have no humour, you say?" repeated Father Sermoise, his whole body shaking. "Let's see how much humour you have for yourself! Maybe we should all laugh at your ancient, torn clothing and the ridiculous pretence that you are a nobleman despite coming from a family of impoverished servants of the King."

Father Sermoise was in pure rage and clearly out of order that time. His fury towards François had turned on Regnier instead. Regnier took a long look around the room. He knew that Father Sermoise was only saying something that we were all thinking. No matter how much I enjoyed my cousin's company, he undoubtedly was a typical example of a bankrupt aristocrat who desperately clung to the idea of keeping up his social status.

Even though his father was more than just a servant, and everybody including Father Sermoise knew that, his name had lost its lustre after he followed His Majesty into exile. He ended up losing his inheritance and subsequently all of his savings, but to Cousin Regnier, he was still a hero. Therefore, he rose from his chair, his tall figure towering over the priest, and to prove that he was nobler than us, he placed his foot with his father's red shoe on the table and polished it with a lace napkin. Then he gracefully threw the napkin back on the dining table, bowed to my father, then to me, and strode out of the room and out of our lives. It was the last time he visited our house.

François, being a loyal friend, joined him. He bid a polite farewell to us, which gave me hope that, unlike Regnier, we would be seeing him at our house in the future. I could not bear it if he distanced himself. François was the torch I followed through the twists and turns of my mind. He inspired me and gave me hope that there was such a thing as freedom.

✦

A few days after the scandalous dispute between François and Father Sermoise, my father left Paris on one of his trade missions. This gave me more space and time for my favourite activities, like strolling through the streets for as long as I liked, even after dusk. Thank goodness that our guard Sebastian was so easily bribed, because that particular Corpus Christi day was especially warm and it emboldened me to stay out long past bedtime. Of course, I had Denise by my side, who was not only a housemaid but also a loyal friend who would never miss the chance of a little adventure.

As usual, I wanted to linger in the area of the Saint Benoit cloister, especially near the house at Porte Rouge, François' home. I always hoped to bump into him, and although he was usually busy somewhere else, that day I was lucky. We spotted him sitting on a bench close to the church, chatting with his friends, Cousin Regnier, a young priest and a young lady, if you could call her that, because as Denise pointed out, she was suspiciously underdressed. François' face beamed as usual, and he was probably sharing something exciting with the group, because the three faces were focused entirely on him.

"Let's go and greet the boys," I decided, pulling Denise along with me, but she stopped at the corner, hiding in the street's dark shadow.

"I'm not sure if that's such a good idea, Katherine," she argued. "What would people think if you were seen with someone as vulgar as that girl?"

"Nobody's here," I replied, but as soon as I said it, I spotted a few faces in the windows opposite to us. I hesitated, and before I could make up my mind, noticed that Cousin Regnier was getting up to leave. He patted François on the back and then turned to the girl, discussing something with her. I didn't hear them well and only understood that he wanted her to join him. She shook her head, though, and planted a farewell kiss on his cheek. I had never seen such a gentle expression on his face before and recognised straight away that she was the one he longed for. I felt relieved at the realisation, because at first I thought she was with François.

After Cousin Regnier had left, I stepped forward and was about to greet François despite Denise's disproval. However, my path was soon crossed by a fast-approaching figure: Father Sermoise. He passed by without heeding us, completely focused on François and his friends. His eyes had the same hateful glare as that time at our house. The menace that shrouded him made me shudder. I sensed another quarrel between them, so I retreated and joined Denise around the corner, not wanting to meet François in such a tense atmosphere. I watched as Father Sermoise reached the bench where François sat with the girl by his side. The young priest who stood above them noticed Father Sermoise and nudged François who finally turned to him as well.

"Ah, Sermoise, our holy friend! Come and join us!" He greeted him with a careless smile, which was probably helped by the wine he had been drinking with his friends. "Let's celebrate this sacred evening together!"

Father Sermoise at first responded with a tense silence, then he turned his attention to the girl beside François, and solemnly pronounced, "I thought I was wrong about you and this lowlife, my love…"

I noticed worry in the girl's face who obviously had some private argument with Father Sermoise.

"Have you been drinking?" she asked him.

The priest shook his head, "I have been too busy looking for you, and I have found you at last! Now I denounce God!"

Without warning, Father Sermoise drew out a dagger from underneath his cassock, and was about to attack the girl, but François jumped in to protect her. I gasped in shock, scared to death that he would hurt him. Denise instantly pushed me to the wall to protect me, holding me tight in her embrace, worried that I might do something reckless. I struggled in her tight grasp, watching the scene from around the corner. I saw blood on François' face. I couldn't detect what had happened only that he was bleeding heavily from his nose and lips. Father Sermoise froze at first, but then he roared, "Step aside, you human worm! She will be mine! If not in life, then in death!"

His hand shook as he pointed the dagger at the girl hiding behind François. My heart skipped a beat when François pushed her towards the young priest with the words, "Take her away, Gilles. Quick!"

Just then, Father Sermoise tried to strike him again. François managed to swiftly dodge him while Gilles grabbed the girl's hand and dragged her away. She didn't protest yet kept turning back in alarm. Father Sermoise grinned at François and neared him in a slow, ominous way, like a beast approaching its prey.

"She will follow as soon as I'm done with you," he threatened.

"She is not with me," François reasoned with him. "She is not with anybody, you know that!"

The priest was not giving up, though, so François reached for his dagger as well.

"Let's not do something we will both regret, Father Sermoise. I apologise for all that I have done to you in the past, but you must know that I have never meant any real harm. That's what we do, huh? Tease each other… play these games…"

Blood streamed from his nose and lips and ran down his chin. My soul ached at the thought of Sermoise hurting him even more. I was about to call out to them, stop the fight somehow, but Denise quickly placed her hand over my mouth. That's when Sermoise made another abrupt movement and François panicked, plunging the dagger in his waist. Father Sermoise staggered for a moment then recovered right away. It was as if the sting of François' weapon had stoked the fire. He became even more aggressive and charged after him again.

Terrified by what he had done and scared to do more harm, François decided to run off in the same direction as his friends had a moment ago. Father Sermoise followed him, slower due to his injury, yet persistent as a hawk. When the priest lifted his dagger to strike again, François quickly picked up a rock and threw it at him, but the priest was fearless, driven by some dark, latent power, hungry for vengeance.

Even after they disappeared from sight, Denise kept holding me tight, comforting me. Time froze there in the lengthening shadows of that Corpus Christi day. The people who had peered from the windows before seemed to have vanished and a dreadful silence filled the air. It felt as if we had just watched some dramatic street performance that nobody else had attended. It was hard to come to terms with what had happened, because whether Father Sermoise killed François or François killed him, both options would result in a tragedy. Even if the priest survived, François would still be judged, and I didn't even want to think of the punishment he would receive for stabbing a man of God.

CHAPTER 6

THE SEARCH

After the terrible accident, François disappeared and Father Sermoise ended up at the Hotel Dieu hospital, fighting for his life. I prayed that he would survive, mainly for François' sake for he was a wanted criminal already. Each time I heard someone talk about the case, I couldn't help but remind them that François was only protecting a girl who had been viciously attacked by Father Sermoise. I also described the whole scene to the provost, Robert d'Estouteville, who was relieved to finally receive the confirmation he needed. He said that a certain young priest and a girl had witnessed the same, but had not been taken seriously by the authorities. He said that he would try to help

François, however, he also informed me that if Father Sermoise died, he would stand little chance of being pardoned. Not even the Benefit of Clergy would be useful in such a serious matter.

"So you did go to the provost after all?" asked Denise when I told her about it. She worried about me and didn't want us to be involved, but I didn't care. I only cared about François' safety.

"I wouldn't be able to live with myself had I not told him what really happened. It's more important than my reputation or Father's admonishment. I'm thinking of visiting Father Sermoise at the hospital today. I have to know if he injured François after we lost sight of them."

"Have you lost your mind?" she said, speaking as a friend, not a maid, which I was already used to. "That would only upset him, Katherine. Remember that if he survives, so will Villon."

She was right, yet I had to know if François was still alive. Therefore, I decided to attend Mass at Saint Benoit Church and visit Father Guillaume afterwards. He looked unusually dispirited, which was understandable given the circumstances. We all knew that François was like a son to him and he always stood by his side.

Even before I met François, Father Guillaume had been my favourite priest. There was a certain child-like quality to him despite his ripe old age, and his short, slender disposition fortified the impression. He was the epitome of a kind-hearted, wise old man who never hesitated to help someone in need. When I had explained why I had come, he smiled.

"It's good to know that François still has some good friends. You would be surprised how many people wish him eternal damnation now…"

"Well, I know that he acted in self-defence," I remarked, which made him look up to me in surprise. "I was there. I saw him protect that girl from Father Sermoise's blade."

Father Guillaume squeezed both my hands in his and said, "Regnier said the same. The girl is their mutual friend…"

Although it was not the right time to be jealous, her connection with François troubled me nevertheless, and Father Guillaume noticed, so I tried to hide my discomfort behind the most crucial question I had come to ask. "Do you have any news of him?"

The knowing expression in his eyes made me blush. He must have sensed that my feelings for François were deeper than friendship, but I couldn't care less at that moment.

"I know only what Regnier told us," said Father Guillaume, "which is that he was not injured too badly and is now in hiding. He didn't want to involve his mother and me in the crime, that's why he didn't come home after the accident. He went straight to Regnier. He has become a better confidant to him over the past few years… He understands what he has been through after the tragic street battle with the sergeants. I think he never fully recovered from it. His mother and I have always disapproved of the reckless lifestyle the two had become accustomed to after leaving the Sorbonne, but we try to respect it. François needs more freedom than anyone I know."

With these words, Father Guillaume looked me in the eye. I read the warning in his look; he wasn't the first and certainly not the last person to warn me about François Villon. It was as futile as ever, though.

Father Guillaume sighed and cupped his smoothly shaved chin in his hands as he began to mull over the situation.

"Thus far, I have never interfered. It has been enough for me to know that he's well and happy, but it has proven to be a mistake. I have been too lenient with him. His mother often reminds me of all the mistakes I made during his upbringing, but should a priest know how to raise a young man? They don't prepare us for such things…"

I could tell that during those difficult times he had needed more guidance than the people coming to him for confession. I wanted to help him somehow, make him feel better, and so I said, "From what I have seen, you raised him quite well."

He couldn't refrain from smiling. "Really?"

Upon seeing his bemused reaction, I had to smile back. We both knew that he wasn't the greatest example of an obedient son.

"Well, he is who he is, he is undoubtedly unique," I said.

"That's true," agreed Father Guillaume. "That is one of his qualities that I have never doubted: his uniqueness."

We parted with the promise that we would keep praying for François and keep our hopes up, yet I left the church with a heavy heart. A part of me sensed that things would never be the same from then on, and I feared that I would never see François in Paris again. I needed to know more, perhaps even try to see him.

Since my father was still out of town, I decided to visit the man who knew most about François' whereabouts – Cousin Regnier. I went to the monastery where our mutual cousins lived, having heard that Regnier had found shelter there after he graduated from the Sorbonne. They seemed bitter towards him and said that he was most likely to be found at a tavern called Margot's Inn.

"If you find him, please tell him to pay his debts," they asked me politely before I left.

The news about Cousin Regnier didn't surprise me. I had heard rumours about him owing money to people and wasting his time with society's lower classes. I knew well that I shouldn't pursue my plan to seek him out at the edge of the city, the forbidden area where all the dubious taverns and establishments were located, yet I did. I knew that Denise would be strictly against the idea, so I went there on my own.

The district made me feel uncomfortable despite my effort to blend in. I wore an old, shabby overcoat that I had found in Father's closet so as not to draw too much attention to myself but people stared at me, nonetheless. I was feeling insecure about seeing all the beggars, vagabonds and sparsely dressed women, so I avoided eye contact with them and hurried to find the famous Rue Bordelle.

Once there, I found myself overwhelmed by the colourfully painted signs and frescos. Never had I seen such vulgar, disturbing images, which I could only hope were an artistic exaggeration of the real act of physical love. The narrow space was crammed with even more prostitutes, and among them, I noticed the girl that Father Sermoise had attacked. I froze to the spot when she looked at me, but her kind, welcoming face surprised me. She seemed concerned, sensing that I needed help, though I assumed that in her eyes, it was a different kind of help.

"Hello, lovely," she addressed me with an amiable smile, "are you all right?"

A part of me hated her for causing François so much trouble, another part was jealous, and the biggest part was curious. François was protecting her, which implied that he liked her. The question remained: how much? I approached her and asked, "You are friends with François Villon, right?"

The girl narrowed her eyes, pondering something, but then started to walk away. I quickly caught up with her and tried to explain myself.

"Wait, I'm his friend too. I'm just trying to find out what happened to him after the accident."

"I don't know anything," she said, "and even if I did, I have no reason to trust you."

She was right to judge me. We were from entirely different worlds, and knew nothing of one another, yet I was willing to take my chances.

"Please, at least tell me whether he's safe," I pleaded with her. She reacted to my urgency and as did someone else.

"Katherine?"

The familiar voice made me turn around in relief. Cousin Regnier strode towards us, confused to see me in his favourite Parisian neighbourhood.

"Cousin Regnier," I exhaled in excitement and hurried to greet him. "I've been looking for you everywhere."

He looked around at our surroundings with a frown. "I should take you home."

"Not before you talk to me about François," I insisted.

He leaned closer to me and whispered, "Don't be stubborn, Katherine, I'll tell you everything I know on the way."

He then raised a warning brow and offered me his arm. Before I accepted it, I turned around to say goodbye to the mysterious girl but found she was already gone.

"That girl... She was there on that night..." I stammered softly, careful to not be overheard.

"How do you know that?"

"I was in a nearby street with Denise when Father Sermoise emerged out of nowhere. I witnessed everything from afar," I admitted.

Regnier shook his head in disbelief. "How strange. It seems that everybody but me was there... How I wish I hadn't left their side. Things would be very different now."

"Or you would both be in trouble."

"Maybe, but then *I* would be the hero who saved her."

He gave me a look that spoke for itself.

"Isn't she a..."

Regnier nodded, sparing me the shame of saying the word aloud.

"Sermoise wanted Isabeau only for himself. He has been jealous of Villon and I since she became our friend..." He paused, weighing his words, but finally decided to tell me the whole truth for he must have known that I wasn't as judgmental as my father.

"I have been trying to turn her into an honest woman for years, however, it seems that I don't stand a chance."

"Do you think François does?" I dreaded asking it, but I simply couldn't contain myself.

Regnier turned to me. "Are you jealous, Katherine?"

"Jealous of her?" I let out a false laugh. "Cousin Regnier, please!"

Regnier saw right through me as always and didn't shy away from stating the obvious. "I know you have an eye for Villon, Katherine. In fact, I think he is the only one unaware of your feelings for him."

The remark baffled me. How could he be blind to my endless, longing looks? Could he be as inexperienced as I was when it came to romance? Hardly. François was a known heart-throb.

"It doesn't really matter now, does it?" I sighed, my thoughts bringing me back to the present.

Regnier shook his head. "I have to say that I'm impressed with you, Katherine. You care about him no matter how low he sinks, huh?"

I gave him a frustrated look. "Did you think I was so superficial? Of course I care about him and about you."

Regnier touched his chest gratefully. "Then I'm honoured. It's good to know I have at least one family member on my side."

I squeezed his hand and said, "Of course, I'll always be on your side. I know you are a decent man, no matter what they say about you."

He gave me a wan smile and took a deep breath before he finally broke the tension. "I'm glad you take an interest in Villon. Unfortunately, I can't tell you where he is, as I made a promise to him not to tell anyone, but I can assure you that when I last saw him, he was alive and healthy. After the assault, he came to Margot's where the girls helped stitch up the wound. He has a deep, ugly scar between his nose and lip now."

"No other injury?" I jumped in impatiently. He smiled at me and shook his head.

"He escaped Sermoise before he managed to strike again."

"That's good," I said, elated to hear he was doing well for the time being. "So I suppose all there is left to do now is to pray for him."

"Or pull the right strings," remarked Regnier. "The more people who believe in his innocence the better. He wrote an official appeal to the King and I helped him deliver it. If the King still remembers him or at least the poem he composed for him years ago, he might be merciful..."

"It was smart to deliver it personally. I bet your father's connection to the King helps as well."

"I wasn't allowed to speak with him directly, but judging from the amicable behaviour of the guards, they knew who I was. What helped Villon the most, however, was that Sermoise finally admitted that he was the perpetrator and Villon his victim."

"He truly did that?"

Regnier nodded. "He even pleaded with the authorities not to prosecute Villon and claimed that he forgave him."

"Why would he have such a sudden change of heart?" I wondered, still feeling suspicious about the priest.

"I suppose we have Isabeau to thank for that. She visited Hotel Dieu and reasoned with him. She wanted to let Sermoise know that there was no romantic connection between her and Villon. She forgave him and implored him to forgive Villon in return. I suppose she also felt sorry for him, despite the fact that he tried to kill her. I personally don't understand why, but I suppose one's heart softens when the enemy lies on his deathbed."

"Don't say that," I shook my head in distress. "Father Sermoise must live."

Regnier didn't appear very hopeful, though.

"He's in a very pitiful condition. Isabeau said that the hospital care seemed inadequate, but she sensed a whiff of death in the air and it confirmed her foreboding. You see, she's a palmist, and she saw a premature death in his lifeline when they first met..."

I narrowed my eyes, struggling not to give in to despair. I couldn't stand the thought of François ending up on the gallows and neither could I make peace with the possibility of him escaping to some distant land. Never seeing him again seemed unbearable.

"Don't worry, Katherine," said Regnier, sensing my fear. "There is still hope for him."

I nodded and tried to quiet my worries. Instead, I thought of our King, Charles VII. He must have remembered François, his unique charm and his clever poetry. However, I also couldn't help but think of the person he used to be fond of and failed in the end: Jean d'Arc. I heard that when she faced her final trial, a local bishop beseeched the King to save her from the enemy's hands, but he ignored the plea and let her burn at the stake. If he didn't help his faithful ally, why would he help some random Parisian student whom he had only met once? Nevertheless, I kept repeating Regnier's words in my mind, *There is still hope for him,* and from then on, I prayed that the King would show François Villon mercy.

Chapter 7

My Love, the Murderer

Paris, October 1456

Cousin Regnier promised to let me know of any developments regarding François, however, many months passed and there was no word from him. Each time I went to Saint Benoit for confession, I asked Father Guillaume about him, but all I took home with me was the confirmation that the father was suffering more than I was. Nobody knew anything about Villon's possible amnesty either. The only news was that Philippe Sermoise had passed away, as Isabeau predicted. I began to lose hope of ever seeing François again, and supposed that he had journeyed into some distant lands. I wished I could show my palm to Isabeau myself, let her read my destiny, but was timid about mingling with Regnier's friends. We were simply too different.

One sunny afternoon, however, fortune smiled upon me. I was at the port market buying fresh goods with Denise when I noticed a familiar figure out of the corner of my eye. It took me some time to grasp that it was truly François. He was wearing a brown, tattered coat and looked more dishevelled than usual. His curls reached his shoulders, his face was partly mutilated, but his eyes had that same old spark that had the power to light up my spirit. Without hesitating, I followed the glow, and left Denise's side to greet him.

When François noticed me, he stopped, curiously waiting for me to approach his side. I could see he was surprised, and although I couldn't detect whether this was in a nice way or not, I didn't really care. It was enough to know he was alive and back in Paris.

As I came face to face with the big scar on his upper lip, the indelible mark of Sermoise's blade, it dawned on me that he was scarred for life, not only on his skin, mainly in his soul. I tried to imagine what he had been through. Not only was he trying to protect his life, he also had to deal with his conscience. I realised that all the while I was praying for his safety, I had forgotten to pray for his soul. After all, he was not just fighting for mercy, but mainly for forgiveness. How much an unfortunate deed like that must change a man, I thought to myself, even such a strong and lively one as François. Still, to me, he was a hero who had risked his own life to protect a friend so I wouldn't ever consider judging him.

"Good day to you, Katherine," he said, hiding his misery behind a polite smile. He was about to say more, but paused when he noticed that my eyes had welled up with tears.

"What's wrong? Do I look so pitiable?"

I smiled through my tears, glad to catch a glimpse of the old François shining through the dispirited figure standing before me. I shook my head and said, "I'm just glad to see you alive and well…"

I was unable to hide my emotions behind a light-hearted comment like I used to. I surprised myself with my honesty just as much as him.

"Don't tell me you were worried about the fate of a *priest killer*?" he said, as though it was hard to believe.

"I know what really happened, François."

He turned away when I mentioned the accident. "Well, still," he said, his eyes vainly locating some safety point in the distance, "a man is dead by my doing. What does it matter who started the fight?"

"Whatever happened was not your fault. You must know that."

"It doesn't make it any better," he said with a wry smile, "but thank you for being so nice to me, Katherine."

He sighed and looked around. "I wish more people were as kind and understanding as you…"

I followed his gaze and only then noticed the disapproving faces and scowls all around us. Outraged swearing, curses, and slander carried on the air. A few people even spat on the ground at the sight of him. I shuddered, realising that in the eyes of the public he was just as he said – a priest killer. Then I spotted Denise standing nearby looking worried. "Perhaps we should go home now, Mademoiselle Katherine," she suggested.

I turned back to François who nodded in agreement. "That's most certainly a good idea," he agreed with a polite nod to Denise before he turned back to me. "It was nice to receive such a warm welcome from you, Katherine. I appreciate it from the bottom of my heart."

He bowed and was about to walk away. I almost let him go, but then something within made me call out. "Wait!"

I didn't care how many faces looked my way at that moment. All that mattered was that he was one of them. The astonishment in his eyes was worth the disrepute. I had his full attention and that gave me the courage to suggest, "Why don't you join us on our way home? We are heading in the same direction, aren't we?"

He wavered for a moment then put on that rebellious grin I adored and offered me his arm. I accepted it despite Denise's disapproving frown, and we left the gaping faces behind. I felt as free as I never had before as I fell into step with him, not minding Denise's sulking or the chorus of slanderous whispers following us. I was proud to walk with François no matter how he was perceived by the public. There was no shame in letting him know. After all, up until that day, I thought I would never have the chance to see him again and regretted that I had never let him know how I felt about him.

François remained quiet for some time, eyeing me with a curious smile. I enjoyed having him focus solely on me instead of his usual playful teasing or poetry.

"The King must have really taken a liking to you," I said after we had become accustomed to people staring at us.

François shrugged. "Perhaps, but it could have been just a coincidence. It's hard to believe I could make such an impression on him after just one meeting and remain imprinted on his memory for all those years. Then again, people tend to surprise me these days." He gave me a friendly wink and continued, "I suppose I underestimated our friendship, please forgive me for that. I always thought that I was just someone you liked to chat with, someone whose verses amused you, but someone who had no significant place in your heart. I thought you would turn your back on me now along with most others."

His words surprised me. Did I really seem so vain to him? Denise once told me that I came across as a cold queen to some, especially to my suitors, but François was never one of them.

"It pains me that you would think that," I admitted. "I have always thought of you fondly and enjoyed your company mainly because you are so different from everyone else I know."

He gave me a warm smile. "If that was ever a benefit, now it feels more like a curse."

I shook my head. "Don't worry, the situation will calm down. Most people will forget about you as soon as the next drama comes along and, as we both know, these sorts of tragedies are like daily bread in Paris."

"I hope you are right," he said, "mainly for your sake, Katherine. Being so friendly to an outcast like me is not the best reputation for you and your family."

Denise coughed behind us, agreeing with him. François smiled at that then turned to me. "And how have you been during the past few months? I bet men still stalk you like hungry wolves."

I waved my hand. "Once life has begun to mark me with the wrinkles of time, they'll soon stalk someone else."

"You want to wait so long to get married? That will drive your father mad!" he grinned.

"I don't care how long I wait, I won't give in to pressure."

"Speaking of pressure..."

François nodded towards our house where Noël Jolis stood like a silent guardian, waiting for me with a reproachful frown. I froze, dreading meeting him. He was the last person I wanted to see at that moment. Not that I disliked Noël completely. He was undoubtedly a good-looking, decent man whose family had always been fond of mine, although they could have been competitive instead. However, that day he was about to end the beautiful conversation I was having with François, and that was simply unacceptable.

"Although I hate to say it, he may be better company for you than me right now," said François.

He was about to bid me farewell, so I quickly asked, "Will we be seeing you at our house soon?"

François hesitated in his response. Finally, he just took my hands into his, kissed them, and gave me a grateful smile. "Thank you, Katherine. I will never forget your kindness."

With those ambiguous words, he set off in the direction of Porte Rouge. I sensed Noël's angry gaze on me, so instead I watched François leave. Judging by his fast pace, I assumed he felt lighter than before.

"How come he's not in prison?" asked Noël who had hurried over to join Denise and me. I rolled my eyes before I turned to face him with a polite smile.

"Because he's innocent."

"Villon is anything but innocent."

"Tell that to our King," I said, "he granted him mercy."

As I supposed, that information left Noël stunned. "He must have some powerful connections then."

"Why do you always see the worst in him?"

"I'm sorry, Mademoiselle Katherine, I know you are fond of the man, however, in my opinion, he had never proven to be anything but a big mouth who likes to associate with people of low class."

"Do these *people* include me and my father?" I asked with a hostile expression.

Noël stuttered. "No… of course not… I didn't mean it like that. What I meant was that he's just a vagabond and you are a lady. He could never make you happy."

"I find it quite curious that you should know what makes me happy, Monsieur Jolis. I don't mean to be rude, but the fact is that you don't know me very well at all. You are familiar only with the mask I wear, not the complex features beneath it. And something tells me you never will be."

I bowed to him and was about to leave, but he grasped my arm and spoke as if in fever. "I wish nothing more than to know and cherish those features, Mademoiselle Katherine, no matter how unattainable they are. Although I'm not a man of words like Villon, I'm reliable and love you deeply. I just want you to know that I will always be here for you, even if your virtue is tainted by someone like him."

No matter how earnestly he meant it, his words disgusted me. The fact that he assumed I wanted to or already had taken François for a lover was just too insolent. Without saying more, I twisted my arm from his grip and grabbed the basket Denise had been carrying. "You must excuse us now, Monsieur Jolis. We have to put this food to use."

"I understand," he said, and moved aside so that Denise and I could enter the house. As soon as we did, I shook off my fury and squeezed her hand.

"I'm so happy," I beamed. "Is it just me or does François look better than ever?"

"Yes, the scar is very becoming," remarked Denise darkly.

"I like him even better with it," I said with determination. "It's as if he has matured somehow… and he seemed so much more interested in me too…"

"That's because you are one of the few people who talk to him now."

"I don't care for your scepticism today, Denise," I said, overjoyed. "My prayers came true! Nothing else matters."

Denise sighed. "Well, let's see what your father thinks of his return."

"He will be just as impressed. The King believes in his innocence! Doesn't that speak for everything?"

However, a part of me realised I was just being a romantic fool. All I had focused on was François' inquisitive, tender eyes. I felt that he had begun to see me as a woman, not just some girl he knew once, and that filled me with excitement. I focused on the warmth that had spread across my heart, and began to consider whether my fondness for him had developed into real love. I could not tell, because I had never been in love before, all I knew was that he made me feel as light as a dandelion puff. I did not care if he was an offender, even a murderer, as in my eyes he was better than anyone else and if he asked me, I would be his, even if it meant going through hell and back.

CHAPTER 8

MIDNIGHT WALKS

Once I realised how deep my feelings for François were, I was especially cold to Noël, but he clearly hadn't picked up on this, as he invited himself over right after my father returned from one of his trade missions. If that wasn't enough, he also said mean things about François.

"People say that Regnier de Montigny became part of a gang after he left the university and Villon will probably follow in his footsteps soon. The two have always been up to no good." I flashed him a look of annoyance. He pretended not to notice, and continued, "When I think of how the two treated that poor priest, I realise it couldn't have resulted in anything else but tragedy."

Father was pensive, and at times it seemed as though he was not even listening to Noël, but then he said, "Yes, François Villon has disappointed me. As opposed to Regnier, I always thought he had a bright future ahead of him. I suppose you were right, Monsieur Jolis, the company we keep builds our characters."

I wasn't surprised to hear my father speak so harshly about Cousin Regnier because he never believed in him, he usually stood up for François, though. The thought that he would condemn him like the rest of society distressed me.

"You judge them both unfairly!" I protested. "You don't know about the hardships they have been through. I know their way of living is unimaginable to you, Monsieur Jolis, since your family has always supported you, but you shouldn't be so critical of something you don't understand. Just be glad that you have never found yourself in such despair."

"That's enough, Katherine."

Father gave me a firm look, which spoke for itself. I had gone too far and what I said might have come across as an offence. Our family reputation was of utmost importance to Father, so he didn't care what the King thought of François: public opinion mattered more. I could tell that he had more on his mind, but he waited until Noël left so as not to embarrass me.

Right after Noël exited, he started. "Katherine, you are not to be seen conversing with or meeting François Villon again. We don't want to make people think we are still friends with him."

"Are we not?" I gasped in disbelief. "How can you be so cruel, Father? He has been our friend since forever…"

"That was mainly because Father Guillaume brought him along a few times. Since he started coming over with Regnier instead, he has been a good source of entertainment, but too many unforgivable faux pas…"

I couldn't give him that awful promise, so I remained silent. That's when his voice turned gentler.

"Please try to understand my concerns," he reasoned with me. "Even though he has the King's protection now, people still talk and spread rumours. No matter how it happened, he will always be a priest killer in their eyes. You know very well that Parisian homes are the only source of our income. I'd rather lose the friendship of François Villon than all of our customers."

I didn't want him to see how upset I was, but he knew me too well, and there was no reason to hide what had been obvious for years.

"Katherine," he went on in a softer tone, "Although François may be charming, you know that he has always caused trouble. Just remember all the escapades back at the university. He may make you laugh now, but he would ultimately make you cry. Life with him would be a disaster for both of us. I think someone like Noël would make you much happier. Please try to give him a chance. He has proven to be so loyal over the years... I have never met a more patient man."

I looked away from him, unable to argue back. I knew he would not even try to understand. That's why I preferred to remain quiet and hope that he would change his mind with time. He would not dare to promise me to Noël without my consent, he loved me too much for that.

✦

The fact that my busy mind wouldn't let me fall asleep that night ended up being a blessing. Had I not been awake, I would not have heard the stones François threw at my window. I often imagined him climbing up to my chamber to rescue me, especially after one of my disputes with Father, but I became used to it being just a dream. Seeing him standing there waving at me to come down and join him filled me with unknown happiness.

I gestured at him to wait and turned back to my room in a panic. I worried that he would wake up Father or Sebastian and they would send him away, so I didn't even fix my hair and quickly ran out of my bedroom. I carefully descended the narrow staircase, aware of the dim surroundings. I assumed that everyone was sound asleep, so I took a deep breath and unlocked the door. I came face to face with François leaning against the doorframe with that irresistible smile that made all the girls blush.

"Katherine," he nodded in greeting, "I'm sorry to wake you."

"I wasn't sleeping," I whispered, and looked back inside with apprehension.

"Really?" he raised an eyebrow. "What is a chaste maiden like yourself doing up so late?"

I blushed, as telling him the truth would mean declaring my love for him, so instead I turned the question around. "What makes *you* disturb this chaste maiden at night?"

"I had a few drinks at a nearby tavern," he said, "and I couldn't stop thinking about how nice you were to me the other day..." His voice wavered with emotion and he checked my reaction before he continued speaking. If I weren't already, I was certainly blushing then. My heart bloomed at the thought of him expressing what I yearned for, but instead he said, "I came to say goodbye."

"Why?" I exhaled in angst. The thought of being without his company again seemed too cruel to be true.

"I thought about what you told me before: that I should wait until the dust has settled. Perhaps I should do it elsewhere, though. Returning to Paris right after my pardon has proved to be a mistake. I'm thinking of visiting my uncle in Angers…"

I shook my head in disagreement, quickly mulling over what to say to change his mind and suddenly I remembered something that Regnier told me once.

"I thought you were married to Paris. If she is the greatest love of your life, you can't leave her…"

He became nostalgic at the thought. "Oh yes, we used to say that, didn't we? It's just hard," he admitted after a pause. "Being confronted with so much hatred stirs up my guilty conscience… It's enough to deal with it in my mind, but having people remind me of it every day makes it unbearable. I have this restless feeling inside of me, a need to escape it all."

I nodded with empathy. "I understand. I too long for an escape sometimes…" My confession confused him, so I went on, "I know I have a wonderful, comfortable life, which I'm very grateful for, but that doesn't change the fact that I feel like a caged bird. No creature likes to be trapped. No matter how admired and pampered, life behind bars is not really life, is it?"

He agreed. "Not to mention it's so short. You deserve to live as you like, Katherine. If this house feels like a cage, you should allow yourself to break free from its walls."

I sighed. "I suppose I could, but life in the streets is not fitting for a woman like me. I wouldn't last a day out there."

He narrowed his eyes then extended his hand to me. "You would if you had a guide and a protector."

"What are you proposing?"

"An escape."

"Are you serious?"

"Don't worry. It's just for tonight. Unless you get a taste for it."

I felt my body shiver as his idea hit home. My reason knew well enough that accepting his offer would lead me down a dangerous path but my soul couldn't resist it. I had never been fond of taking the rational approach, so I accepted his hand. François happily squeezed it then looked me up and down.

"I think you'll need to wear some warmer clothing, though."

That's when I realised I was wearing just my nightgown. I gasped. The irresistible fever I felt in his presence had made me forget about the cold or how revealing the fabric was. I quickly covered my chest with my arms, hoping he hadn't seen anything, but judging by the grin on his face, the opposite was true.

"Wait here," I said in distress. François kept on smiling, and I could feel his gaze follow me as I ran up the stairs to my chamber.

In my haste, I grabbed some warm undergarments, a not very flattering winter dress and a velvet overcoat with a long, pointed hood. I checked myself in the mirror and decided to keep my hair loose this time. It suited a free spirit. I also didn't forget to pinch my pale cheeks to make myself look more alive. After all, it was almost midnight, and I was used to resting at that time. Then I hurried back down, hoping it was not just a dream and that he would still be there when I returned.

Because I was rushing, I managed to stumble and bang into a large chest in the hallway, making the old wooden floor creak. Denise, who slept in the chamber beside me, peeked out with tired eyes and asked, "Mademoiselle Katherine, are you all right?"

I became speechless and so did she when she spotted François waiting for me at the entrance. She frowned in confusion, but before she managed to say anything, I placed my finger over her lips and implored her, "Please lock the door behind me and wait for me. I'll be back soon."

My nervous face was pleading with hers as I joined François below the stairs. He nodded to Denise before he closed the door behind us and turned to me with an impressed smile. He offered me his hand and asked, "Where would you like to go, my lady?"

"Wherever. You are the guide tonight," I said, beaming like a little girl as he squeezed my hand in his.

The excitement in his face filled me with even more courage. I could tell that I had managed to surprise him once again and made him more interested in who I truly was. He led me through the streets at a fast pace and though at first I kept nervously turning back, checking to see if anyone had seen us, with a stronger grasp of his warm hand I let go of all worries. Instead, I gave in to the anticipation of what our midnight walk through Paris might bring.

✦

We carried on through the dim streets lit only by the full moon and the occasional torch. I still felt worried, but François' confidence put me at ease. Unlike the bird used to living in a cage, he was born free and I trusted that he knew what he was doing. He continually checked on me with a wink or a smile, filling me with gratitude and joy. He must have already known that I would follow him anywhere and never grow tired of his company. With every step we took, I began to feel more unfettered, and decided to enjoy it while it lasted.

The houses were quiet. People like me were already tucked up in their beds and people like him rested with their heads on tavern tables or the bosoms of beauties. There was only one person we met on our way, a very old, frail woman who was wandering the affluent neighbourhood, vainly begging for food. The poor thing was skin and bones, but appeared lively, nevertheless. The cordial way François greeted her made it clear that they were acquainted. He apologised for not having any food for her, however, he pressed a few coins into her palm, and encouraged her to go to Margot's before she froze to death. I remembered the name of the establishment, because I had been there to meet Regnier.

"They say freezing is the best way to go!" she called out chirpily, but then thanked him and planted a grateful kiss on his cheek before she set off with what seemed like a generous donation.

"Who was that?" I asked as she blew him another kiss.

"They call her the Crone Armouress, and she's the oldest prostitute in Paris. She got the nickname after the law tried to push the girls off the streets. They had to work in disguise as shopkeepers, so she pretended to be an armour seller."

I knew that François and Regnier were fond of the seedier establishments in the poorer districts, and I had never minded it before, but right then I couldn't help but feel jealous. It made me wonder how many girls he had been with and how many he still frequented.

"She's an admirable soul," he went on while I pondered his licentiousness, "and she was the most desirable beauty a few decades ago before she fell in love with a pimp who robbed her of everything including her heart. She never gave up on life, though, and still tries her best to live it to the fullest. I wrote a poem to her once…"

"Really? Do you remember how it went?" I asked as I knew he was used to memorising his poems. François thought about it and finally said, "Actually, I think I do remember that one…" He cleared his throat and began:

Oh how merciless aging can be
Changing a girl before she's ready.
What still keeps me here in this damn town?
Who'd care if this sack of bones tumbled down?

The crone has stolen my high hand:
Beauty, the only power I ever had
Over merchants, nobles, holy men
Back in the day, there was not a lad
Who wouldn't give me all he possessed
For a moment alone with me
Although he would later repent
As he knew that no whore is free.

I refused many of my suitors
Even if it made no sense whatsoever
For what? The love of a deceiver

An impoverished roué, a nonbeliever
And even if I went with others
I swear, I loved him dearly
Even if he liked to make me suffer
And cared only about money.
He could sweep the floor with me
Kick or beat me, I loved him still
Even when he tried to break me
If he asked for a kiss, he had his fill
I always forgave everything
To the bloody scamp who had cruel whims
Made me live like on a swing
And left me with nothing but shame and sin.

It has been thirty years since he perished
And I keep on crying for him, old and weary
Saving the memories that I cherished
Remembering who I used to be
But now when I see the new me
I curse time for being so nasty
For leaving me wretched and bony
I can't help it – it drives me crazy.

The poem made me forget all about my jealousy.
He coloured the story behind that loose woman so
well that it made me empathise with all of her kind.
What touched me most, however, was how well he
could describe the aching soul of an elderly woman
longing to turn back time. I liked all his poems, but

that one was a hundred times better than the ones I had heard before.

We passed through countless streets, archways, nooks, and crannies, and ended up by the riverside. It was cooler there, but François seemed to have a secret plan for us, so I followed him without complaint. We stopped by a tiny lane hemmed in by a wall of stone where Francois instructed:

"Wait here, I'll be right back."

I nodded and watched as he disappeared behind the wall. I felt a bit anxious to be left there by myself, but I soon overheard François' hushed voice so, curious, I followed it. Behind the wall, I saw him talking to a man. He was a strange character. He had a long, braided beard, bare head and curious eyes that eventually fell on me. I quickly hid behind the wall, worried that the man was some kind of criminal that François had to meet with that night.

Soon after, François returned and pointed at a small boat tied to the shore and said, "That one is ours."

"Does it belong to the man you just spoke to?"

"No, he's a river bailiff. I just wanted to make sure we were safe at his bailiwick tonight," he explained, then grabbed my hand again and pulled me towards the shore. I supposed it was not the first time he had borrowed a boat and wondered how many girls he had tried to seduce with a secret midnight boat trip. It reminded me of the moment when he had risked his life for one. François could tell I had something on my mind, and so before he helped me into the boat, he asked, "Are you afraid?"

I shook my head. "No… It's just that I've been meaning to ask you something. I keep trying to understand the reason behind… Well, I've been wondering why you protected that girl from Sermoise."

He smiled, probably guessing why I asked. I didn't mind, though. I was never any good at hiding the fact I was attracted to him. On the contrary, I had always challenged him to react to it, but with time, I learned to understand that I simply was not interesting enough for him.

"Isabeau is our friend," he said. "She has helped us out many times, especially during our student years. She's a very nice girl. I would do it for anybody, though, it was pure instinct."

The answer satisfied me. I stepped into the boat and sat down opposite him. He took hold of the oars then looked at me from beneath his brows. "And to answer the underlying question, it was not because I fancy her."

The sudden heat in my cheeks made me realise that I was blushing again. A familiar fever spread over my body, keeping me warm in the cold river breeze. François noticed and put on an amused smile as he began to row so I couldn't help but smile back.

Although I had never been on a boat before, I sensed it was most magical at night. As we floated away from the mundane world, we lost ourselves in the mysterious skies and their reflection below. The river of stars cradled us in an unforgettable moment, one that I would treasure in my heart from then on. The realisation made me feel equally as content as worried. The worry came mainly from the fact that I didn't know why he was suddenly so keen to spend time with me. Was Denise right? Was it because all the other girls were now avoiding him? I hoped it was not the case, yet I had to consider it.

As if reading my mind, François suddenly said, "I apologise if I was ever rude to you, Katherine. Like the time I brought you that poem as a birthday present, remember? I wish I had behaved differently back then. I should have written something about you instead of rambling on about the vanity of Parisian ladies. The truth is, I never realised how different you were..."

"In what sense am I different?" I asked, as no matter how much I admired his straightforwardness, it sometimes mystified me.

"I don't know how to describe it. I just feel it."

"It's hard to believe you would have trouble describing something or someone."

"Yet I do when it comes to describing you," he said. "You are not like any other woman I know."

His pensive eyes bore into mine and he held my gaze until it made me nervous. Even though I wanted him to say all those things and give me the attention, I was not used to it. That's why I looked away and changed the subject.

"Have you been working on any new poems lately?"

He sighed at the mention of his poetry. "No, unfortunately, I am not myself these days."

I noticed his face was tinged with the same gloom as it had been that time at the market.

"I hate to see that deep sadness in your eyes. It doesn't belong there."

"Maybe it does," he argued. "It would be strange if I remained the same after I had killed a man, don't you think?"

I shrugged and looked down, not knowing how to respond, but he didn't mind my obvious discomfiture and continued, "Regnier told me that you went to the outskirts of the city while I was gone, asking about me."

"Yes, my father and I were very worried for you."

"I doubt that your father was aware of your visit there," he challenged, prompting me to tell him the whole truth.

"You're right. I was worried that I would never see you again. You must know that I have always enjoyed your company."

I noticed his eyes sparkle. "I will be back," he assured me with a gentle smile, but that didn't satisfy me. I was desperate to make him stay in Paris, so I tried to change his mind again.

"What if you were needed here?"

"By whom?"

"By me," I said bravely, yet panicked as soon as he leaned towards me. The expression on his face spoke all the things I longed to hear, only I wasn't ready for it. I knew not why, because I had craved it for years. I must have been scared that I wouldn't live up to his expectations when it came to intimacy.

"Yes. I need a teacher," I explained with a shaky voice, making up the first thing that came into my head. "I need someone to teach me how to read."

He pulled away, laughing. "Really? You keep surprising me, Katherine! I had no idea you were interested in such things."

"Should I be flattered or offended?"

"Oh, be certain that I meant it as a compliment."

"Then you will help me, won't you?" I pressed, sensing that I could really make him stay. "Please, François, nobody else would bother with me. You are the only man who could take this seriously. Others would advise me to stick to embroidery instead."

"Well, judging by your home decor you were never any good at that either," he teased.

"François!" I exclaimed with a laugh, pretending to be upset at the same time.

"Don't worry, you might become a wonderful reader instead," he grinned.

"I might, but only under your supervision."

We exchanged a conspiratorial look. I knew that he liked the idea. After all, he enjoyed anything that was tinged with rebellion. To make it even more appealing to him, I added, "But if we really do this, no one can know about it."

"Indeed," he laughed, "especially if I'm the teacher."

He wavered a bit longer but finally consented. "Why not? I will stay and teach you under one condition."

I clasped my hands together in excitement, waiting for him to finish the thought.

"You'll stay away from me in the daylight. We will meet only at night. It's enough that you greeted me in public the other day. There is no reason for you or your family to be a source of defamation because of me."

The request touched me. I did not expect him to be so invested in my safety and reputation. Lost for words, I could only nod in agreement.

✦

From then on, François waited at our house every night at the stroke of midnight. Denise became accustomed to my secret trips and let me back in before dawn so that Father or Sebastian wouldn't notice. The days turned into a tiresome, dull wait for escape. François often took me to the boat, but once or twice, he even snuck me into his loft chamber at Porte Rouge. He was patient with me and complimented me whenever I made progress. I could tell that he enjoyed our secret meetings and judging by his warm behaviour, he was attracted to me as well. He kept dazzling me with those long, lingering looks of his, but they no longer made me feel insecure because I became used to them. I wanted to know if it meant that he returned my feelings, because if he truly loved me, I would do anything to be with him.

One night, we took a detour on the way back home, and ended up by one of the Parisian city gates dedicated to Saint Germaine. The sergeants roamed the battlements, so we stood far enough away not to alert them as we admired the picturesque countryside through the magnificent archway. For some reason, the sight of the armed guards sent chills down my spine. Sometimes I wondered whether the walls of stone were meant to protect us or keep us under surveillance. The thought made me realise that no matter how freely I could roam the streets I would never be completely liberated from the confines of society.

An unsettling premonition overwhelmed me then and I instinctively moved closer to François. That's when I noticed he was watching me with a nostalgic expression.

"Do you remember that time we met beyond the city walls?" he asked.

I nodded with a smile. "How could I forget? Thanks to you, my nanny never let me play by that old tree again."

We thought back to that moment. It had happened shortly after he had stolen my ball. My nanny and I had taken a long walk beyond the city walls and were headed towards the old oak tree where children used to meet and play. That afternoon, I noticed François there. He was sitting beneath the great branches alone, waiting for his friends. I couldn't refrain from pointing him out to my nanny. François saw us approaching and stood up to greet us. I reminded him of the ball he stole from me last time, but he just grinned and said, "Don't worry, little lady! I can compensate. I have two better ones right here in my pants."

My nanny started after him and he nimbly ran off.

We both laughed at the memory and I couldn't help but ask what I had been wondering for years.

"What happened to that ball?"

"It found its resting place in the Seine," admitted François, "along with many other toys."

I shrugged. "Well, I suppose it served its purpose…"

He became thoughtful for a moment then leaned against the nearby wall and said, "I have finally written a new poem."

"You have? That's wonderful! What is it about?"

"About destiny and appreciating what we have instead of crying over what we have lost… "

He didn't have to say more, I knew why he wrote it, so I just asked, "Would you share it with me?"

He focused his gaze in the direction of the countryside and began to speak:

Fortune: Long ago scholars used to call me by that name
So why do you, François the murderer, insult my game?
You who have no respectful fame?
I have broken greater men than that!
By poverty, hard labour, and torment
Yet, you speak wrongly of me because you live in shame?
Know this: You are not the only one to complain!
Just look into the history and contemplate
The fate of the mighty men that turned still and pale
In comparison with them, you are just a scum
So shut up and learn to mind your tongue
Be grateful, Villon, rather take things as they come!

He turned to me with a bow. "That is it so far. What do you think?"

I smiled and said, "That you're too hard on yourself."

He weighed up my words. "Or on the contrary, I should learn to face my problems instead of running away from them."

We both knew he was hinting at his decision to stay in Paris; neither of us had to verbalise it. Then as if remembering something, he reached into his overcoat pocket and pulled out a scroll of parchment fastened with a red ribbon.

"I almost forgot to give you this," he said. "It's something I prepared to make the learning a bit easier for you."

I wanted to unwrap the parchment, but he stopped me. "Wait till you get home. It's a surprise."

I liked the idea, so I pressed the scroll to my heart.

"Thank you, François."

I planted a kiss of gratitude on his cheek. The way he looked at me afterwards made me linger with my face close to his. He challengingly lifted his brow, expecting me to do more. Not to disappoint him, I kissed him on the other cheek too, slower than before. With his eyes still fixed on mine, he was clearly waiting for something even more daring, something that I would not do even though I was ready for it. Therefore, he guided me back home and said goodbye to me with a polite bow as usual.

Chapter 9

The Dark Side of Love

The nights with François filled me with deep joy, such that I had never experienced before in my life. They also filled me with hope, although I didn't quite know what I was hoping for. Even if I managed to win his heart and change his opinion of marriage, we wouldn't receive Father's blessing. I would have to run away with him and become an outcast myself. It was presumptuous of me to think so far ahead, but I couldn't help myself. I was ready for anything, except being let down. That's why when he didn't show up one night, I began to fear that he had had to leave Paris after all or that he simply didn't want to see me anymore. I couldn't focus on anything, not even the scroll of parchment he had given me which revealed a copy of his favourite Greek legends.

After he didn't show up the following night either, I considered breaking my promise and seeking him out at his home. Denise argued that it might seem desperate and encouraged me to be more patient. I agreed with her and waited until the next day only to be left disappointed for the third time.

A whole week went by and there was still no sign of François until one morning I saw him in the street with Isabeau and another sparingly dressed, voluptuous woman with lustrous golden locks and a set of cute dimples. They didn't notice us, carelessly wrapped up in each other's company. I watched them in consternation as the woman grabbed François' arm and pulled him closer. She whispered something into his ear, and he whispered something back with a mischievous smile. I wanted to walk over to them and find out what was going on but had too much pride for that.

"The vulgar types suit him better," noted Denise upon seeing them. Her words felt like a splash of cold water. I rushed home without turning back, hoping that my emotional reaction hadn't been noticed by anyone else, including him. Denise ran after me.

"I'm sorry for my heartless comment, Mademoiselle Katherine, you shouldn't be so troubled by what you've seen. On the contrary, you should be glad. You know that men go to women like that for practice."

"And ladies go to men like him? You sound like Jolis."

"I thought that was your plan all along," she said. "It's not like you could ever marry him."

I didn't answer and strode on, wishing to be left alone. It felt as if nobody understood me, perhaps not even the man I thought was so different from the others. Denise quickly fell into step with me and begged, "Mademoiselle Katherine, please don't be like this... I apologise for being so rude, you know how impetuous I tend to be with my words..."

"Let's not discuss this any further, Denise." I was too upset to talk. The idea that François would prefer those women to me was simply too painful.

I hoped he would show up that night and put my mind at ease, but he didn't. Jealousy slowly devoured me. I couldn't rest; I just kept gazing out into the night, hoping for a miracle. Despite my pleading with Mother Mary and her angels, though, there was nothing but darkness for me out there.

To turn my mind to something other than the image of François with the loose women, I turned to the legends he had copied for me. The fact that they all spoke of love made me feel a bit better. I wanted to believe that it meant something. I took an immediate interest in the legend of Orpheus and

Eurydice, so I decided to read that one the most diligently. It was a slow process, however, I had many sleepless hours ahead of me to better my skills. After I had managed to read the story, I found myself aching for François even more. How I wished he loved me as deeply as Orpheus loved Eurydice! Would he journey all the way to the underworld to get me back? I assumed he wouldn't. In reality, I would have to save myself. The fact that even mythological heroes made fatal mistakes that cast love back into the shadows proved only one thing: we are all alone on our journey through life, particularly those that lead to the underworld.

The realisation that I had been able to read a full story for the first time lifted my spirit a bit, but after dawn, I fell into even greater melancholy. The lack of sleep and uncertainty had made me restless. I couldn't bear the idea of another day and night of futile waiting. I had to speak with him and find out why he had broken our promise no matter how desperate it may seem. I was to be played by no man, not even one whom I had been obsessed with since childhood. Therefore, I asked Denise to tell Father I had gone to church and headed for Porte Rouge instead.

✦

As I approached the house, I noticed two figures emerging from its entrance and heading towards me through the morning mist. It was Father Guillaume and François' mother, Madame Montcorbier. They were both surprised to see me and even more so once I told them that I was on my way to visit François.

"How nice of you to stop by, Mademoiselle Katherine," said Father Guillaume, "but François is probably still asleep."

"I hope not," argued Madame Montcorbier. "He promised to clean the house and cloister today."

Father Guillaume threw his hands up and said, "François has been very busy lately, he even works during the night."

"Oh, has he found himself some work?" I asked sceptically, sensing that he was probably just busy at the taverns.

"No," sighed Father Guillaume. "He's been trying, but nobody will hire him after what happened. When I said he works, I meant on his latest book, *Tale of the Devil's Fart*. He has been thinking about writing it for years and it seems as if he has finally found his muse now."

The news calmed me down a bit. If he had lost himself in creativity, his distance was quite understandable, yet it didn't excuse his disregard for my feelings.

"If he were paid to write, he'd certainly be a wealthy man already," said Guillaume with that genial smile of his. I returned the smile and longingly peered up to the attic where François' chamber was located.

"Then I won't disturb him," I concluded. "I will come some other time."

Madame Montcorbier hurried to my side.

"There's no need for you to leave. You might be the angel I have been praying for, come to rescue my son from the dark corners of his room. Go to him, Mademoiselle Katherine, he will be happy to see you."

She gently led me to the carved front door and unlocked it for me.

"I wouldn't like to intrude," I reasoned with her, nervous about entering the house by myself.

"You definitely won't be," she insisted. "Isn't that right, Father Guillaume?"

We both turned to him for the final blessing. He hesitated for a moment, but when he met with Madame Montcorbier's obstinate face, he said, "Of course, please be our guest, Mademoiselle Katherine, see yourself upstairs. If he's not up yet, just knock on his door, he certainly won't mind being woken by you."

They ushered me inside, said goodbye, and hurried off to the church. Their exceptionally warm behaviour made me wonder whether they knew something I didn't. The idea that François had shared his thoughts and possibly even his feelings with them delighted me. I entered the house and looked around for him, bashful yet determined. He was not downstairs, which meant he was still asleep in his chamber. I felt too embarrassed to knock at his door as they had suggested, so instead I stepped back outside and pulled on the doorbell. After a moment, I heard his raspy voice call out, "I'll be right there!"

His irritation made me smirk. I took a malicious joy in waking him mainly because of the sleepless nights he had caused me. François came rushing down clumsily dressed, with his hair all messy and face wrinkled from the pillows. When he spotted me standing in the doorway, he stopped in bewilderment.

"Katherine!" he exhaled, quickly fixing his girdle and walking down to meet me. "What are you doing here? You promised you would stay away from me in the daylight."

"And you promised to come over every night."

"I supposed you would have enough to be going on with, with the legends that I copied for you."

"I did," I said, trying to compose myself. "I started with the legend of Orpheus and Eurydice."

"That's wonderful," he smiled. "You learn fast. In no time you won't need me anymore."

His words stung like the dagger he knew how to use so well. I supposed he wanted to be rid of me already, so I took a deep breath and braced myself to leave with some dignity intact.

"Well, I should be on my way then. I wish you good luck with your writing."

"Are you leaving already?" he asked, baffled by my sudden change of heart. "You can't break your promise with such a short visit. Please, come inside."

With those words, he invited me into the main chamber. I could never say no to him, so I entered the small but tidy space which was dominated by a large stone fireplace. The furnishings were simple. There was just a table with four chairs, a heavy cupboard to one side and one simple bench with white, embroidered pillows. Father Guillaume lived humbly as opposed to most clerics, which didn't surprise me. We all knew he liked to give more than to receive.

François reached for a jar of wine and poured us both a full goblet. I refused.

"It's far too early for wine for most people," I said, "but I suppose that for a man free from rules and restrictions it's the right time to start, especially if he has to clean the whole house and cloister today."

He laughed at my sharp tongue. "I can see you met my mother. Now I can definitely quit trying to charm you... What else did she tell you?"

I didn't react to the question, clinging on to the sentence that preceded it.

"Since when have you tried to charm me?"

"Since forever."

He smiled at my honestly perplexed expression and took a sip of the wine, perhaps for courage.

"I admit that the desire intensified upon my return to Paris. No other woman of your status would talk to an outcast like me, not unless she was a precious soul."

I felt a familiar heat rising up my spine and spreading over my skin. I had no idea he thought so highly of me. Before I was able to recover from his confession, he stepped closer to me and said, "I never imagined that I could have a chance with a girl like you…"

I gazed back at him, letting his eyes search out mine. I could see it quite clearly then: he did return my feelings. It didn't matter whether they were as deep as mine or not, because I knew that a spark was enough to start a fire. I wanted to kiss him, but as his face neared mine, I gently pushed him away. There was still something that I needed to ask.

"Who was the woman I saw you with the other day?"

The question surprised him. He tried to remember, and when he finally did, he just threw his hand up with a smile. "Oh, you mean Margot? She's a good friend, but not someone I think of at night."

"Who do you think of then?"

He hesitated, joining my game.

"It would not be polite to say."

"Politeness doesn't suit you anyway."

I bit my lip as soon as I realised that I might have gone too far with my flirtation. He seemed to like it, though. In fact, he took it as an invitation, and without any warning, he suddenly pressed his lips to mine. I tasted the wine, savouring it as if for the first time. I leaned in for another taste, already intoxicated, addicted. I brushed my lips against the rough scar, encouraging him to react in any way he liked. He held me in his arms and gave me an even deeper kiss. I melted into his passion, but the fervour with which I returned it was unbefitting for a woman of my upbringing so I had to stop myself.

"I should go," I whispered, as soon as our lips parted. The way he made me feel surpassed anything I had experienced before, however, I couldn't lose control, not if I wanted him to come back for more.

"Are you sure?" he said softly, his face nearing mine again. I trembled as his lips reached my ear and he whispered, "I could teach you more than just how to read, Katherine…"

I felt the irresistible fever rush through me. My body was ready to follow him to his chamber, but my principles were stronger than that. I knew that I would be just another one of his female friends had I given in.

"Please tell me, where do I stand with you?"

"That depends on where I stand with *you*, Katherine."

I was tired of fooling around, though, so I said, "I'm serious, François."

"Me too."

"Well, you know where you stand. I keep refusing Noël Jolis because of you, but I'm afraid that one day Father will stop being as tolerant as he has been thus far and marry me to him…"

"Do you want my marriage proposal then? Despite my reputation?"

"Not necessarily."

"Just tell me what you do want," he asked earnestly. "Do you want us to run away together?"

"If we loved each other, I would definitely consider that option," I admitted.

"So how do we find out if we do?"

His closeness disorientated me so I stepped aside, leaving him to face the wall instead. I had to be sensible. I couldn't let him ensnare me without having some assurance that I wasn't more than just a fling to him. François seemed to understand as he turned to me with empathy and said, "Don't be scared of me, Katherine. I will be respectful of your wishes, no matter what they are. I will gladly kidnap you, take you far away from here, even marry you if your heart calls for it, but you would have to give me some time."

Although I wanted nothing more than to hear him say such sweet things, I couldn't help the troubling thoughts that came rushing into my mind.

"I wish I could trust you," I sighed, yearning to hear the confession of love I was still waiting for.

"Have I ever been dishonest with you or anybody else?"

"No, but the truth is that I don't know you very well, François…"

"We have known each other since childhood," he objected, missing the point.

"You know what I'm trying to say. I know the mask you present to the world, not the man you keep so well hidden from others."

"I'm not even certain I know that person myself," he argued. "All I know is that I'm unable to be the man you deserve, at least at the moment, especially after my chances of establishing a decent life vanished with that one swing of a dagger."

He looked at me with the kind of urgency I had never seen in his face before and said, "They won't employ me anywhere, Katherine. I have no place to go, the only door that remains open to me is here at Porte Rouge, but I believe that things will change." He paused then and continued in a merrier tone. "I still think about what you told me upon my return to Paris: I have to wait it out."

Although I had dreamt of bewitching his heart since what seemed like forever, it was hard to believe he could truly be mine one day. At that moment, however, I desperately wanted to believe it, so I moved closer to him and caressed his face. He read the desire in my eyes, and before I knew it,

I was drowning in his kisses again. I was unable to imagine there could ever be a time when such passion was not the norm between us. It became the most natural thing for us to do, so I continued to drink my fill from the sinful cup.

✦

I couldn't stop thinking about those passionate moments François and I had shared at Porte Rouge. I assumed that many girls lost themselves in his embrace and dreamt of being more than just a momentary whim, but I felt that I was special to him.

The fact that François promised to return the same night filled me with the thrill of anticipation. I knew I would be too weak to resist him the next time he tempted me and supposed that it didn't matter. I had nothing to lose but my virtue, which was already compromised anyway. Even though it was considered a sin, I knew I would never feel that way about anybody else, and I would rather give myself to the man I loved instead of living in regret for the rest of my days. Therefore, I promised that I would welcome him into my arms without shame. *There is no sin worse than not following one's heart*, that's what my mother used to say. She was a romantic soul like me. Father often talked about her philosophy on life and said that we would have been best friends if she hadn't passed away before I could even lay eyes on her.

Denise noticed how happy I was, but didn't ask why. She knew there was no use in reminding me of her opinion. I was used to deciding things on my own. Therefore, I spent the whole day in solitude, preparing for the night ahead and imagining what it would be like to lie beside François. I had never taken a lover before, though many people assumed I had because of my countless suitors. I had refused everyone because of the one I adored, but since learning that he ached for me as well, I was ready for anything.

As if sensing my bold plan, Noël paid us a visit later that day. Father was on the road again, so I was the head of the household for the time being and decided to act like it.

"I'm busy today, Monsieur Jolis, please come another time," I said with a polite but detached look.

"I understand, Mademoiselle Katherine, I won't trouble you for long," he argued with a suspiciously victorious expression and handed me a scroll of parchment. "I'm just a messenger today."

I accepted the scroll, confused. "What is this?"

"I'd rather you find out for yourself as I would not want to embarrass you. When your father returns, he will surely read it for you."

I didn't bother telling him that I might not need help with that anymore. Unlike François, he wouldn't understand why a woman wished to read and write. He was like Father in that way. According to them, a woman like me was raised to be a good wife who may indulge in crafts, singing or dancing, but God forbid if she showed any sign of intellect.

"I wouldn't be able to live with myself had I not presented you with an example of who the real François Villon is. I hope you forgive me for this one day, Mademoiselle Katherine."

With these chilling words, he gave me a courteous bow and set off. I looked down at the scroll in my hands and hesitated. Noël clearly wanted to tear François and me apart, so I wavered over whether to read it or throw it in the wastewater where it belonged. I was too curious, though. How bad could it be? I reckoned that if I was willing to accept François despite his reputation and misbehaviour, nothing could surprise me. I expected to laugh at Noël's naivety, so I unwrapped the scroll.

Because of the collection of Greek legends François had copied for me, I recognised his handwriting straight away. The parchment revealed a poem addressed to a certain "chubby Margot". I instantly thought of the woman I had seen him with the other day and began to feel apprehensive. I leaned against the wall for support and started reading:

Because I adore and serve this beauty
Do you deem me a fool or a scoundrel?
Her fine skills put me straight into duty
For her love, I use my shield and dagger.
When customers come, I fetch a decanter
And pour them wine, acting nice and steady
I offer water, cheese, and bread in plenty
Then if they pay well, I politely say:
"Come back again when you are horny
To the brothel where we hold our state!"

But afterwards, there may be some ill-will
If Margot comes to bed without a penny;
Then I can't stand her; I could easily kill
So I grab her coat, belt, and all her daily wear
Threatening that I will keep them as my share
With hands on her hips, she yells: You Anti Christ!
And swears me revenge in the name of Jesus Christ
So I grab a shard and near her frightened face
Scarring her nose to have it in writing
There, in the brothel where we hold our state!

When we make peace, she lets out a big fart
Bloated like some venomous beetle
She sits on my crown, laughing, riding hard
Then slaps my thigh and calls me a weasel
Like two logs, we fall asleep after we grow feeble
But at dawn her belly wants me to recruit
So she sits on top of me to not waste her fruit

Her weight flats me down, satisfying my taste
Until there is no more lechery left to tease
There, in the brothel where we hold our state!

Vending, freezing, no bread, and no shame
I'm a debauchee so debauchees I attract
Lady, neither of us is better, we are the same
Like-for-like, bad rat to bad cat
Only filth suits us, so filth we seek
No honour have we, our future is bleak
In the brothel where we hold our state!

The poem was a dagger to my heart. I couldn't believe that he had written it, so I read it again and again until I finally came to my senses. The meaning behind Noël's words seized my mind then: *I wouldn't be able to live with myself had I not presented you with an example of who the real François Villon is.* That's what he had said and delivered. The realisation that the man who wrote the poem was the same man that I had looked up to for years made me feel unsteady. I fell onto the cold floor below the stairs, unable to cope with the wild emotions that engulfed me. Not only had he used that vulgar poem to declare his affection for another, he had also admitted to being a violent pimp – the lowest of the low, just like everyone said. Suddenly, I was unable to fathom why I had ever admired him or his poetry. The core of his soul that I so desperately longed to reach was darker than I could ever have known.

My initial panic was soon replaced with fury. I squeezed the parchment in my hand with all the power I had left in me. The idea that I wanted to be his that night made me shudder in disgust. He would probably turn me into one of his whores afterwards. *Freedom is not free*, that was what my father told Regnier once, and he must have known what he was talking about. How could I have been so foolish as to think that François Villon wanted to rescue me? He probably just wanted to lure me into a trap. I would end up on the streets with him, scarred in body and soul, prostituted for his pleasure. I couldn't believe how easily love could turn to hate. I welcomed it with open arms, filling my heart with its pain. Hate was all that was left in me at the thought of François Villon and it was the only emotion I allowed.

I couldn't rest another moment, consumed by the desire to confront him. I couldn't let him see how hurt I was, though, he didn't deserve that. Therefore, I promised myself to be strong and keep my distance. I had to treat him as the person he turned out to be – someone who was not worthy of my attention. Still, I didn't want anyone to know the truth. I couldn't bear to admit that they had been right all along so I locked myself in my chamber and let nobody in, not even Denise. I had to fight this strange illness on my own.

Despite the unbreakable fortress I had built around my heart, it almost stopped beating when a stone hit my window. François came as he had promised, but it was too late. I thought back to the smiles, kisses, promises, and suddenly wanted to forget that it had ever happened. I buried my head in my hands, unable to even shed tears. He had depleted me of everything.

Another stone hit my window, then a third and a fourth. He was persistent, emboldened by what I had allowed him to do earlier. I had to slap my own face to stop myself from going to the window. Although the idea of him leaving was painful, the idea of letting him break me all over again was even worse. A fifth, sixth, stone hit my window and each strike felt as if it was aimed straight at my heart. Then, to my horror, the sound of our house bell reverberated through the walls. I froze, unwilling to believe he would be so daring. Did he know or sense that something was wrong? The part of me I detested was glad that he wanted to see me so badly, but the rest of me dreaded it.

Someone's steps made me jump up in fear. I ran to the door, pressing my ear to the thick wood to eavesdrop. I heard Sebastian's voice reminding François that it was too late for a visit. He was clearly not willing to give up though and after a short quarrel, I heard them running up the stairs. Sebastian was asking him to leave again, but François banged on my door nonetheless.

I clawed at the doorknob, hesitating about what to do next. The situation had become too serious.

"Katherine!" he called out in despair. "Please open the door! We need to talk!"

"You should come back when Monsieur de Vaucelles is back home," insisted Sebastian firmly. "It's impolite to visit a lady at such an ungodly hour."

The rest of the house was quiet. Denise was probably locked in her chamber, too worried to even steal a peek at what was happening in the hallway.

"I'm not going anywhere!" snapped François, then he addressed me again. "Katherine! I must explain something to you!"

A breath of hope swept through me, but I shook it away with stubborn determination.

"Regnier told me that Jolis went to Margot's to find some dirt on me and found the poem I wrote years ago. It was just a whim of a young mind, please don't take it seriously!"

Hearing him admit to writing the poem destroyed the last bit of hope I had left, the secret wish that Noël had hired someone to fake his handwriting.

"You can see the funny side, can't you?" he asked through the wall that separated us. The idea that he thought we could laugh at it together fired me up. I unlocked the door and stood before him with the coldest look I could conjure.

"It's all right, Sebastian," I nodded to our faithful servant. "This is Monsieur Villon's last visit to our house, so we might as well let him say what he must, and then we can all go back to bed."

Never had I seen François so shaken, so upset. His eyes were pleading for mercy and for a moment there, I thought it could disarm me, but then I recalled the rhymes I had been re-reading the whole day and pursed my lips. "So speak and spare me the details, please."

He took a deep breath and started on his excuses. "The poem was nothing but a depiction of what the pimps I know behave like. Margot always says that she's her own pimp, so it was meant as a silly provocation. I didn't even know that she had kept it."

"Is it the same woman that I saw you with in the street?" I asked, barely breathing.

"Yes, we are friends."

I let out a derisive laugh. "Friends? Like that other prostitute you risked your life for?"

"Is it so hard to believe I have female friends?"

"The fact that you write such poems for your female friends doesn't make it any better. Who would want to be one of them?"

The shock on Sebastian's face made me realise that I had let my emotions take hold of me again so I forced myself to remain firm. "Certainly not me."

"I told you that you are special to me, Katherine. I am trying to be a better man for you. I am done with all of that whoring and drinking."

I wanted nothing more than to believe him, but my pride was stronger than I had thought. "Yet you still meet with whores."

"I do, but in all innocence, I swear. Since I realised that…" he looked at Sebastian and wavered for a moment then turned back to me and said, "I'm all yours if you still want me."

The sight of Sebastian's petrified expression set things straight for me. I suddenly saw François from his point of view and saw him for who he truly was – a known criminal who had broken into our house at night, spoken of despicable things and hinted at an affair with Lady Katherine de Vaucelles. A shiver of repulsion ran down my spine. I could simply not see him in the same light as I used to.

"It doesn't matter whether or not you meant the words you wrote, Monsieur Villon," I said with a voice that I didn't even recognise as my own. "You wrote them – that is all that matters. One's fantasy precedes one's deeds."

"I beg you to let me talk to you in private, Katherine." He took a step closer to me. My heart wanted to give in, but my reason won over and I turned away from him.

"Sebastian," I addressed the confused servant. "If Monsieur Villon does not leave on his own, you may use all the force at your disposal to see him out."

For once, I was the one who disarmed him, not the other way around. The hurt in his eyes struck me. I could not bear the sight of the inner torment I had caused him, mainly because it reflected everything that I had pined for all this time: his love for me. I once thought it was all that I could ever want, but I was just a naïve girl then. The cold queen within me had defeated her, so I looked away and put an end to this unreal fairy tale. Somewhere deep within I sensed that someday I would regret the disdain I showed him that night. I already foresaw the older me: a woman disappointed by life and love, dreaming of what might have been had she behaved differently at that one crucial moment. Yet I stood my ground.

For a moment longer, he held my gaze, but then he swiftly moved aside. He left faster than he came, and the house fell into a tense, dreadful silence that overpowered the sound of his receding footsteps and the voices of Sebastian and Denise who were trying to console me. As always, I did not listen and did not care about what they had to say. It did not matter to me. I had lost the man that I loved, the man who probably never even existed, for he was just a romanticised hallucination.

PART THREE:

MARGOT

To my chubby Margot
The sweet, devoted creature
Whom I love, swear to God
She understands my nature
As well as I do her curses
If you ever find her venture
On one of her adventures
Read her the following verses:

Because I adore and serve this beauty
Do you deem me a fool or a scoundrel?
Her fine skills put me straight into duty
For her love, I use my shield and dagger.
When customers come, I fetch a decanter
And pour them wine, acting nice and steady
I offer water, bread, fruit, and cheese in plenty
Then if they pay well, I politely say:
"Come back again when you are horny
To the brothel where we hold our state!"

But afterwards, there may be some ill-will
If Margot comes to bed without a penny;
Then I can't stand her; I could easily kill
So I grab her coat, belt, and all her daily wear
Threatening that I will keep them as my share
With hands on her hips, she yells: You Anti
Christ!
And swears me revenge in the name of Jesus
Christ
So I grab a shard and near her frightened face
Scarring her nose to have it in a written form
There, in the brothel where we hold our state!

When we make peace, she lets out a big fart
Bloated as a venomous beetle
She sits on my crown, laughing, riding hard
Then slaps my thigh and calls me a weasel
Like two logs, we fall asleep after we grow feeble
But at dawn her belly wants me to recruit
So she sits on top of me to not waste her fruit
Her weight flats me down, satisfying my taste
Until there is no more lechery left to tease
In the brothel where we hold our state!

Vending, freezing, no bread, and no shame
I'm a debauchee so debauchees I attract
Lady, neither of us is better, we are the same
Like-for-like, bad rat to bad cat
Only filth suits us, so filth we seek
No honour have we, our future is bleak
In the brothel where we hold our state!

Extract from *The Testament* (1461-1462, François Villon)

CHAPTER 10

THAT DAMN KATHERINE

Paris, December 1456

So I gave in to his charms again, I sighed to myself when I woke up beside the infamous François Villon. He still did it for me, even though the scar on his lip was decorated with morning drool and he snored louder than the old priest who had bedded Isabeau next door. I praised the Lord for sending that girl into my path, as her unique allure made our brothel more prosperous than the others, thereby allowing us to live comfortable lives. Thanks to her, I was still able to start choosing my customers instead of the other way around. Villon never paid, though. He was one of the lucky few who managed to win me over without money for he was one of those rare, genuinely good-hearted men.

I have had a soft spot for him ever since he first showed up at our inn. He was still young and innocent back then, but he learned fast and in no time, he was drinking plenty and entertaining my customers with his poems. I took him under my wing right away. I was his first lover and enjoyed educating him in the art of physical love. He had a God-given talent for pleasuring a woman of high demands such as myself, so I tended to treat him as my private pet. He didn't seem to mind and I could tell he preferred me over the other girls.

After the brawl with Sermoise, I cried myself to sleep, scared that I was going to lose him. Although we all assumed he would end up on the gallows, he surprised us with a victorious return. I offered him a private celebration in my chamber, but he wanted only wine. It was the first time he said no to me. I knew that a woman had something to do with it, so I respected his decision.

I sensed that with time he would come crawling back to good old Margot anyway, as he was not the type to settle down. The parting must have truly hurt him, though, as he hadn't been himself since. He used to call me many names, but he never called me Katherine before. That Katherine must have taught him a lesson and the wicked part of me was glad, because it brought him back to my lair.

I watched him grimace as the sunlight tickled his face. He scratched his nose, then covered his eyes and groaned.

"Margot?"

"Yes, my love?" I answered gently, almost forgetting that I was nothing but a warm body to him.

"Pull the curtains, will you?" he asked and turned his back to me. His lazy attitude irritated me so instead of closing the curtains, I pulled the blanket aside and kicked him out of my bed.

"I don't have all day for you, Villon! The customers are waiting."

"Let the girls deal with them," he rasped as he crawled back for warmth. "I know you prefer staying here with me anyway…"

"Don't flatter yourself," I hissed. "How about cleaning the fireplace, starting the fire and telling me what happened. I've been trying to get answers the whole night but all I received were drunken sobs and vomit."

He fell silent for a moment, so I thought he had dozed off again, however, then he grumpily murmured, "There's nothing to talk about…"

"Really? Then why were you crying for someone called Katherine the whole time?"

Her name woke him up. He sat up in bed and held his head in pain.

"For devil's sake don't mention that name," he complained, then started to cough. "Could I have some water, please?"

I reached for the carafe on the table but paused before I handed it to him.

"Only if you tell me who she is."

He gave me an irked look, his eyes unusually puffy and sad.

"Does it matter? She ended it before we even started anything."

He tried to stand up but fell back on the bed right away. I laughed while he moaned, "By God's loins! How much wine did I have last night? I must have spent my last sou here."

"Don't worry about that," I said, "Montigny paid for everything. He seems to be doing well now that my brother-in-law is keeping him busy."

"That's how it goes with gangs," noted Villon. "First you receive a golden necklace then a filthy rope."

I have never heard him speak so darkly. He managed to make me take pity on him, and I rarely pitied anyone, including myself. With a deep sigh, I handed him the carafe and even a plate with some leftover cheese and bread.

"Eat, you need to gather your strength," I instructed, but he only took the water and set the plate aside.

"Take while I'm giving, Villon!" I insisted, worried that the heartache would drive him to starvation.

"If you make me eat this, I'll spew it right back along with last night's dinner."

I smiled at the comment and gave him a friendly pat on the back. "That's the Villon I know!"

He just shook his head, though. "Oh, how I wish to return to that dream…"

"I hate lovesick men," I whispered, trying to hide my envy. That Katherine of his had managed something I hadn't and probably never would. I had his body, but she had his soul.

"I thought I'd never be one of those fools myself," admitted Villon, suddenly pouring out words as if in the confessional. "You know I never considered things like marriage before. I thought my greatest love would forever be Paris, but then she proved to be more than the unattainable fantasy of my early youth. She could have changed me. She could have made me into a decent man… Without her, I don't even feel like trying."

How nice of you to share that with me, I thought to myself, wondering why I still wanted to know more about Katherine if I despised her already.

"It was like a dream," he continued. "The girl that I have always admired turned into an angel, welcoming me into her arms despite all my flaws, but then suddenly throwing me into a hellish pit and letting me suffer in the shadows of what could have been…"

"Why?" I asked, trying to remain disengaged. "Did she find out that you have no money?"

He shook his head and faced me with the saddest expression.

"What then?" I pressed. "Did you do something to her? Did you try to get under her skirts too soon or something?"

He laughed in pain and after a moment of sulking, he admitted, "It was because of you, Margot."

For a moment there, I thought he was going to declare his undying love for me, but instead he disappointed me all over again.

"Jolis gave her that poem I wrote for you years ago, remember? She's more innocent than I thought, Margot, she couldn't see the funny side of it… She actually thought it was the truth, not just my imagination."

Silly Margot, I rebuked myself, *how could you even think that he would be interested in you? No matter how nice or compassionate you are, you have always been just a friend to him.* I quickly recovered from the distress he was causing me. I never wanted to repeat the same mistake as I had with my late husband who tormented me until he died from an excess of food, wine, and orgies. The fact that I made our home into a brothel was really a tribute, not some kind of low revenge like most people thought. Our marriage was the best thing that ever happened to me. Although he didn't love me as much as I loved him, he always made sure that I had everything I needed. Even on his deathbed, he asked his brother to let me do whatever I wanted with his property.

"You should have told her that you would make an awful pimp!" I laughed, though I couldn't help but wonder how I would feel about the verses if I were a virginal maiden who compared all men to her papa. I supposed Katherine wanted to love Villon the troubadour, not Villon the rowdy fiend that I adored.

"Can you believe that Jolis won?" He gave me a forced grin that made his scar expand into a grotesque grimace.

Seeing him so troubled made me suggest something that I instantly regretted. "Would it help you if I talked to her?"

Luckily for me, he shook his head. "I'm afraid that would only put more fuel on the fire."

I shrugged and turned away, suddenly feeling a bit strange about the whole situation. Villon must have noticed, as he reached for my hand and squeezed it.

"But thank you for the offer, Margot, you are sweet..." He sized me up with those dreamy eyes of his and smiled. "The morning light suits you. You look like a Venus..."

I checked myself in the mirror opposite. My ample curves looked enticing covered in nothing but my golden curls, yet it didn't seem to be enough.

"...so why does my heart ache at the sight of your beauty?" he added, spoiling the compliment with his misery.

"I hate her, Margot. I hate her more than I hate myself."

And I hated them both, yet I didn't have the heart to let him know. His pain was too real. Therefore, I sat by his side and let him rest his tired head on my pounding chest. In no time, he was asleep again, drifting off into a dream in which it was probably not I who cradled him, but that damn Katherine.

✦

From then on, Villon abandoned his chaste life at Porte Rouge and stayed at my brothel instead. He avoided sobriety as that led him to think of Katherine. It pained me to see him that way, but the tavern and brothel kept my mind occupied with more than his piteous love life. December had always been a busy time, especially as that was when the Coquillards stopped roaming the streets and retreated into my warm haven to plan new thefts. Regnier de Montigny had joined the gang not long ago, and that was beneficial to both of us as he had become an extravagant customer ever since.

He organised glamorous events and bought nice presents for my girls. We all knew why he was so prodigal with his first big earnings. He wanted to impress Isabeau who he hoped would be his someday. I often wondered why Isabeau didn't take the chance, because I could tell that she liked him too. So when I noticed her follow him with her eyes again, I couldn't help but ask, "Why do you keep tormenting the poor man? He's no longer just an awkward student who pretends to be a nobleman even though he still wears those ancient red boots of his."

"It's even worse now," she argued, "he's a criminal."

I laughed at her fruitless worrying. "We are all criminals here, Isabeau!"

"What are you trying to say? That a thief and a whore make a good match?"

"Yes! A well-established criminal is better than some incorrigible vagabond," I argued.

"Like Villon?" she teased. I responded with a reproachful frown. I didn't like it when my girls made fun of me, not even Isabeau who I considered my best friend.

"Don't take this the wrong way, Margot," she continued with a friendly nudge, "you know better than anyone how eternally grateful I am to him for saving my life. It's hard to watch him pay such a heavy price for it, but I have noticed that he has been taking advantage of you and Regnier. I'm quite certain he doesn't even realise it for he's unable to think straight these days. That's why he needs your merciless honesty more than ever now. He can't go on like this forever. The sooner he stands on his own feet the better for all of you."

We both looked at Villon who had his arms round Regnier de Montigny and Colin de Cayaux and was waving at us to bring them more ale. As I gazed at his empty face, I realised that Isabeau had a point. However, it was hard to tell him the truth, mainly because I knew he would decide to do the right thing and leave. I procrastinated, but only until I saw him grope Rose. I knew he couldn't afford her and didn't like the idea anyway, and so I roared, "Villon!"

Everybody turned to me in an instant. I smiled to myself, as I enjoyed having such respect at my establishment. Even the Coquillards feared Madam Margot, particularly if she raised her voice. They knew only too well that I wouldn't hesitate to punish those who disrespected my authority. Moreover, I had the protection of my brother-in-law, Wolf, who happened to be one of the most feared man in the whole of Paris, and his companions in crime, the Coquillards.

"We need to have a word," I insisted. "Come with me."

He was not too drunk to obey, so I took him outside into the snowy night and without further ado, simply expressed what was on my mind.

"I'm done with hosting you for free, Villon."

At first, he was taken aback by the news, but then he thought about it some more and nodded.

"Very well then," he agreed in all seriousness. "I know I have been living off you and Regnier for the past few weeks, and please know that I intend to pay you both back."

"How?" My voice sounded colder than usual. "You can't seem to find any work in Paris and you don't want to join the clerics or the Coquillards."

Villon leaned his back against the wall and said, "You are completely right, Margot, this way of living leads nowhere but down…"

He took a deep breath, letting the cool air refresh his mind.

"I have been trying to make it work here in Paris, though everything has been pointing in another direction. I can't wait around for Katherine's change of heart forever. All I need to do is pay my debts, make some money for the journey, and then I'll leave the love of my life behind…"

A year ago, I would understand that he meant Paris, but after what had happened with Katherine de Vaucelles, I could not be sure anymore.

"She has made her choice. You have to live with it."

I was referring to the fact that Noël and Katherine were engaged. The reminder made him drop his head into his hands, so I punched his belly in frustration. "Man up, Villon!"

"I know I can use a good kick in the arse, Margot, but not into a belly full of wine," he complained. I crossed my arms, unwilling to listen to the pathetic sobs any longer.

"We have all been through hell in life," I said firmly. "Moping around is for the weak and nobody likes weak men."

He gathered his composure and smiled at my sharp comment.

"I agree. That's why I have to leave as soon as possible. I can't be strong in a city where Katherine Jolis walks down the streets."

"Nonsense," I scoffed at the silly talk. "Paris is filled with heartbroken men and women. Imagine what would happen if they all ran away. Only the heartless bastards would remain."

He gave me a gentle, apologetic look. He must have known that all the while Katherine was trampling on his heart he was stomping on mine in return.

"Thank you for all your help and support, darling Margot, however, I had made up my mind before you even brought it up."

"What about your mother and Guillaume?"

"I know they love me," he said, "but I only bring them shame and worries. Imagine Guillaume's inner struggle with the fact that I killed a priest! And my mother? Ha, she prays for my soul every day and fears that the devil will ensnare it." Then he locked eyes with me and added, "Also, we both know that you'll be better off without me."

I narrowed my eyes at him and remained quiet for a while. He was right in a way, but I was too dependent on the pain he caused me. I punched him again, knocking the breath out of him.

"What was that for?"

"For being so miserable all the time!"

I was ready to leave him, but his hand stopped me.

"Wait. I have just had an idea."

I melted at the sight of that familiar, excited spark in his eyes. That was François Villon – a man full of excellent ideas and zest for life.

"What if I turned that poem I wrote for you into reality?"

I frowned in apprehension. "What do you mean?"

"I could be your pimp."

"How many times do I have to remind you that I don't need any pimp? I have said it a thousand times already: I am my own pimp!"

He gave me a crafty smile. "Yes, but you also often say that you deserve wealthier, more generous customers. I know such men, however, these men would not risk their reputation by going to brothels. They stopped inviting me to their get-togethers because they think of me as a lowlife now, but I could use that to our advantage. Think about it, Margot. I could be a discreet middleman between you and all of those shy nobles, family men or bishops…"

"And who would be opening her legs to these potential customers you speak of?" I asked, wondering where he was heading with it.

"Anyone you like, of course," he said evasively, calming me down a bit.

I began to consider the suggestion. The truth was that I had found some exquisite beauties among the street sluts and Isabeau was the best example. Arranging private meetings at affluent homes was not a bad idea at all.

"I'll ask Wolf what he thinks about it," I promised.

It was good to see him smile again. He kissed both my cheeks and beamed.

"Wonderful! This way, we will both make enough money and I will pay off my debts before I leave Paris. I could also start helping you around the tavern if you like. Give me any work you like, Margot, I'm at your disposal."

"You can start by taking out the chamber pots," I said out of spite. Villon didn't even take it seriously, though. He just laughed at me.

"Oh, Margot, thank goodness I have you!" He wrapped his arms around me, snaring me with his charm as always.

✦

Right after Wolf gave his blessing to the proposal, Villon increased his debts by inviting everyone at the tavern to drink with him. He said he had to celebrate properly and so he did. After midnight, the gang decided to take their boisterous drinking outside. I joined them, mainly because I wanted to enjoy Villon's company while I still had the chance. However, I didn't expect to end up on the Right Bank in front of the house of Katherine de Vaucelles where Villon, already drunk as a lord, began calling out her name. His faithful friends Montigny, Tabary, and Cayaux jeered along with him and Montigny's hound joined in by barking like mad. As usual, I had to be the smart one and persuade them to leave before her angry father or servant came down to confront us. Villon was in enough trouble already and had made a complete fool of himself that night.

Montigny's hound was the first to obey me and soon afterwards, his master joined us as well. Cayaux and Tabary reacted only when I pulled on their ears, but Villon needed a big slap. Although he usually handled my physical assaults well, that time he collapsed to the ground. Whether it was the slap or the barrel of wine he had drunk, he was completely out of it. We tried to pull him up, but he insisted on staying put and kept muttering the name that I simply couldn't stand to hear anymore.

I was fed up with his never-ending whining, and decided to leave him there and let him suffer through it on his own. Taking care of him hadn't paid off so far so I prompted the drunken fools to go on and followed them into the dim streets.

"What if he does something reckless? We can't just abandon him," argued Montigny, tottering by my side.

"If he needs a tough lesson so be it!" I said determinedly, pulling him along with me like a rag doll.

Nevertheless, I did turn around to check on Villon before we disappeared around the corner, and I saw him crawling back to Katherine's house. He sat up and rested his head against her door, mumbling something under his breath. Then I caught a glimpse of a female figure in the window above him. She drifted past like a malicious apparition. It must have been the cold queen herself. I spat on the ground, hoping she would get the message.

✦

The following morning, Isabeau and I had to clean up the mess after the wild celebration.

"I preferred them when they were students," I complained to myself, cleaning up their vomit. "At least they had better manners. Now they are all just cocky criminals!"

"I know that you like them nonetheless, Margot," said Isabeau with that wise smile of hers. "This all is just a part of their charm."

"This?" I lifted the dirty rag and shook my head.

She laughed but froze when the door swung open. Villon rushed inside naked, covering his crotch with his hands. I couldn't help but clasp my hands together and cry out, "Have you gone completely mad, Villon?"

He just stood there, shivering and out of breath. Thank goodness he at least had his shoes on. We hurried to him with blankets and wrapped him up like a baby. His teeth were chattering as he explained.

"I woke up like this at Katherine's house. Someone must have stolen my clothes, and I was too wasted to notice. I woke up frozen to the bone and to my horror saw Jolis approaching. He thought I had undressed myself as some kind of provocation. I was unable to argue with him. My head was spinning – I was in shock. The whole situation seemed absurd. I wanted to leave, but tripped over, and that's when he took off his belt. He started to whip me! Can you imagine? He whipped me all the way here, as if my humiliation hadn't reached its peak already!"

He wheezed and checked our reaction. Isabeau and I looked at each other, both imagining him running through the streets of Paris like a biblical Adam after the expulsion, followed by gasps and cheers. The vision made us both burst out laughing and we could not stop ourselves. The scoundrel had it coming! I was glad someone had finally woken him from the unattainable dream he kept clinging to. Villon frowned at us both at first, but in the end, he began laughing along with us. At some point, I wasn't certain whether he was actually crying as well, but it didn't matter. We all knew that if he survived the day without fever, he would only grow stronger.

CHAPTER 11

VILLON THE PIMP

Noël's lashes seemed to have whipped Katherine from Villon's mind. He no longer spoke of her or drowned his sorrow in wine, and most importantly, he kept his promise. He had successfully arranged us some wealthy customers with whom I supplied my most beautiful, well-mannered girls. Everything was organised discreetly, in the privacy of their homes. One day, Villon came to my chamber with a daring proposal.

"There's this one honourable nobleman," he started while pouring us both the Gouais Blanc, the only wine he could afford to buy himself. "He's a young, handsome widower who lives in one of those affluent stone-built houses on the Right Bank and who hasn't been with a woman since his wife passed away. I have never met a more sophisticated and wiser man in my life, well, except for Guillaume who would never indulge in such…"

"What are you trying to say, Villon?" I interrupted him, as we both knew what he was building up to.

He smiled at my understanding and said, "His wife was similar to you in some ways… a curved belle with lustrous locks and forget-me-not kind of eyes…"

"Flattery will get you nowhere!" I warned him.

"Ha, it has got me to wondrous places before," he teased, finishing his wine in one gulp. Then he jumped up and threw me on the bed with a playful smile. I felt joy pump through my veins at the sight of his jolly face. He was finally acting like the man I fell for years ago. However, after we finished our routine of wearing each other out, he suggested, "How about meeting the widower tonight?"

I pushed him away and crawled out of the bed.

"Stop acting like a pimp. I thought we both agreed you were just a matchmaker."

He smiled and reasoned with me. "Come on, Margot, we both know that you'll be horny again in two hours."

I hated how easily he turned from a sweet boy to a cunning rogue. I threw his clothes at him and pointed at the door. "And by then you'll be finished sweeping the floors!"

His smile faded. He knew I was not toying with him anymore and so he agreed.

After he left my chamber, I began to mull over his proposition, and finally decided to do it. It was for the silliest reason. I wished to make him jealous, although I knew painfully well that I could never be the next Katherine.

Despite my misgivings, I let Villon take me to the widower the following day. I wore my finest gown, a modern hat Wolf gave me, and even shaved myself for the occasion. The "hairy cunt" fashion was long passé and everyone preferred the new look not to mention better hygiene. To my disappointment, Villon showed no jealousy on our way to the widower's home. He was happy and talkative, boring me with unnecessary information about the man. I didn't bother listening to it, too busy regretting the stupid whim already.

As we neared our destination, Villon suddenly became quiet and serious, and I soon realised why. It seemed like some kind of cruel joke that of all people, Katherine de Vaucelles and Noël Jolis were walking towards us, staring at us like a pair of statues. Jolis, the sly bastard who snuck into my chamber and stole the poem I treasured, looked as disdainful as ever. On the other hand, Katherine seemed inwardly tormented, just like Villon. The situation was truly absurd. We were the poem she dreaded brought to life, although Villon would never dare to lay a hand on me. The look Katherine gave me that day shook me to the core. I didn't see the icy queen in her face, just a disappointed maiden whose romantic vision of love was completely shattered. However, she soon looked away from me and tortured Villon with her gaze instead. Their eye contact was intense but short because Jolis hurried her away as fast as he could. I had to hold Villon tightly by my side so that he wouldn't do anything foolish like run after her or fight the man who treated him so deviously.

"Let her go, my poet," I whispered into his ear comfortingly. Katherine turned around and stole one last glance in his direction. I sensed that she still loved him. Why wouldn't she? He was an adorable rascal who had a way with words and his hands, although he was tormented by heartache, debts and a bad reputation. However, I still had high hopes for him. He was a special breed, such that even God must favour.

The encounter with the newly engaged couple reopened Villon's old wounds. After that, he walked beside me like a living corpse and recovered only once we arrived at the widower's house. He was waiting for us and seemed uneasy and shy just like I imagined him to be. Coming face to face with this desperate man made even the desire to make Villon jealous fade. I felt like a mercenary in a way. Before I followed him inside the large, well-built house, I kissed Villon on the cheek and said, "Wait here for me, I will make you forget about her as soon as I'm done."

Villon forced a smile and then drew away to a nearby alcove.

After the widower had fed me some delicacies and dressed me up in his wife's clothes, he proceeded to expend his long-suppressed lust on my reclining body. While he thought of his dead wife, I thought of Villon, and Villon thought of Katherine. How pathetic! I missed the times when his mind belonged only to me. I was not just a substitute back in the day. I was his favourite whore, and that was something.

✦

To cheer Villon up, I drank and danced with him and his friends all night. Villon clung to me, Montigny to Isabeau, and Cayaux to Tabary – just like back in the days when they had come to my tavern after school. And just like then, Villon decided to share one of his newest poems with us. He entitled it *The Ballad to Lovers* and explained that it was mainly a personal declaration. He claimed that he was finally done with love, and for some reason considered that a good thing. The band played a cheerful tune to set the tone as he jumped on the table and theatrically began reciting:

So go on fall in love all you please!

Celebrate it on gatherings or fests
Just be ready to lose it all for a tease
As all you'll bang is just your head!
Foolish love turns us into beasts
Just look at Solomon and his queen
Or Samson who lost sight quite literally
Lucky the man who escapes it!

And now about my poor lot I shall scribe:
I was beaten like laundry in a stream
Completely naked too, why would I lie?
And who made me eat that putrid cream?
No one else than Katherine de Vaucelles!
And Noël, the damn third wheel
Lucky the man who escapes it!

The following day, we learned that Katherine de Vaucelles and Noël Jolis were officially wed. Villon feared that his heart would not survive it and therefore began to write his last will in a way that came most naturally to him – in verse. He retreated to his home at Porte Rouge, and returned only when he was finished. He paid off all his debts like he promised and announced that he was finally ready to start anew in a place where his name was not stained with gossip and hatred. He chose Angers, as that's where his father's brother resided. It didn't worry him that it was the same man who had kicked his mother and the young Villon out on to the streets once before. He said that had happened due to an unfortunate misunderstanding. His uncle assumed that his mother had started an affair with his neighbour and there was no reasoning with him back then. Only the many years apart and after a few warm letters had been exchanged, the two made peace and all was forgiven.

We all supported his decision to begin again somewhere else, even me, since I came to realise that it was the only way for him to be happy. The only trouble was that he needed more money for the journey. His friends were trying to come up with ways to help him, but since he wasn't willing to join the Coquillards like them, there was not much they could do. However, Cayaux's new friend, the emaciated bandit Petit Jehan, who was known as the best picklock in Paris, arrived with an intriguing proposal one evening.

"I have had my eye on the fine treasures stored at the College of Navarre for quite some time but have been waiting for the right accomplices. Ex-students would be a perfect fit, don't you think?"

"We studied at the Sorbonne, not Navarre," noted Cayaux.

Petit Jehan smirked. "I know that, and I also know that the College of Navarre has always been in competition with the Sorbonne."

"We hold no grudges, though," said Villon firmly, clearly opposed to the idea already. He was never as big a crook as everyone thought. His ethics were definitely stronger than the rest of the crowd. He would never cause any harm to his friends or people he respected. Petit Jehan ignored him, and went on reasoning with them.

"You have been inside its halls, though, so you know your way around, right?"

"Forget about it," laughed Villon. "My friends and I would never join you in a crime against any university."

I noticed the way Cayaux and Tabary exchanged a look. They seemed to have formed a pact already, but Villon was oblivious to it.

"Are you such a loyal student?" sneered Petit Jehan.

"What if I am? The university gave me years of wonderful experiences not to say providing me with financial support and the best status I could ever ask for. If I had ever abused it, it was due to necessity. I'm grateful for my student years and will always appreciate what they gave me."

I watched Villon with pride whilst pretending to dry the bowls at the next table. Petit Jehan was suspicious of my presence at first, but he stopped eyeing me as soon as Villon told him that I was their friend.

"Forget about sentiment, Villon. We all know that the universities and the Church are the biggest criminal cliques," argued Petit Jehan again and Cayaux chipped in soon after.

"Indeed. They have plenty, and we have nothing. If they were true benefactors, they would have provided us with better prospects for our future, but look at us today – what have we become?"

"What we have become is our own fault," said Villon. "And by the way, Tabary has found himself a good job so don't include him in your generalisation."

We all looked at Villon as if he had been sleeping for a year and had just woken up, which might have been true in a way. Suddenly, it dawned on him and he turned to his younger friend with a look of disappointment.

"Don't tell me you joined the Coquillards as well!"

Tabary didn't dare to reply or even look at him. Villon was someone he had always admired despite having a worse criminal record than all of them put together.

"Of course he did!" answered Cayaux for him, "and if you were smart, you'd be joining our brotherhood too instead of running away like a coward!"

Villon glared at Cayaux but didn't argue with him. He was wise enough to know that like all his friends, Cayaux just desperately wanted him to stay in Paris.

"I thought we all learned our lesson five years ago when our classmates lost their lives at the hands of the law. We promised not to test our luck anymore. I know, I may seem like the last person to lecture you after all that I have done, but that is exactly why you should take it from me: it's no fun waiting for the axe to fall, and trust me, there are many free spaces at the Gibbet of Montfaucon."

The young men grew silent, all except for Cayaux.

"But Wolf has taught us how well crime and the law connect," he argued. "He has shown us how to go about it without being caught."

Villon laughed at his blindness. "Are you serious? Then tell me where Wolf was when our friends were bleeding to death on the bridge? Hiding at home along with Montigny and me! You must be stupid to think that he would ever help you when it comes down to it!"

Cayaux fired back straight away. "And where was our beloved alma mater that day, huh? They raised us like an obedient herd of cattle. They fed us nice, fresh treats, but only because they were raising us for the slaughter!"

Villon lost his cool and grabbed Cayaux by the collar. "Stop with all the insults! Don't you recall all those carefree years we had? It was the best time of our lives!"

Then he stood up and walked away from the table, heading straight for the door. I shot Cayaux a threatening look and went after Villon. Outside the inn, we met Montigny who had just thrown some butter on one of his red boots and was letting his hound lick it off.

"My new invention," he explained with an oblivious smile. "The boots have never been cleaner!"

He threw some butter on the other boot as well so the hound couldn't decide where to lick first. Although Villon was still visibly upset, he couldn't help but smile at the sight of his friend.

"Ah, Montigny!" he patted him on the back. "I will miss you."

Montigny gave him a disapproving glance. "You promised not to bring it up anymore, Villon. You know how much it upsets Estienne de Montigny II."

Villon laughed and patted the poor hungry beast as well.

"Maybe you should ask Wolf for help instead," I suggested. "He is more experienced than that shady bandit inside."

"Oh, you mean Petit Jehan?" asked Montigny. "Cayaux told me about his idea. It would be a clean theft, no strings attached, and it's not like it's the Sorbonne."

"That doesn't matter," insisted Villon. "You wouldn't do it, would you?"

"I don't have to," he said proudly. "Wolf has finer work for me."

"Really? Like robbing a rich widow after banging her all night?" I sniggered at him. "That's fine work indeed!"

"Like your work is any better," muttered Montigny, which made me slap him and exclaim, "Our work is as fair as could be and you know it, so don't you dare insult me on my doorstep!"

Montigny touched his cheek, complaining, "I don't know why you women treat me like dirt. That shrew you just mentioned made up the story about me raping and robbing her. You give me a hard time whenever I see you, and Isabeau – don't even get me started on that!"

"What are you talking about? Isabeau is a good friend to you," I argued.

"Pfft, I have enough friends already! She can stick her friendship up that lovely arse of hers."

"Have you ever considered why she goes with everyone but you, you fool? Don't forget that with us prostitutes it's all reversed," I said, dusting off his shabby overcoat as an apologetic gesture. I enjoyed teasing and occasionally even beating the poor man, but I still liked him best of all Villon's friends. Montigny thought about what I had said and absentmindedly dropped another piece of butter on top of his red boot to employ his loyal hound again. I shook my head.

"That poor beast is as skinny as you, Montigny! Bring him inside, I'll give him some kitchen scraps."

"See, Estienne?" he addressed the hound with a loving smile. "She is finally showing you some sympathy. Let's hope I'll have the same luck."

"You can share the scraps," I said, prompting the hound to follow me.

Villon laughed, but Montigny just pulled a face. While the hound and I retreated into the inn, the two men stayed outside, discussing crimes that I was grateful not to be a part of. Luckily, I never had to steal anything but asceticism or innocence.

✦

Villon didn't come to my chamber that night, however, he returned the following day, requesting a jar of his favourite burgundy and my full attention.

"I have just said goodbye to Guillaume and Mother," he said with a tormented expression. "I didn't realise it would be so heart-wrenching. Guillaume pleaded with me to become a cleric like him, Mother cried… The poor woman has shed too many tears for me. I hope she will have less worries now that she won't have to deal with all my wrongdoings."

"When do you plan to leave?" I asked with a heavy heart.

"Tomorrow morning."

"So soon?" I was unable to hide the wild emotions rushing in. He stroked my face and smiled. "Only if tonight's robbery goes well."

"I hope you don't mean the College of Navarre?"

He wavered, then had a big gulp of the burgundy and looked down at his feet. I could tell he was ashamed, even in front of a woman who always tolerated his misbehaviour.

"I need to pay for the trip to Angers. I can't live off my uncle, it's enough that I'm still indebted to Guillaume. I despise the idea of robbing a university, but Cayaux is right, it's better to steal from a rich institution than from an individual. The treasure there would probably be used for superficial indulgences anyway..."

"Still, this is going to change everything," I reminded him. We both knew that despite the student pranks he had initiated in the past, he had never wanted to become a thief like his friends.

"I know, please don't remind me," he begged, drowning his bad conscience in the burgundy. I poured him some more, thinking of another way to help him. Although I had been warned not to, I suggested it anyway. "I could lend you money. I have some savings that nobody knows about..."

Villon grasped my hands and kissed them with the gentle attention he used to shower me with before Katherine bewitched him. I sensed that things might change for us with time, but what good was that if he had to leave?

"You are the kindest and most generous woman I have ever known," he said, looking gratefully into my eyes, "but I promised myself to never take advantage of you or anyone else ever again."

I sighed. I knew he would do the right thing for us all in the end, even if it went against his morals. As he himself wrote once: *Necessity makes people vile, just as hunger drives wolves from the wild.*

Chapter 12

Villon the Thief

The five brothers in crime, Petit Jehan, a newcomer called Dom Nicholas, Colin de Cayaux, Guy Tabary and François Villon, returned shortly after midnight, and judging by their mysterious behaviour, the robbery had been successfully completed. I kicked out the last few drunks who were still lingering at the tavern so that we could discuss what had happened. Montigny joined us soon afterwards, as he was also curious about how Villon's first organised crime had gone. We all knew well that it was the last night we would be together, for Villon's plan was to leave before dawn, and so we turned the secret meeting into a private celebration. Only one member of our group was still missing, but we expected her to be back soon. Isabeau was at a nearby house with another one of those rich customers that Villon had arranged for us and since he was so busy that night, Wolf had promised to look after her in case there was trouble.

I wanted to enjoy the last few hours I had left with my poet and therefore acted as host to the company, supplying a generous amount of ale, wine, and food. However, since I was hoping to invite him to my chamber one last time before he departed, I made sure that he didn't drink too much. Luckily for me, he agreed with me, mainly because he needed to be prepared for the early morning journey to Angers.

"So tell me all about the robbery! And don't leave anything out," I commanded once our bellies were filled with enough ale. Villon didn't seem keen to talk about it, though.

"Why would we discuss it? It was the lowest point of our lives."

"Speak for yourself," argued Cayaux. "To me it was the other way around!"

Despite his initial bashful approach to crime, Cayaux had become the proudest Coquillard over time. The other men cheered him on while Villon turned away from them and gulped the last of his ale. Cayaux meanwhile started telling us the story.

"To our surprise, it all went rather smoothly. We started by climbing over Robert de Saint-Simon's house, and in the courtyard, a tall ladder waited for us, perfect for reaching the second storey of the college. Tabary held the ladder and a small lantern, which provided enough light for us to see, but not too much to alert the neighbours. Thank God, the moon was hidden behind the clouds the whole time, so if anyone saw us, they probably made out only five indistinguishable male figures."

"Still, we had our faces partly covered just in case," added Tabary with wide-open, exhilarated eyes.

"Let me speak, will you?" Cayaux hushed him. Tabary pulled a face and let him carry on.

"We broke in through one of those creaky old windows and moved through the darkened hall. Dom Nicholas and Villon clutched their weapons in case anyone surprised us while Petit Jehan and I prepared our lockmaster tools. The college was quiet as a tomb, so we quietly snuck to the vestry entrance, which Petit Jehan masterfully unlocked."

"He didn't even need your help with it," jumped in Tabary again so Cayaux angrily elbowed him. "Stop interrupting, you idiot!"

The two were like an old married couple, probably because they were so unlucky with women.

"However, once we had found the chest with the treasure, I showed off my own lock mastery as well," crowed Cayaux. "It had four heavy locks: three for a big key and the other for a tiny one. It was very difficult to work on that one, but I managed it quite quickly, right?"

"Yes, only we almost fell asleep while you were doing it!" laughed Tabary and the two started arguing again.

What an odd group of criminals, I thought as I observed their childish dispute. Most of them seemed immature and witless yet they knew how to skilfully rob a university.

"Anyway," continued Cayaux when they were done quarrelling, "when I unlocked the big chest, I found out that there was another, smaller chest inside it. Even though it had fewer locks, it was still an unexpected complication. Dom Nicholas and I began to feel nervous, so we peeked out into the dim hall to make sure we were not being spied on. The halls were clear, but after a moment of careful listening, we heard a squeak. It made us all worried, though it was probably just the wind. If someone saw us, he must have disappeared in fright, and waited until we were gone."

"He was right to be afraid," noted Villon. "God knows what else we could have sunk to…"

I turned to Villon with an exasperated glance. His dark attitude worried me, and I hoped he was done with all the sulking. I prompted Cayaux to tell us more. "And then?"

"Well, Petit Jehan and I helped each other to unlock the smaller chest to reveal the heavenly glitter of the treasure! Five hundred golden crowns, one hundred for each of us."

"Let's stop chattering and put these filthy earnings to use instead," said Villon. "I want to make my last night in Paris memorable."

His words brought sadness to our faces, as we all dreaded the fact that he had to leave.

"Maybe we should all leave Paris," suggested Tabary. "This town will not be the same without you anyway so why stay behind?"

Villon smiled at his young friend. "You will soon forget about me, you'll see."

"Hardly," smirked Montigny, "we are loyal beasts."

He winked at his hound but avoided eye contact with Villon. We all knew that Montigny was taking his escape the hardest of us all. The two had been inseparable since childhood and despite never saying it aloud, I knew they loved each other like brothers. Villon patted the hound and said, "Take care of your master, will you? He's not as bad as he pretends to be."

We all noticed the gloom in Montigny's expression, though he tried to hide it behind a brave face. He broke the dismal atmosphere himself. "Let's get wasted already! I need to stop my mind from rolling tonight."

We were all cheering when suddenly we were disturbed by a loud knocking. I had locked the door that night in case someone was looking for the thieves. However, a different tragedy was about to play out. As soon as I unlocked the door, Wolf stumbled inside with Isabeau in his arms. He was out of breath and she was motionless, her face and dress covered in blood.

"Take her from me," wheezed Wolf. "I carried her the whole way…"

We all rushed to his aid at once. Montigny took her into his arms and when he noticed the deep cuts on her listless body, his face flooded with pain. She was still alive so I tried to wake her, but she must have fainted, for she didn't react at all. Wolf had meanwhile collapsed on the chair, trying to catch his breath in order to explain what had happened. I quickly checked the injuries on her arms, legs and belly. I knew we should treat them as soon as possible if we wanted her to survive, so I looked at Montigny and said, "Take her upstairs. I'll bring some warm water and cloths. We need to clean and stitch up the wounds."

Villon helped Montigny carry Isabeau up the stairs and as soon as they had disappeared, I turned to Wolf and demanded to know what the client did to her.

"She wouldn't say. I broke into the house when I heard her scream and found her tied to the wall with a rope! I knocked the bastard unconscious, freed her and took her away from his lair as fast as I could."

I patted his arm. "You've done well, thank you, Wolf."

He shrugged at the comment. "They are my girls too, remember?"

His reminder of the fact that I was not the owner of the house irritated me. However, despite our occasional differences and competition, he was the only family I had left. I fetched him some ale before I hurried upstairs to help Isabeau.

Unfortunately, there were many such brutes out there, and so I was used to healing my girls when it came to the physical and emotional repercussions of such horrendous assaults. I always cursed while doing it and this time was no exception. I blamed myself for letting Isabeau go to that devil's house in the first place and promised myself to never risk anything like that again, and take my girls only to the customers we already knew.

Villon brought me some more clean water and a goblet of aqua vita for disinfection. The intense smell brought Isabeau back to consciousness, but her mouth was swollen from the beating so I advised her not to speak. I encouraged her to stay still and let me take care of her. Judging from the ugly bruises on her neck, I could tell that the bastard had even tried to strangle her, probably when she fought back. He must have been whipping or cutting her while she was tied up. I treated the wounds with care and diligence to prevent any possible infection from spreading.

Montigny insisted on staying with us and helping me so I made him useful. He asked about the man and where he lived, immersed in the desire to punish him for what he had done to Isabeau, but I knew it would only get him into trouble, so I didn't tell him.

"These things happen to women like us, Montigny," I said. "It's not the first or the last time, so just let it be before you do more harm."

"It could be the last time," he objected, referring to his desire to take Isabeau under his wing.

"Like that would make any difference!" I laughed at him, but Isabeau squeezed my hand, her eyes pleading with me to stop giving him such a hard time.

"I would never hurt a woman," continued Montigny, offended by my comment. "You know very well that the obnoxious rape story was made up by that horny hag after I stole her husband's gem collection!"

Isabeau couldn't help but smile despite her pain, and seeing her reaction made me smirk as well.

"I was just toying with you, Montigny," I said with a friendlier tone then. "Now you should give us some privacy. I need to check the rest of Isabeau's body."

Montigny agreed, however, he couldn't refrain from stroking Isabeau's hair first. "If she is too rough with you, call me, I'll be waiting outside the door and will remain at your service for as long as you need."

Once he had finally left, I tended to Isabeau with the gentle, loving part of me that I showed to no one but her. "I'm so sorry. I never wanted you to go through something like this."

"I know," she rasped and helped me undress her aching body. The cuts were worst on her back and buttocks and must have hurt badly when I treated them. She was brave, though, and trusted my skills. She once said I was like an older sister to her and I wished to be just that to all the poor souls who still roamed the streets, selling their bodies for the price of a slab of butter. Whenever I saw potential in one of those street strumpets, I offered them a way out. Most of the girls hoped that my establishment would be a step closer to a normal life, but none of the visitors ever showed more than just a physical interest in them. That's why I couldn't help but marvel at that one exception: Regnier de Montigny. Although he was a criminal, life with him would surely be a better option for Isabeau.

"Montigny really cares about you," I said, to keep her mind occupied during the worst procedures. "I think you should at least give him a chance."

She didn't respond at first, so I thought that I had upset her even more, however, after a moment of contemplation she finally confided in me, in spite of the pain.

"Do you know why I keep refusing him? It has something to do with why I stopped giving palm readings years ago... I had an awful vision when I looked at Regnier's lifeline. I saw death, Margot. I saw him swaying on a rope at the Gibbet of Montfaucon and it scared me even more than my feelings for him. I was afraid to give into it and my apprehension intensified after he joined the Coquillards. I began to fear that it had sealed his fate. I warned him about the gang many times, but he didn't listen. How could I live with a man whose death I had foreseen? His passing would break my heart now so imagine what would happen if we were lovers..."

I thought about it. Although I had never taken her palmistry skills seriously in the past, she had already proved to be right on a few occasions. Like the time Agnes found her lost husband or the time Rose gave birth prematurely. The prediction that I would love only two men in my life seemed quite believable as well. Nevertheless, what she told me about Montigny that evening sent chills down my spine.

"Even if that vision came true, isn't it better to enjoy the time you have left with him rather than dismiss the feelings altogether? Love is a miracle, Isabeau, especially when it's mutual."

She gave me a painful smile, but I could tell that nothing would change her mind. The poor soul had lost her family when she was very young and I knew that due to that, she had always tried to detach herself emotionally. I was the only one she let into her heart and that was probably just out of despair. I too clung to my girls like they were my own kin.

✦

After our company had dispersed and Isabeau fell asleep with Montigny by her side, Villon and I retreated to my chamber to spend the short time before his carriage arrived alone. Instead of seducing him like I was used to, I couldn't help but worry about the possible consequences of the robbery. What Isabeau said about Montigny made me remember all the times I had joined Wolf at the gallows, witnessing the executions of his fellow criminals. I couldn't stand it if Villon suffered such a cruel end.

"We left no traces behind," he said, trying to calm me down, "and most likely they won't even notice that the money is gone until a few months later. It was part of a reserve that is rarely checked. With hindsight, I have to admit that this was a masterful plan."

Although he might have been right, I was still apprehensive. Villon poured us another glass of the delicious burgundy and prompted me to have a drink with him. We toasted each other, trying to remain optimistic like we used to be.

"To your first robbery then!" I said before I had a sip.

He gave me a sad look and added, "Let's hope it was also the last one."

Then he rested his head on my pillow and began to confess. "As we ran through the dark streets, I realised that no matter how fast I run or how well I hide, I will never escape the stigma of what I have done. The Devil's Fart was just a student prank and the murder of Sermoise self-defence, this, however, was an intentional crime."

"You are too hard on yourself," I said, and for some reason, the words made him sit up. He looked away, as if remembering something he wished not to be reminded of. I sensed that it had something to do with Katherine but didn't want to ask as I knew it would spoil the time we had left together.

"I feel like a complete failure, Margot," he admitted. "I failed those I love and mainly myself. When I was younger, I imagined that my future would be something spectacular... My mother and I were so relieved and moved when Guillaume arranged for me to study at the Sorbonne. It was a dream come true for a boy from such a poor background. I really wanted to make him and my mother proud, yet I couldn't stop that strange restlessness within me, and ended up being nothing but a disappointment.

"I could never lie to them, so they know everything about me, even the things they would rather not. They have never said it to my face, they love me too much for that, but I know what they really think of me. Those two are the only real Christians that I know, and there are some things that they simply can't understand…"

"Like this moment?" I guessed, seductively leaning closer to him, showing off my deep cleavage. Although he gave each of my bulging breasts a kiss, for some reason he didn't initiate anything more.

"I don't want a taste of something that I will be deprived of from now on," he said, but I didn't believe him. I knew he was thinking of Katherine. Since she had become Madame Jolis and thereby officially closed the door on their short-lived affair, he had become distant with me again.

"Cayaux, Dom Nicholas and Petit Jehan will also leave Paris for a few months," he said after a pause. "We have all decided to lie low just in case there is a commotion. Only Tabary plans to stay behind, but he should be safe. He was just the lookout man anyway, and nobody would go after such an innocent-looking fella." He smiled to himself.

"Don't underestimate the least suspicious brother in crime," I warned, intuiting that something could go wrong, mainly because Tabary had such a big mouth. Villon just shrugged, though.

"I trust he will control himself when it comes to such a serious matter."

My throat tightened when the church bells struck four, as it announced the hour of his departure. After he had packed up the few things he owned, he reached into his overcoat for a scroll of parchment tied with a red ribbon.

"I wrote you a new poem," he said, handing me the scroll. "It's more than just a joke this time, and it's meant only for you. Let Montigny read it to you when I'm gone."

He wasn't much for goodbyes, so he just squeezed me in a tight embrace and rushed off, leaving nothing behind but that scroll of parchment and a broken heart.

CHAPTER 13

THE RED BOOTS OF REGNIER DE MONTIGNY

The house felt dreadfully lonely without Villon. I missed his laughter, poetry and even his occasional broodiness. I kept telling myself that I should simply focus on my everyday tasks and avoid thinking about him, but it was hard when every corner of the tavern was imprinted with the memory of him. I often lost myself in reverie, remembering the way my world lit up when he came in. I kept picturing his face so as not to forget a single wrinkle, yet time began to erase it bit by bit anyway.

Isabeau was still recovering from the horror she had been subjected to and although her physical wounds were healing fast, it was too soon to deal with the emotional repercussions. From what she had told me, I fully understood why she was so afraid to return to her duties. The monster had strapped her down, whipped and raped her. Although Wolf tried to break inside as fast as he could, most of the damage was already done when he finally reached her.

She tried to go with one of our regulars a week after the accident, but began shaking uncontrollably as soon as he undressed, so I advised her to work only down at the tavern from then on. I even began to consider whether it would be better if she stopped selling her body altogether. I knew it would be a shame since she was the fairest of our girls, but she could help us in other ways. I sensed that she might ultimately accept Montigny's offer and become his wife, as the way he had been taking care of her after the horrendous experience made her believe in their love, no matter how short lived it might be.

We hadn't seen him around for quite some time, when one early morning he burst into the tavern with a crazed expression. He just stared at us while his hound barked as though he was trying to speak for him. When I noticed that his hands and clothes were covered in blood, I quickly called Isabeau and we both hurried to his side. Her presence seemed to make him even more distressed, though. Since there was no one else around, we seated him at the table and checked whether he was injured or not. He had a few scratches on his arms, but nothing that required immediate attention. Isabeau stroked his cheek as if hoping to see into his faraway look.

"It's all right, Regnier," she said compassionately, "whatever you tell us stays between the three of us."

I thought he might be more communicative after he had had a drink or two, so I offered him someone's leftover ale. He gulped it all thirstily then took a deep breath and stammered, "I... I think... I think I killed him."

He and Isabeau locked eyes with each other in a panic.

"Who, Regnier?" she inquired with a quivering voice.

Montigny turned away from her, struggling with distress and deep regret.

"I finally found out who he was and where he lived..."

I buried my face in my hands at the realisation. We should have known that he would do something foolish to avenge Isabeau. I immediately blamed myself for being oblivious to it. Since Villon had saved her from Sermoise, Montigny had been struggling with senseless jealousy. He wanted to be the hero in her eyes, the one who risked his life for hers.

"How could you have been so stupid, Montigny!" I cried. He looked away from us again, but I couldn't stop myself from rambling on. "What were you thinking? You should have known that this would only bring us more misery! Do you even realise how serious this is? The man was a noble, damn it!"

"He was a monster!" roared Montigny.

"Yes, but couldn't you have just beaten him up, cut off his balls or something? Why on earth did you have to kill the man?"

"I only went there to rob him," he argued, the need to defend himself bringing him to his senses.

"I snuck into his house while he was still asleep, but before I had even managed to go through his valuables, he appeared in the doorway... I took out my dagger, he took out his, and we fought for what seemed like eternity until suddenly he was on the ground and I was standing above his motionless body..."

"Did anyone see you leave the house?"

"No... Well, maybe... Some people saw me in his street... I don't know. I panicked and ran off..."

As he stammered the words out, I checked on Isabeau who had been suspiciously quiet since he began confessing to us. I noticed that she had turned pale and was shaking like an aspen leaf so I grabbed her round the waist in case she fainted.

"Calm down, Isabeau. Wolf will take care of this, don't worry."

Montigny supported Isabeau from the other side and we helped her sit down. Her reaction surprised him for no words could have shown her feelings for him better. He began to lose himself in her face, so I shook him and asked, "Have you spoken to Wolf yet?"

He quickly recovered and said, "No... I thought he'd be here..."

"Then I'll go and find him, tell him to arrange a carriage or a boat for you straight away. We must help you escape Paris."

"Maybe it won't be necessary," he argued, looking at Isabeau. "I have talked myself out of trouble before..."

"Wake up, Montigny! This is far worse than some burglary! You can't just count on luck this time."

I quickly threw on my cape and instructed him to hide in my chamber and have some more wine to calm down. Montigny nodded, but Isabeau just stared at me, desperately seeking some comfort.

"And give her some as well," I advised, sighing at the sight of the two unfortunate souls.

✦

Isabeau had been impatiently waiting for my return and as soon as I walked into the tavern, she pulled me aside from the other girls and customers and begged, "What did Wolf say? Is he able to help him?"

"He is arranging a boat for him," I said softly, carefully scanning the room. There could have been sergeants here already, working in disguise, eavesdropping.

"He ordered me to let him stay here until he comes over to fetch him. We can definitely count on his help, Isabeau, you know how fond he is of Montigny. We should not give in to fear, and do anything we can to keep him safe in the meantime."

Isabeau's cold hands clasped mine. "All right, we will do that, but tell me, was there a commotion in the streets?"

I nodded, unable to lie. The situation was indeed serious. The sergeants were already roaming the nearby streets, investigating the crime and questioning the neighbours. I looked around, worried that someone might overhear us, however, our guests were busy with the girls. Some of them had even started to mess around right there in the main room so I had to raise a warning finger that sent them to the upper floors. I didn't tolerate such behaviour at my brothel.

"We have to find a better hideout for him now," I whispered to Isabeau once I had finished admonishing them. "When they find out his identity, this place will certainly be their first stop."

"But where should we take him? Nowhere is safe really…" she whispered, anxiety clutching at her throat.

"I'd suggest the cellar or the loft. Let him
decide."

I could tell that Isabeau was about to burst into
tears soon, so I squeezed her trembling hands and
encouraged her, "Hurry. Go to him and try to
remain calm. That's all we can do for now."

She nodded in distress and ran up the stairs
while I turned to my customers with a forced smile.
I took some new orders and encouraged my girls to
attend to the newcomers. I tried to pretend that it
was just another one of those normal busy days,
but my chest tightened as I remembered the fate
that Isabeau had foreseen in Montigny's palm. I
was terrified that it would come true as many of
her predictions did. I thought of Villon and
wondered what he would do in my shoes, how he
would behave in the tense situation, but my mind
seemed to be as numb as my heart. I couldn't and
didn't even want to imagine the world without
Regnier de Montigny in it.

After some time had passed, I noticed that Guy
Tabary had walked in with some new
acquaintances.

"Margot!" he waved at me, pretending to be a
venerated regular. "Fetch us some fine burgundy,
will you? I bring you special guests today!"

I fixed my hands on my hips and scowled. He
had never ordered me around before and after
what I had planned for him, he would never dare
to again. I assumed that he just wanted to impress

his companions as he had back in the days when he used to follow around Villon, Montigny and Cayaux. Since he was Villon's friend, I decided not to embarrass him and keep the punishment until we were alone. Therefore, I quietly led Tabary and his friends to the gang's favourite table. I didn't like the way they were surveying the space as though we had something to hide. I wasn't used to such suspicious behaviour, my customers usually went straight for a drink or a girl. One of the men noticed me eyeing him and he gave me an inquisitive look.

"Where would I find the man of the house?" he asked.

"Woman of the house," I corrected him, but he just laughed, which upset me even more.

"What is so funny? I do look after this place!"

"But surely there must be a…"

"The owner has entrusted me with his property. He is absent at the moment," I explained curtly.

"It's true," chipped in Tabary and grabbed me by the waist. "This beauty is the madam of the place!"

My silent glare made him take his hands off and watch me from a respectful distance like he was used to doing.

"If you wish to speak to the owner, you'll have to wait until he returns, though that could take many hours, even days. Nobody knows where he went and how long he'll be gone."

"The owner is Jean de Loup, alias Wolf," added Tabary. "He's a good friend of mine."

His newly found assertiveness faltered again when he saw my grave expression. I didn't like him bragging about the details of our establishment to complete strangers. The man noticed our exchange and gave me a sly smile.

"Very well then, I'll wait for this Jean de Loup… And if you would be so kind and bring us some cheese and bread with the wine, madam?"

My eyes bored into each one of them including Tabary. I didn't like these dubious men one bit. As I walked away, I heard him excuse my temperament.

"Margot is a highly esteemed woman around here. Even the toughest individuals don't dare to test her patience, she likes me, though, so no worries, my friends."

I smirked at his foolishness, but right away wondered whether to take him aside and tell him about what had happened to Montigny. In the end I decided not to. The boy was such a big mouth that he would probably do more harm than good.

So I prepared them a leftover mixture of random wines, scraped the green mildew from the cheese block, and found some hard bread for them as well. I was unwilling to share anything better. I also decided to cut the loaf at their table in order to eavesdrop on their conversation.

"I'm a fine locksmith myself, but I can also recommend the two finest ones in town to you," boasted Tabary as I struggled to cut into the hard bread. "They can deal with any kind of lock. I was there when they opened the most complicated one I had ever seen! However, they are not in Paris at the moment, so you would have to wait for them to return."

I couldn't believe it. Was the imbecile really thinking of introducing them to Petit Jehan and Colin de Cayaux just to make himself look important? I stomped on his foot to warn him, but he yelped as if I had plunged a hot piece of iron in his arse. I pinched him to be quiet, but he yelped again.

"Oh, did I step on your foot? I'm so sorry, Monsieur Tabary, I'm just so busy today. Actually, I could use your help with something outside."

"Can it wait, Margot? I'm in the middle of an important conversation here."

"Unfortunately, it can't wait," I insisted with that threatening voice of mine that made everyone obey. "The new load of herrings has just arrived. You wouldn't be so cruel as to let a woman of my delicate disposition carry it by herself, would you?"

I knew they would laugh at me, but I didn't mind. I was proud of my delicious, shapely figure and was not afraid to show it. Therefore, I turned to the chuckling herd and said, "As Monsieur Tabary mentioned, he is one of my favourite regulars, so he often helps us with practical matters…"

A flash of worry crossed Tabary's face. I rarely spoke kindly of him so he must have thought that I planned to mock him in front of the men he was trying so hard to impress. He gave me a worried smile and quickly stepped in.

"Margot is just trying to say that she goes crazy for my skills. This won't take long, my friends!"

He winked at his companions and hurried after me.

Once we were outside, he looked around and then at me, confused. "So where are the herrings?"

I gave him a proper slap. "What is wrong with you, you imbecile?"

"What's wrong with you?" he argued. "Why do you keep embarrassing me today?"

"Because you are sharing our secrets with complete strangers!"

He finally understood. "Oh, you don't need to worry about that, Margot. My new friends are criminals like the rest of us, but they are new in town, so they need some advice from an experienced local."

He smiled confidently, clasping his belt.

"How well do you know them?" I asked softly, very careful to not let anyone in the street overhear our conversation. "They could be investigating the burglary."

"Ah!" he threw his hands up carelessly. "There has been no hustle around the College of Navarre yet, you know that, Margot."

"That may be true, but some people operate in disguise," I said, "so stop being so damn reckless!"

Tabary sighed, disappointed to lose his chance to show off, so I pinched his buttocks again to make my advice clear. "Do you understand me?"

He didn't yelp that time, just frowned and nodded.

"And get those vermin out of here! I don't like them one bit," I ordered him before I headed back inside. Tabary went to follow me so I quickly stopped him.

"Where do you think you're going? You're supposed to be helping me with the herrings, remember? You must wait out here a moment longer."

He rolled his eyes but obeyed like they all did when Margot got fired up.

"And be glad that I let you go without punishment this time," I added, before closing the door. "Nobody treats me the way you just did at my inn!"

✦

The evening became busier, and I was running back and forth attending and serving my customers. Meanwhile, I kept checking on the stairs, wondering whether Isabeau had taken Montigny to the loft or decided on the cellar instead. I checked the cellar first, as I had to fetch some more wine anyway, but just found some drunken fool urinating in the corner. I kicked him out and was attempting to clean the mess up when suddenly I heard loud voices and footsteps coming from the main room.

I quickly ran back up, hoping only to witness a regular brawl, but instead I found myself in the scene I had been fearing the whole day. A group of sergeants were arguing with my girls, demanding to search the house. I quickly ran over to them and tried to reason with the tallest one who appeared to be their leader.

"How may I help you, gentlemen?"

"We are looking for Regnier de Montigny. We heard he's a regular here."

"Oh, Monsieur de Montigny? I haven't seen him around for ages! Is he in some kind of trouble?"

The sergeant didn't reply, just looked suspiciously around the tavern.

"It's our duty to find him," he said firmly and headed for the stairs without my permission. I spotted Isabeau standing on the first floor, gazing down at us like a frozen angel, so I quickly tried to block their path.

"There is nothing to find there but my girls satisfying their customers and I can assure you that

Regnier de Montigny is not one of them, so please let us get back to our work."

The leader must have sensed my nervousness, because he resolutely pushed me aside and ordered the others to search the upper floors. Although I wanted nothing more than to behave like the madam of the house and fetch my weapons, I knew I wouldn't stand a chance against the representatives of the law, so had no choice but to clench my teeth and let them do as they pleased.

I ran behind them, meeting with Isabeau who appeared strangely calm. What I found even more baffling was that she had Montigny's hound by her side. She was patting his head and calming him down as he softly growled at the sergeants. I leaned closer to her as soon as they began searching the chambers, finding nothing but shocked, naked figures inside.

"Where is he?" I whispered in her ear.

She just put her finger over her mouth and kept stroking the hound that stood by her side as if she was his new master. I could tell that her seemingly placid behaviour was really just a reaction to the unbearable stress she had been experiencing. I also assumed that something romantic had happened between her and Montigny, because she was wearing her nightgown. Whether it was for the better or worse I couldn't tell; all I knew was that it must have made Montigny's last moments with her even more precious.

After the sergeants left, Isabeau quickly explained that Montigny had escaped through the window as soon as they heard them coming. We tried not to despair. There was still hope that he would reach the boat that Wolf had arranged for him or that his life could be spared due to the Benefit of Clergy. It had helped Villon before and Montigny had been down a similar route many times. He was often imprisoned and released due to his good connections at the King's court. However, he was strictly warned that the provost would not be lenient with him forever just because of his fine background and we all knew what happened to those who were considered to be beyond redemption.

Montigny's hound became restless once Isabeau stopped patting him. He started to whine and run around, anxiously looking for his master. Isabeau forbade me to set him free into the streets, because she had promised Montigny to keep him safe.

"We must take care of him until Regnier returns," she insisted. "He would never forgive us if anything were to happen to him."

I agreed with her although we both sensed that we were only fooling ourselves and that we would be stuck with the poor animal from then on.

✦

Unfortunately, Wolf returned with dreadful news that night: Montigny had been caught and imprisoned at the Châtelet. For the two weeks that followed, we prayed that he would be absolved, but neither his privileges nor benefactors could save him this time. Isabeau tried her best as well. She went to the Châtelet determined to explain the reason for the accidental murder and beg for his release, however, the sergeants just laughed at her and refused to let her meet the provost. Had Wolf not gone with her that day she would have probably ended up being raped again as well. Since we had exhausted all our options for helping our friend out, we were left to pray and hope for the best outcome possible.

One day, Tabary burst into the pub with terror in his eyes and announced, "They are taking Regnier to Montfaucon!"

With that shocking news, he rushed off to see his friend one last time before the executioner broke his neck. He expected us to follow him and support Montigny in the final moments of his life and I was ready to do so until I saw Isabeau's ghostly face. I realised she could not bear to watch him die. Therefore, I embraced her tightly and let her know that I understood.

"Let's stay here and pray for him like we have thus far. He wouldn't want you to see his public humiliation anyway."

I knew it might not be true, and that perhaps it would give him more courage to pass away with dignity, but I had to console her somehow. Even though her heart was breaking, she didn't shed a tear during the hours that followed. She just stared fixedly at Montigny's hound. He too had stopped barking and was resting by the door, slowly giving up on the hope of ever seeing his master alive again.

I kicked out all the customers and closed the tavern, unable to concentrate on anything else but my friend that day. We all felt powerless, and sought comfort in each other's arms. Most of the girls joined us in our prayers, asking for Montigny's fast, painless passing and a safe journey to heaven. Though I was not used to all the praying, such tragedies naturally make one turn to higher powers for help.

At one point, Isabeau fell silent and after a moment of fixedly gazing ahead, she whispered, "I felt him. It's over."

My chest tightened at the sight of her ashen face. She was still so strangely calm and resigned, but it was only the quiet before the storm. At that point, she had not yet fully comprehended what had transpired. The pain would strike only later, enveloping her in all its shades and shattering her to pieces. I knew that she would never be the same again. It had happened to me. When my husband died, I forgot about all the heartache he caused me during our marriage and only focused on the love that it all started with. That's what mattered the most in the end.

After our silent exchange of empathy, Isabeau stood up and addressed the hound. "Come, Estienne de Montigny II, now we can go to your master."

I couldn't let her go alone with the animal; she needed human comfort by her side as well, particularly at such an awful place as Montfaucon. Since I was the only one who knew just how much she cared for Montigny, I ordered my girls to keep the tavern closed and hurried after her.

Our trip to Montfaucon was quiet, filled with sorrow and regret. We passed a few familiar faces on the way and assumed that they were just leaving the savage spectacle. Who would miss the chance to witness the degrading end of such a well-known Parisian criminal? Among the faces, I recognised Katherine de Vaucelles. She didn't notice me as her head was bowed and her eyes filled with tears. I knew that Montigny was her cousin, but Villon never told me that she actually cared about him. From what I heard, most of his family members had turned their backs on him during his most prosperous criminal career. She seemed to be different, though, and that made me see her in a new, better light.

As we reached the foot of the hill, we looked up, daunted by the sight of the ominous, three-sided

stone structure which was used to kill the most
dangerous criminals or display the bodies of those
executed elsewhere. It functioned as the largest city
scarecrow, meant to deter us sinners, but it didn't
have that effect on everybody. We still misbehaved,
acted on our impulses and pushed boundaries just
to see what lay beyond them. I never spat or cursed
at the gibbet like some other, heartless people did.
How could I if we were all the same? I had
sympathy for those who hung on the filthy nooses,
as I was a part of the same breed: I too was one of
those who lived in dirt and disgrace simply to
survive.

The screams of ravens shattered the formidable
silence. The voracious birds surrounded the
monstrous gibbet from above, welcoming the fresh
prey they could feed on. Isabeau grasped my hand
tightly as we both looked up, searching for
Montigny's body among the rotting corpses. We
couldn't locate him at first, but suddenly the
desperate hound rushed off and without having to
check, simply lay down beneath a figure who hung
at the lowest level. The tall, willowy man was
wearing nothing but rags and a pair of red boots.

Isabeau gathered her courage to look at the
lifeless face that gaped down at us, its fate etched
into its features. That was the moment when she
was plunged into those dark streams that I knew so
well. She knelt beside the hound and joined his
howling, crying hot tears for the man she hadn't

dared to love until that fateful moment. Despite the tough armour I was used to wearing, I too could not control the emotions rushing in and started to weep.

At first, it seemed that we were alone there. The executioner had long finished his work, the sergeants returned to their duties, and the audience had witnessed enough cruelty for the day. However, at one point I noticed that there was another person there with us: a stoic priest whose chin rested on the top of his praying hands as he whispered something to himself. I recognised him. It was Villon's guardian, Guillaume. I smiled to myself through my tears and slowly clasped my hands together, joining the priest in prayer. I asked the angels of mercy to guide Regnier to the home we had all come from, but also prayed for his best friend whom I never wanted to see suffer the same lot – François Villon.

PART FOUR:

GUILLAUME

Item: To my more than father
The rare, loving soul, Guillaume de Villon
Who has been as gentle as a mother
And fed me when I was skinny as a scallion
He helped me through my foolish rebellion
And though I know this shall make him grim
I have to fall on my knees and implore him:
To leave all of the worries to us hellions.

I leave him my library
Including the "Tale of the Devil's Fart"
Copied by Guy Tabary
The loyal follower of my written art
It's on my table by the notes and cards
And no matter how harsh or crude
The core is strong and not too rude
Which makes up for the weaker parts.

Extract from *The Testament* (1461-1462, François Villon)

CHAPTER 14

THE RETURN

Paris, June 1461

Three years had passed since we received any news from François. The last time he wrote us a letter was shortly before he left his uncle's home in Angers. We kept praying for his wellbeing, but were growing more anxious every day, sensing that he might have got himself into some kind of trouble again.

One afternoon, I received an invitation from the provost, Robert d'Estouteville, asking me to meet him straight away. I knew very well that he must have had something important on his mind, because we only ever spoke at social occasions, and I therefore reached the Châtelet greatly distressed. The provost had been fond of François since his school years. Like most people, he admired his wit and compelling personality, however, François mainly won him over by honouring his marriage to his wife Ambroise with a beautiful poem.

Robert d'Estouteville behaved in a respectful manner as usual, and offered me some fine burgundy, remembering that it was my favourite. After a little small talk, he finally addressed the main issue.

"I wanted to inform you of some troubling news regarding François' classmate, Guy Tabary. As you may know, we have been investigating the College of Navarre robbery for quite some time but we haven't made any progress until recently. A certain prior called Pierre Merchand came to Paris in disguise to investigate the robbery, and overheard Tabary talking in a tavern about some brilliant locksmiths he knew.

"Merchand then pretended to be a criminal seeking experienced brothers in crime for some grand theft and asked Tabary to help him out. Tabary swallowed the bait and started to be of service to him. With time, he began to trust Merchand and eventually disclosed his participation in the College of Navarre robbery. He was taken to the Châtelet for questioning right away and had been there ever since."

The woeful expression in the provost's eyes alarmed me. I could sense that the boy was in deep trouble and was probably not the only one. The provost paused for a long time before he continued talking.

"Father Guillaume, I know that Tabary was a good friend to your adopted son, and he proved that by not naming him as an accomplice during the first round of interrogation. Only when more drastic methods were applied, he finally revealed the names of all his accomplices: Petit Jehan, Dom Nicholas, Colin de Cayaux, and François Villon."

I shook my head in disbelief, trying to find a reason behind the boy's ludicrous statement.

"You know what people are capable of during torture, Monsieur d'Estouteville," I argued. "They lie just to make the pain go away. Even the bravest souls are broken during such cruelty. I hope you aren't taking his claims seriously."

"It was also hard for me to believe it at first, Father Guillaume, and I can't imagine how upsetting it must be for you, but it seems that François truly was involved in the robbery somehow. Although I have no doubt that it was an act of pure despair, it's quite understandable why he would do it. Imagine the situation from his point of view. He had to leave Paris because of his bad reputation without any financial security…"

I couldn't listen to the preposterous allegations anymore so I interrupted. "Had François needed money for the trip, he would have come to me. He knew I would support him as I had thus far."

"Maybe he was ashamed," suggested the provost with an empathetic look, "and he probably did not want to be a burden to you. We both know you are not a wealthy man, Father Guillaume."

Although he may have been right, I was unable to accept the idea of François robbing an institution that had provided him with education and safety during his adolescence. I knew him better than anyone. I had been his closest friend since he was seven years old and was certain that he would never lower himself to such a level.

"You don't have to worry, Father Guillaume, I have not issued an official arrest for him yet, I just wanted you to know that it might come to that."

"I don't know where he is," I stammered out nervously, sensing that was why he wanted to talk to me, although he must have realised that even if I knew I wouldn't tell him.

"I believe you," he assured me, "and I have not asked you here to pry." He gave me a secretive look then lowered his voice. "In fact, it's quite the contrary…"

I finally understood. He wasn't about to interrogate me, he actually wanted to warn me, but he couldn't be completely direct as that would compromise his career.

"You know I have always been fond of François. He's an intelligent man who had a bright future ahead of him before that terrible accident with Sermoise. Of course, he attracted some trouble during his school years, but you know very well that even then I was lenient with him. That's why I wouldn't want to see him follow in the footsteps of Regnier de Montigny."

The mention of Regnier made me shiver. I still had the vision before me: his uncontrollable shaking as he was dragged to the gibbet, the frantic look in his eyes when they put the rope around his neck, the pleas he yelled as I stood there unable to do anything but pray for his fast passing. I still couldn't forgive myself for looking down at his swaying red boots instead of holding his terrified gaze until the very end. Had it been François up there, it would certainly break my spirit, and I couldn't even think what it would do to his poor mother. I squeezed my hands together in an attempt to compose myself.

The provost noticed how perturbed I was, so he poured me some more wine before he continued speaking.

"The others, Dom Nicholas and Petit Jehan managed to escape, however, Colin de Cayaux was caught in Senlis and condemned by a secular court. He escaped the noose there by pleading the Benefit of Clergy, but not here in Paris. He will be hanged at the Gibbet of Montfaucon."

My heart ached at the thought of Colin facing the same fate as Regnier.

"If Guy Tabary survives the consequences of the interrogation," continued the provost, "he will have to face the same ordeal…"

I turned away, overwhelmed by the rush of emotions. I felt sorry for the boys I had watched grow up, especially after learning that one of them so bravely protected François during the torture. Back in those days, most people thought that Guy Tabary was just a witless wimp, but he proved to be a hero in the end. I took a deep breath for courage and asked, "If it comes to that, may I be his last confessor?"

The provost nodded in sympathy. "Of course. I will keep you informed about the situation."

I stood up, impatient to be alone to digest the disturbing news. "Thank you," I said earnestly, "for everything."

He smiled, knowing full well what I meant and sealed the silent pact between us with another friendly warning. "I need you to know one last thing, Father Guillaume. If François returns home, my hands will be tied. I can't protect him forever…"

I nodded, knowing very well that if he saved François from execution again, he would put himself into a very compromising position.

After I said goodbye to the provost, I rushed to Saint Benoit Church. I needed to ask God for guidance and help, but mainly the strength to endure the worry. Unlike François, I had been clear about my mission after I graduated from the

Sorbonne. I always wanted to be a priest. It gave me the opportunity to focus solely on theology and philosophy, my two greatest passions in life, such that allowed me to escape the cruel world I was born into.

There had been a dark cloud over Paris after the Hundred Years War. First, we were struck with an unstoppable plague and then, with the extremes of summer droughts and winter freezes, a large-scale famine had spread over the land. During those dark times, only the strong ones survived, but those who were under the protection of royalty or the Church had better chances than the ordinary citizens like François' father. I often spoke to the man in my mind, asking his spirit to guide me and help me become a decent surrogate. There was never a time when I would not feel honoured to be raising his son, even when it became so hard.

✦

I cloistered myself in my church for the rest of the day, praying for François' safety and for heaven's forgiveness in case he truly did rob the university. He had sinned greatly many times before, but the angels of mercy must have known that there was never any wickedness behind his deeds. With a heavy heart, I realised that I should stop praying for his return because then he would surely be imprisoned and sentenced to death like his companions. I kept Colin de Cayaux and Guy Tabary in my prayers too and implored the Lord to take them straight to heaven upon their last breath so that they would not have to join the lost spirits that roamed the Gibbet of Montfaucon trying to disconnect from the horror.

I remembered how François came to befriend Guy Tabary. We were enjoying one of our city walks when we noticed a group of older students harassing a younger one. They had surrounded him like a pack of wolves, shouting insults, ridiculing his short stature and childlike appearance. As he tried to free himself, daggers were drawn. They were about to injure him and that's when François stepped in. He was ready to fight them, but had I not taken command of the situation with my quiet authority, he wouldn't have stood a chance. They ran off because they knew that hurting a priest would land them in a great deal of trouble.

Since then, François had become Guy's hero. Although Regnier and Colin were bothered by him following them around, they tolerated his presence for François' sake. He developed an almost fatherly affection towards Guy, and in his eyes, he was a loveable, honest berk. Now the boy was suffering in a cold cell at the Châtelet without any hope of salvation. Nobody could help those who were pronounced beyond redemption and robbing a

Church organisation such as the College of Navarre was considered a greater crime than murder.

It was a hypocritical way of thinking, of course, as everyone knew that most criminals could be found among the Church members themselves. I often struggled with this because I too was a part of the institution, and knew that the Church had the power to do whatever it liked. People were just loyal sheep to them, and no rebels had managed to break that system, not even the most devoted Christians. All we could do was pray that true Christianity would not disappear beneath the strange dogma that had formed around it.

Because of the seriousness of the situation, I decided not to tell François' mother, Magdalene, about the robbery. I couldn't stand to see her even more worried than she had already been for all these years. I knew she would overhear people talking about the case in the streets, but I wanted her to consider it just slander. After all, without François here to explain himself, we could not be certain that it was actually the truth.

Just as I finished praying and was about to return to my clerical duties, I heard a soft feminine voice addressing me from a polite distance.

"Father Guillaume?"

I turned to face Katherine de Vaucelles, now Jolis. It took me by surprise, because since the quarrel she had had with François, I had met her only out and about, and once at Regnier's execution. I supposed she avoided our church and its vicinity, but she had chosen a peculiar time to break that habit.

"Madame Jolis!" I was as friendly as I always had been. "What brings you here?"

She fidgeted a bit, looking around to see if we were alone and only then dared to take a step closer.

"I came for a confession," she said in a timid voice, perhaps unsure if I would accept her. How could I not, though? I was always true to my mission and provided guidance to everyone, and anyway, the dispute between her and my adopted son did not involve me.

"Have I come at a bad time?" she asked, deducing that something was not right.

"No, please, come with me." I nodded to her with a polite smile, encouraging her to follow me to the confessional. I noticed a spark of determination in her eyes that shone through the obvious nervousness which intrigued me.

"What troubles you, Madame Jolis?" I asked once we were seated. She was quiet for a moment, gathering her thoughts, so I waited patiently, trying to chase away my prejudices in order to remain unbiased. Not that I ever blamed her for marrying a more prosperous man. Life with an untamed spirit such as François would certainly not be easy. I knew about his love of drinking and whoring, and was even aware of the poem that had caused the end of their blossoming affection. To him it was nothing but a silly, vulgar joke, however, to a gentle maiden like Katherine it must have been an utter disappointment. She surely needed time to look at it in a more detached way, to understand that it was an exaggeration of the truth.

"I fear that God is upset with me," she said out of the blue.

"Why would that be?" I wondered.

"Because I married a man I never loved."

I finally understood why she had come to me for a confession that afternoon. She was hoping to receive some information regarding François or perhaps hoped that through me she would get to the truth in a less scandalous manner. I was glad she had taken such a brave step, but it pained me to consider that perhaps she was too late. Still, I had to help the burdened soul somehow, so I thought about what to say while she continued.

"I married a man out of spite. I realised how wrong it was, yet I did it anyway. I behaved like a reckless fool, overwhelmed by confusion and a childish thirst for revenge. I thought I would hurt the one who had hurt me, but ended up hurting myself."

She took a deep breath before she continued, the words suddenly flowing like a waterfall. "I'm reminded of the mistake every day, and it pains me so much that it even hurts to breathe sometimes. I do care for my husband, Father Guillaume, he is a kind and generous man, but my heart belongs to another. A man I despised for so long that I forgot how I truly felt about him. I see certain things differently now. I have begun to realise that I may have been imprudent in certain judgments... My husband senses that I never truly belonged to him, and I fear that God is punishing me for the years of deceit by not blessing us with a child..."

The words she planned on adding trailed off, disappearing back into her heart. Although I was touched by her honesty and strength at that moment, it didn't surprise me all that much. I knew that François would not fall in love with just anyone; it had to be a strong, one-of-a-kind personality. Katherine waited for my response with her gaze lowered, so I braced myself to come up with some comfort. I had to be objective, therefore reminded myself to act like a priest, not a confidant.

"God does not punish," I started then hesitated, as the way I viewed God was a bit different to most people. Only Magdalene and François knew that I was a secret admirer of Marguerite de Porete, a philosopher who was burnt for her views on Christian mysticism, and who viewed God as Love. To me, God was definitely not the merciless ruler that the Catholic Church presented to people.

"God has no judgments, only ever-spreading love for us," I said. "You may be punishing yourself, but do not fear punishment from God. Love is not a sin. Love is a blessing even when it seems to be a curse sometimes. Only reason stands in the way of love and as one wise woman wrote, *Reason, you'll always be half-blind…*"

I smiled at the wise lines written by Marguerite de Porete then explained my thoughts on the conflict between her and François more bluntly.

"Sometimes we think we are doing the right thing and stop following our true heart's calling, other times, crude humour is just a mask for an inwardly troubled man."

I wavered over whether I was being too direct, as I was clearly hinting at the ballad that François had told me about, the one that made Katherine behave so coldly towards him. She did not respond at first, which filled me with apprehension, but to my relief, she finally said, "Thank you, Father Guillaume."

I nodded and since she had become pensive again, I asked, "Was there anything else you wanted to talk about, Madame Jolis?"

She hesitated for a moment then stammered out nervously, "Well… I… thought that… I wondered whether… if you have any news about François?"

"Unfortunately not," I replied. "I suppose all we can do is pray for him."

"I shall do that. No matter what has happened between us, I still think of him fondly."

I wished François could hear those words, as I knew that they would heal his wounded heart. I recalled his dramatic declaration as though it had just happened: *I will never love again!* We both knew he was lying, and mainly to himself.

✦

I felt tempted to tell Magdalene about Katherine's surprising confession but had to remain loyal to the priesthood. Sometimes it was hard, especially if someone confessed to a crime, however, I promised myself to never let any soul down. My visitors had one thing in common: they were able to reflect upon their deeds and take responsibility, which showed that they wanted to change for the better. I often prayed that I never came across a sinner who could pose a real danger to somebody, as then I would have to break my rule and my oath.

Magdalene made us one of her simple, tasty meals, using the humblest ingredients to produce a delicacy, and we joined in prayer before we sat down to enjoy it. As always, I did not forget to thank God for having that woman by my side. She was a living angel, though she liked to boss me around and her words stung like needles sometimes.

My affection for her was not always a blessing. The troubling thoughts and dreams that made me think of her as more than a friend were difficult to control. Sometimes I sensed that she returned my complicated feelings, but I would never dare to address the issue. We were too accustomed to the way things were. Although we lived under the same roof, many people thought there was more to it than that, but we never gave in to temptation. We kept our physical longings at bay, and instead enjoyed our unique spiritual connection.

As we dined that evening, my gaze kept falling on the empty chair that François used to occupy. The visit to Robert d'Estouteville had disquieted me, and the fact that I could not share the information with Magdalene made me feel terribly lonely inside. Upon finishing my third goblet of burgundy, I noticed Magdalene's disapproving frown. She hated it when I exceeded my limit.

"I have had a hard day," I explained. "Would you bring me some more, please?"

"No," she snapped at me, "you've had more than enough."

"Just one more," I reasoned with her, but I could see from her strict expression that she would not oblige. I never understood why I let the woman control me like that. I supposed it was because she often knew better.

"I can always pour myself some more after you fall asleep," I said grumpily. "There is no one to have to set an example to here anymore..."

I realised the comment may have been hurtful, so I shot her an apologetic look. She was wise enough to understand, though, and in fact, she sensed that I was not myself that day.

"Tell me what's wrong, Father Guillaume."

"Nothing," I replied curtly, trying to pretend that I had everything under control.

"Has it got something to do with someone's confession?"

Avoiding the question, I went to fetch myself more burgundy. She watched me with that adorable reproachful look of hers, so I responded with an impish smile and suggested, "Why don't you have some with me, Magdalene? I can see you could use a drink to calm down."

Her eyes pierced me through, yet I poured her a goblet anyway. As usual, she pretended to not care for the enticing liquid at first, but I knew that she would start sipping on it once she had become distracted.

"I've had a difficult day as well," she admitted. "It may have been because I didn't sleep well last night."

"Why is that? Did Father Laurens have female company again?"

Father Laurens lived next door to us, but the wall between Magdalene's and his chamber had a large crack, so she often heard him with his lovers, one of them being the infamous Widow Bruyer. François once found him roaming the streets in confusion, naked and drunk, so he helped him home to where Madame Bruyer lay, also tipsy and without her gown on. He wrote a whimsical poem about it, which started the whole Devil's Fart escapade.

Magdalene smiled at my comment and finally had a taste of the wine. "To my surprise, Father Laurens seems to lack female company these days. It was François who kept me awake. I heard him calling out to me, crying for help. His voice sounded weak and anguished, as if he had not much power left in him…"

"Was it a dream?"

"Yes and no," she said with a troubled frown. "It was hard to tell, it just kept spinning in my mind like an unstoppable, merciless wheel. I can feel that something is wrong. Every mother senses when her child is in danger."

I sighed, worried that she may be right. She had another sip of the wine, crossed herself, and looked me in the eye. I knew what it meant. She was about to confide in me.

"I feel terribly guilty about it, Father Guillaume, but sometimes I wish François was different… All I ever wanted was for him to lead a comfortable life, have a good job, a kind wife, children, a home of his own. His career looked so promising. Why did he change so much after he graduated? From then on, all he cared about was his friends, taverns and, well, you know." She crossed herself and lowered her gaze, feeling ashamed for bringing it up. "I can't help but think that it's all my fault. I spoilt him after we lost our family, and in the end, all the good you have done for him has gone to waste."

"Oh, don't blame yourself, Magdalene. The more love you give the better, and we both know he has always appreciated your kindness. Who's to say he wouldn't have rebelled even more if you tried to control his free spirit? He has always wanted to live life to the full, not get bogged down in prayers and the mundane like the two of us."

"I just wish he were safe and not always attracting trouble."

"Nothing and no one is safe in this world, Magdalene. This world is one big battle between good and evil, and we all fight it differently."

Magdalene didn't like to philosophise about things like that. She liked her world simple and clear.

"We must pray for François, that is all we can do," she said.

I nodded, although I had a feeling that it wouldn't be enough. He needed to change his ways before it was too late, however, that was an inner struggle that he had to face on his own.

✦

Paris, October 1462

It was a cold, foggy October night, and even the animals were reluctant to stray abroad. Magdalene and I were already tucked up in bed when a knock at the door startled us. I supposed that something had happened, as no one would dare to disturb me at such a late hour, therefore I anxiously hurried downstairs. Magdalene peeked out of her chamber as well, but I gestured at her to stay put in case there was some danger. One never knew because Paris was filled with all kinds of individuals, even those who had no respect for the clergy. The banging grew louder with every step, so I called out, "Calm down! I'm on my way!"

There was no need to wake up the neighbours and cause even more of a disturbance. I almost slipped as I hurried to the door to check the scene outside through the peephole. A strange man stood there, rain pouring down his scarred face and braided beard. He looked upset and was impatiently looking behind him into the darkened street. Waiting nearby was a carriage with two horses, the driver's seat empty.

"Father Guillaume?" He addressed me through the thick wood that separated us, his voice sharp as a blade's edge.

"Yes," I replied, worried that he would try to break in and assault Magdalene.

"I was going to take care of him myself, but he insisted on being brought here…"

It was only when he said this that I noticed there was another man with him, clinging to his body for support, his hooded head hanging down. As the strange man supported his body to help him straighten up, I caught a glimpse of a deep scar above his lip. My chest tightened at the realisation. I hastily opened the door and checked his face. He was unrecognisable: skinny to the bone, bald, ashen, and almost unconscious, but it was truly him – it was our François! Before I could think about what I was doing, I held him in my arms and the strange man jumped on the driver's seat of the carriage and rode off into the mist.

CHAPTER 15

FRANÇOIS' WILD JOURNEY

François was delirious, suffering from a high fever. He didn't recognise me, just kept muttering nonsense until an ugly, rough cough silenced him. He coughed for a long time and when it was finally over, he wheezed in pain and fell back into a slumber. I couldn't recover from the shock of seeing him in such a poor condition and couldn't keep my eyes off the tormented face that concealed many dark secrets. It seemed as if he had aged twenty years instead of six. He must have been through something unimaginable.

Only upon hearing Magdalene's gasp was I able to free myself from these troubling thoughts. With her hands over her mouth, she kneeled beside him.

"François?"

He didn't answer, so she stroked his face, hoping to revive him. Like me, however, she soon came to the realisation that even a slight touch hurt him, so she looked at me in despair.

"Let's take him inside," I said, quickly closing the door, making sure that nobody had seen us. Magdalene helped me support him and together we dragged him to the main room where the fire still blazed. We laid him on the bench and looked at each other in bewilderment. Magdalene was seized with panic so I had to be the strong one.

"Why don't you bring a bowl, some water and more blankets? We should let him sweat the fever out."

She nodded and hurried to fetch all the necessities. I meanwhile undressed him to check if he was wounded. Luckily, I found just a few old scars on his chest, so I reached for a warm woollen blanket to cover him when all of a sudden, his hand grasped mine tightly. He half-opened his eyes and mumbled, "Please have pity, have pity on me and my folly…"

I could no longer contain the emotions rushing through me and broke down in tears.

"Oh François," I whispered with a heart-wrenching premonition, "what have they done to you?"

As he lay there feverish and helpless, I recalled the first time I had met him. It was twenty-three years ago by Saint Benoit Church. I noticed a young but feeble woman begging for help by the unconscious body of her son, a boy of six or seven years. I took them in and learned that they were all alone after the plague had killed the boy's father and most of the woman's family. She said her brother-in-law took them in, but after a dispute, they had ended up in the streets, going around towns in search of a new home. She introduced herself as Magdalene and the boy as François, and since she was so distressed, I provided them both with food and shelter. However, there was not much more I could do for François, since the fever would not go down despite all the healing methods I applied, and he was growing weaker by the day.

Magdalene needed a friend to lean on during those difficult times, so I was there for her, offering confession, sometimes even a shoulder to cry on. She felt indebted to me, so she began helping me around the house and cooking me the most wonderful meals. When I realised that I had begun to develop romantic feelings for her, I decided that it would be best to let her go, whether François had recovered or not.

To my relief, however, he woke up without any fever one morning. I found him at the window, gazing out into the streets with an excited expression. He was like a bird locked in a cage waiting to be released.

"I love Paris in the springtime!" he exclaimed upon seeing me, without the need to know who I was.

"Me too," I chimed in and went to stand beside him. The sunbeams caressed our faces as we looked over the stone buildings and crooked chimneys.

"I heard all the stories you read for me while I was in a fever," said François and looked at me with his curious eyes. "Although I could not respond, I loved to listen to them. I especially enjoyed the one about Diomedes and King Alexander the Great."

I was surprised that he remembered so I smiled and nodded. "Yes, that's also my favourite one."

"I could imagine it so vividly," he continued. "The best part was when the King asked Diomedes why he was a thief and he replied that had he not been born so poor or been through so much misery in his life because of it, he would not have been driven to steal. The King was wise to change his fate instead of executing him."

"Indeed," I agreed. "Making a poor thief an honourable, wealthy man to see if his character would change was a very compassionate step."

"And it worked," said François. "What do you think happened then?"

"Well, I think the two became friends."

He nodded. "I think so too."

With those words, I began to sense that God had sent the boy into my path for a reason. Perhaps I was called to service, to give him a second chance by providing him with a good life. He reminded me of myself when I was his age, but there was one significant difference: he had a special glow about him. It was like a blazing fire that either has the power to enlighten the spirit or to burn it up. I tried to guide him towards a safe, clerical life, but he was not content in the world of philosophy like me; he sought real adventures in the streets of our beloved city. I learned to respect this with time and gave him the space to find his own path rather than force him to follow mine. Despite our worries for him, I knew he was born to experience life with all it had to offer, and I felt that it would make him into someone special.

✦

Just like all those years ago, one morning François woke up feverless and simply came down to have breakfast with us. He was still weak, but his eyes had the same spark again. Magdalene ran to him straight away, touched his forehead and turned to me in surprise. "This is a miracle!"

François smiled at her enthusiasm and embraced her when suddenly he became woozy and leaned on the wall for support. His face contorted in a grimace of pain as another nasty coughing attack took hold of him. Magdalene stood aside, patting his back for comfort. We exchanged a worried look, both realising he was not as healthy as it seemed. When the cough subsided, François touched his chest and wheezed, "By God's loins, will this cough ever leave me?"

Those typical swear words of his made Magdalene cross herself every time, but to me it was just an innocent provocation. I was well aware that like me, François believed in a God who had a good sense of humour.

"You should rest," reproached Magdalene and was about to hurry François back to his chamber.

"I feel much better now, don't worry," he protested with a tired, raspy voice and instead headed towards me to give me a hug as well. "You can't imagine how happy I am to be here with you two again," he said, his voice more emotional than usual.

As I held him in my arms, I smiled at Magdalene. We were both thrilled to have him back. However, his condition perturbed me as much as the secret information I had received from the provost. I guided him over to the bench and wrapped him in a woollen blanket by the fire.

"I'll bring you some stew," said Magdalene, but François protested.

"Oh no, please don't!"

He winced and I knew well why. Magdalene's "fever stew" as she called it was basically a thick onion and garlic broth, and as much as we usually loved her food, that one was very hard to keep down. Magdalene pretended to be offended, although I could see the amusement in her face. François had brought back the light we were missing, therefore we both ignored the fact that he looked so worn and haggard.

"But I could do with some wine, how about you?" he suggested.

"You two are just the same," complained Magdalene, though she didn't have the heart to refuse his wish. Her boy was back home, and she would do anything to make him stay. While Magdalene went out to fetch some burgundy, François gratefully squeezed my hand and said, "I don't know how to thank you for taking me in again, Guillaume."

"You thanked me already by getting better. Remember that this door will always remain open to you."

He smiled as he eased himself down onto the bench. He gazed at the burning fire for a moment before he turned back to me and asked, "How have you two been?"

"Ah, nothing has changed." I gestured with my hand, keener to hear what he had to say.

"That's true. You haven't aged a bit compared to me."

The comment made me realise that he was still able to take things lightly. Before I could ask about his journey, however, Magdalene came forth with a jar of wine and asked, "Would you like anything else?"

"No, thank you, Mother. Why don't you have some with us?"

Magdalene shook her head, but we both knew that she would eventually join us. François took a sip of the wine and rolled it on his tongue, savouring every drop.

"You can't imagine how much I missed this!"

He then turned to Magdalene and planted a grateful kiss on her hand. She gently stroked his bald head, enjoying the moment she had been waiting for all those years. Her eyes were filled with love and devotion, yet they couldn't conceal the worry that filled her mind.

"What happened to you, son?"

"Nothing, I just spent a few months in a prison vault, that's all." He confirmed what we had feared, and looked away as he admitted, "I suppose it wouldn't be me if I hadn't got into some sort of scrape."

"You were in prison, and you call that a scrape? asked Magdalene. "I don't believe this! Hasn't my brother-in-law taken good care of you?"

"He did. He was very kind and generous, but as I wrote in my letter, I couldn't stay with him any longer."

"I don't understand you." She shook her head. "Your uncle's home was the safest place for you at that time."

"Safest maybe, but utterly boring."

The scar on his lip stretched as he grinned. Magdalene clasped her hands together and exclaimed, "Good Lord in heaven, please make me understand why my son prefers trouble over comfort!"

"I'd like to hear that explanation myself," noted François.

Upon seeing him lower his head, Magdalene calmed down and asked more gently,

"Why did you end up in prison, François?"

"To explain how I landed in that hellish dungeon I have to start with the brighter part of my trip. I spent almost a year at Blois, at the palace of Charles d'Orleans."

Magdalene and I gasped at the news. François was managing to impress rather than distress us at first. We knew that the Duke of Orleans had been very popular since he had returned home following twenty-four years of British captivity after the Battle of Agincourt.

"The Duke took you into his palace?"

François nodded, enjoying the sudden change from worry to pride.

"Charles d'Orleans is known for supporting artists," I remarked, giving Magdalene a smile to lift her spirits. What I failed to add was that he was also known for his mischievous, vulgar poetry. I supposed that's why François and him got along so well.

"After his imprisonment, the Duke returned home to finally enjoy life to the full," explained François further. "He has always wanted to spend his days surrounded by the beauty of nature and inspiring people. That is why he hosts many artists... well, but that's not how I ended up at his palace. It was just an accident really." He checked Magdalene's reaction and hesitated, weighing something up before he continued, "It was because of a woman."

"Really? You met a girl there?" beamed Magdalene. "Who was it? Was she nice?"

"She was an obnoxious shrew," answered François taking another swig of wine. "You may not like hearing about this incident, Mother, although it's actually the best part of my trip. I met this woman at a market in the beautiful town of Blois. She said her name was Macée, but who knows whether she lied about that as well... Initially, she struck me as one of those cheerful, easy types – well, an ideal girl for me at that time. She seemed to enjoy my company as well, so I thought it would be nice to spend a night in someone's warm embrace as opposed to some chilly stable or archway."

François ignored Magdalene crossing herself again, and went on with his story.

"I used my old wine trick at a local shop and stole us some white wine. We drank until the streets became dark, but after arguing with a few locals, we moved our private celebration closer to the palace. We walked alongside the palace walls and when the time was right to kiss her, she suddenly challenged me. She said that she would let me lie with her only in the palace gardens. I was feeling brave due to the slight intoxication, so I agreed."

François paused to have another sip of the burgundy, oblivious to Magdalene's reaction. He was always like that. He rarely shied away from sharing the things we would rather not hear.

"I helped her climb over the wall, and as she balanced on my shoulders, I stole a peek under her skirts, which made me conclude that the trespassing was truly worth it."

I couldn't help but laugh, which made Magdalene turn to me with a reproachful frown.

"If you don't mind, Guillaume, I'll cut the story short, for Mother's sake," he said. "We spent the night in the palace gardens and in the morning, I woke up with nothing but my pantaloons on. She had taken my boots and my money belt, along with the few coins I had in it, and left me in the middle of the palace gardens alone. The guards found me and no matter how eloquently I tried to reason with them, they insisted on bringing me to the Duke.

"However, to theirs and my own surprise, Duke Charles actually believed me and was amused by what had happened. That's when I realised that the rumours I had heard about him were probably true: he had a good sense of humour. I also knew that he liked poetry so I tried to use it to my benefit. I told him about the new book of poems I had been working on, the one that I intend to be my last will and testament. I admitted that I hadn't been able to write for quite some time, but that the unfortunate escapade in his gardens had given me an idea for a few new verses. Charles asked me to recite them, so I did:

> *To the accountants I leave empty scrolls*
> *And a place where they can hide*
> *And to those with enflamed arseholes*
> *A chair with a solid hole inside*
> *Provided that Macée of Orleáns is found*
> *She who took all my money*
> *Let them hunt her down with feral hounds*
> *For she is a stinky little harpy.*

I thought the verses may seem too rude or rough, but I took my chance and it paid off. The Duke exploded in raucous laughter and asked the guards to provide me with a chamber and some clothing. He said that he would pardon my break-in if I were to stay and entertain him with more of my poetry. You can imagine how relieved I was."

"So you became his court poet?" marvelled Magdalene.

"You could say that."

"You ended up offending him in some way in the end, didn't you?"

"No, the whole stay was a wonderful experience, but it turned out not to be for me."

"What do you mean? This was the best thing that has happened to you since you left the Sorbonne!"

Although François understood his mother's frustration, he simply couldn't lie. "I'm sorry, Mother, that's how I felt. Something pulled me elsewhere…"

I understood what he meant, because unlike Magdalene, I didn't overlook his true nature. Despite the fact that staying at the court would help his reputation and ultimately even protect him, I knew that he would wither away if he remained enclosed within the palace walls for too long.

"I often regretted my decision to leave his court," admitted François. "I was fond of the carefree lifestyle that Duke Charles indulged in and there were many inspiring artists to talk to. I also enjoyed the plenitude of wine, food, excellent conversation and passionate nights, but most importantly, Duke Charles and I became good friends. I still remember the long, deep talks I had with him. It reminded me of those we used to share, Guillaume."

He paused with a nostalgic glance in my direction then continued, "However, I simply couldn't imagine myself living that way forever. The splendour slowly turned into a tedious routine. I began to feel trapped, restless. I told Duke Charles about it and he understood, even though he initially argued with me. He said that he used to be like me until he became a prisoner of war. Despite spending his years of captivity in comfortable chambers at different castles, he was simply not free to go where he liked. He missed France and began to long for a peaceful home instead of adventure. I sympathised with him but replied that I would never find a place I could call home if my heart still belonged to Paris. He liked my answer and so he let me go, along with a very generous farewell gift. It was enough for me to get by for two or three years… However, for some reason, it lasted me for only a year or so."

"Oh, François," sighed Magdalene, "you're just like your father. He also immediately spent all that he obtained…"

"Well, he was better than me, Mother. I spent even more than I had… I had to borrow a few times as well and sometimes, I couldn't pay people back in full…"

I could tell he was ashamed of it, so I remained quiet while Magdalene pleaded with the heavens to forgive her son. Instead, I couldn't help but think about the College of Navarre robbery. I wondered whether he truly was a part of it and if he knew that Guy and Colin were killed for it, and that

Regnier went even sooner. Did he have any clue that all of his friends were dead? I couldn't talk about it in front of Magdalene, so I had to wait until we were alone together. Anyway, François was not finished with his story yet.

"Shortly after I left the court, I ended up being arrested for some minor theft in Bourges…"

Magdalene's face turned ashen. "Was that how you ended up in prison?"

He shook his head. "No, that time I was released straight away. The judges empathised with me. They knew that if you are as hungry as a wolf you won't shy away from stealing a loaf of bread at a market. It was hard as a rock anyway. I ended up breaking a tooth on it.

"However, fortune smiled upon me once again after that short imprisonment. I was accepted at the court of the Duke of Bourbon who became fond of my poetry and offered me accommodation at his palace."

Magdalene's eyes lit up again, but in futile hope. Given the condition he was in, we both knew that part of his journey hadn't ended well either.

"After having such a good time at the court of Charles d'Orleans, I thought it would be a good idea. However, the Duke of Bourbon was nothing like Duke Charles. We didn't share the same opinions on art and he didn't understand my humour either. He grew tired of my poems and I started to despise him.

"His support for artists seemed to be just a pretentious façade. He thought it would make him popular with the public. Moreover, he only lent money to artists instead of generously gifting it like Duke Charles did. I found it unfair, so I hope he doesn't hold it against me that I never paid him back…"

Magdalene and I looked at each other in disbelief. No matter how far François had fallen after he left the Sorbonne, he had become too accustomed to such ways. I realised that if the dire prison he had ended up in didn't change him, then nothing would.

"After I left the palace, things were good for a few months until…"

With those words, he turned sulky and I caught a flare of hatred in his eyes as he finished, "…until I was thrown to the pit at the Meung-sur-Loire castle."

He pronounced the castle's name in such bitter way that it sent chills down my spine.

"That city was unwelcoming right from the start. There were no cheery companions to turn to, no alluring girls, an overall lack of inspiration. Perhaps that's why I started going back and forth between the local taverns, drowning my boredom in wine. My bad moods continued to weigh me down until I ended up at the lowest point possible…"

His face turned grim. He stopped speaking, taking a moment to gather his courage.

"Could I have some more wine, please?"

Magdalene was more understanding by this point, because we both knew that he was about to share his unsettling experiences with us. She poured us all another goblet and downed hers surprisingly quickly to calm her nerves.

"I ended up in that hellhole because I stole again, this time a silver lamp from a local church. I felt guilty about it, of course, but I had no choice – I would have died of hunger had I not done it. However, that judge was not as sympathetic to my situation as the previous ones. He was the most malicious man I have ever met."

He took another break, had a bigger gulp of wine, and it seemed as if he was swallowing the abhorrence along with it.

"After a few weeks in my cell, he found out that my name, François des Loges, was fake and learned about my criminal past. The fact that I killed a priest made him livid. He didn't believe me when I said that it was just an accident and after that, he turned into the most vicious beast. King Charles VII was already dead, and his letter of pardon expired, therefore Canon Aussigny took justice into his own hands. He wanted to see me suffer rather than have a quick passing. He sentenced me to remain in chains for the rest of my life, rotting away like some undesirable garbage in a filthy prison beneath the castle.

"I can't believe that anything could be worse than that awful pit. The only light coming in was from a heavily barred round window from which the canon often spat or urinated down on me... I had never met such a loathsome man before. He made me harbour so much hatred that I began cursing instead of praying.

"To lie down there with his filth around me was worse than the already dreadful conditions. To imagine living like that my whole life was simply impossible. I hate to admit it, but I often found myself wishing that the guards would lower down a solid rope instead of a chain with a basketful of hard crusts."

I inhaled in shock and noticed that Magdalene was completely speechless, tears welling up in her eyes.

"I saw no chance of getting out," he continued. "Death seemed like the only resurrection from the daily torment. I trembled with chills even when it was sunny outside and when it rained, I had to lie in the cold, nauseating puddles beneath my feet. I suffered with excruciating thirst and hunger all the time. Rotten breadcrumbs or potato peelings became a delicacy down there..."

The memories created a cloud of darkness around us all.

"I realised how foolish I was to ever feel indestructible," he hissed bitterly. "I survived three months down there, but the cold, wet conditions and the malnutrition took its toll on me in the end. I developed this ugly cough, became weak, and worst of all, I began to lose my mind. To keep myself sane, I clung to my memories, although I found little comfort in them. I kept recalling all the mistakes I had made in my life, all the reckless words I had spoken... I thought of how my life could have been had I been a better person..."

He looked at Magdalene with the kind of gentleness he showed only to her. "I thought of your innocent face, Mother, and regretted how much I have disappointed you. I wanted nothing more than to make it up to you one day and prayed that I would be allowed..."

Magdalene was unable to speak due to the flood of tears, so she just clasped his hands in hers. Then François turned to me with the utmost respect. He was not used to verbalising his emotions, but I was always aware of how much he appreciated me.

"And I thought about the many things you taught me, Guillaume, and about how you have always believed in me. I think that the thought of you two was what kept me alive down there."

Magdalene had begun to cry so loudly that François had to comfort her in his arms. I myself couldn't contain the tears any longer, for his confession shook me to the core.

"No matter what has happened or what you have done, dear boy," I said, unable to control my trembling voice, "the most important thing is that fortune had your back once again and that you survived it all. Now tell us how on earth you managed to escape."

François gave us a dark grin and said, "It was the strangest thing... I don't know whether it was destiny, fortune, or maybe even the King himself, Charles VII, looking out for me from heaven, but it truly happened. Our new King, Louis XI and his bride, were passing through Meung, and to honour their union to the fullest, they decided to free all the prisoners on the way. Thank goodness Aussigny was gone that day, probably torturing someone else, as under his watch, the prison guards would not have consented to freeing me as well... Despite my weakness and physical discomfort, I ran for my life upon my release, just to be as far from that place as possible...

"I hurried down the road without any plan, not following any particular direction, and ended up collapsing by a village house. The mistress of the house, a certain Marthe, took pity on me, and because of her diligent care, I began to recover from the worst. For some reason, the woman took a liking to me despite my awful looks and poor health."

"Was she a widow?" asked Magdalene.

"No," shrugged François. "Her husband had gone to visit some distant relatives and left her alone for a fortnight. I had a wonderful time with her before her husband returned and she performed a hysterical pantomime. She claimed that I took her as a hostage and tried to rob them when the only thing I took was her chastity belt."

Magdalene just sighed as she had given up crossing herself long ago.

"I thought I could trust her," he said, "but I woke up from the illusion when her husband ran at me with a dagger. I don't even know how I managed to escape him… From then on, I wandered around the countryside, begging for food and shelter. That was when my cough began to worsen again. After all, the summer was long gone, and I had nothing but a few rags on.

"One day I ended up at a crossroads and noticed a sign that pointed to Paris. The vision of home made me feel alive again. I couldn't resist and so decided that it was time to come back. However, I grew weaker every step of the way, especially when it started to rain. I began to feel the chills of fever slowly overpower me until I fainted. All I remember from that point on is seeing a familiar face above me. It was a man who saved my life once before – Jean de Loup, alias Wolf…"

I repeated the name in my mind until I finally remembered who he was. He was one of the Coquillards, the one who had introduced Regnier to crime. Anxiety took hold of me then. I knew I had to tell François about everything including the provost's warning as soon as possible, but not in Magdalene's presence. She was upset enough, still shaken by all the details that François had just confessed to.

"Maybe one of the angels sent that man on your path," she said in tears, still gently cradling his hands in hers.

François smiled. "Maybe, Mother. I'm beginning to believe in the power of your prayers."

Magdalene smiled back and embraced him again. As I watched the two strong souls, I silently prayed for them and thanked the Holy Spirit for reuniting us. Sunshine had returned to our home that day, but only for a while, for I knew that he couldn't stay if we wanted to keep him alive. We had to hide him while we came up with a plan for yet another escape.

CHAPTER 16

THE PERIL OF MONTFAUCON

I dreaded telling François about everything that had happened while he was gone, but I had no choice. Although he promised to stay at Porte Rouge until he had fully recovered, I knew that he wanted to meet up with his friends sooner or later. So I went to his attic chamber the following night, hoping it would be the right moment for us to talk. I had missed the sight of him sitting at his desk, moving the quill across parchment in the candlelight, focused entirely on noting down his thoughts and verses.

"I hope I'm not disturbing you," I said, addressing him from the doorway.

He turned to me with a distracted look, which showed that his mind was partly in the verses, but he said, "Not at all, Guillaume... please, come in."

He began to cough again so I sat beside him and patted his back. "That cold dungeon really took its toll on you, dear boy."

"It wasn't just that," he wheezed.

My eyes met his in apprehension. What other horrors was he hiding?

"I didn't want to worry Mother even more than I already have," he said, trying to suppress the cough, "so I left out the worst part of my trip."

My throat tightened at the thought of him suffering.

"I was tortured, Guillaume," he said then, corroborating my dreadful suspicions.

He looked down then peeked out from beneath his brow, checking my reaction.

I was stupefied, yet I had to ask, "What method did they use?"

"Waterboarding."

I shivered, outraged by the idea of François being strapped down and forced to swallow litres of water until his stomach expanded to the point of bursting.

"Excruciating pain, the worst imaginable," he added curtly, anguished by the memories. Then he turned away, unable to speak or even think about it anymore.

"I wanted you to know the truth, but let's leave it at that. I wish to forget about it, erase it from my memory forever."

I was not convinced that was such a good idea, as I knew that the more we hide away from the dark corners of the soul, the weaker we get. It was too soon to deal with it, however, so I respected his decision.

"Let's talk about your new poem instead then," I suggested, looking at the verses before him. "If you're ready for it, of course."

He shrugged and said, "I'm only writing down what I have memorised. I carved this poem in the stones down in the pit and promised myself to remember every word so that I could write it down one day. To survive through the darkest times, I turned to the memories of my youth, the times I spent with you and Mother, but also with my friends... We have been through so much together, so many sleepless nights, adventures, we even fought the Grim Reaper herself..."

I smiled at this, as I remembered that François believed the Grim Reaper to be woman who entices her victims to follow her over the threshold between life and death.

"As I lay down there, I wondered where all my friends were when I needed them the most, what they were doing while I was slowly fading away, feeling as lonely as a beast who clings bitterly to his own skin..."

I knew it was time to tell him the truth about his friends, however, before I could say anything, he asked, "Would you like me to read it for you?"

I wavered but concluded that I could wait a little longer, so I nodded. He took a deep breath and began reciting the poem to me:

Please have pity, have pity on me and my folly
Dear brothers of mine, dear friends
I wither under the heavy grates instead of a holly
In this dreaded exile, this futile escape
You know how fortune and God operate
My girls, lovers, my faithful companions
Jolly tumblers, singers, dancers of cotillion
Quick as arrows, fiery, blade-sharp
Your distant voices clear as a harp
Will you leave him down there? Poor Villon!

Hearing the verses made me feel even more anxious than before. I knew it was time to address the important issues. I had already made peace with the idea that he truly did rob the College of Navarre, but a part of me still hoped that he would refute the allegations.

"François, I have been meaning to ask you something." I was brave enough to speak yet scared to know the truth. "And I want you to know that no matter what your answer is, it won't change anything. You will always be my favourite person in the whole wide world."

"What is it Guillaume? Ask me anything," said François, already sensing my distress.

"Did you rob the College of Navarre?"

At first, he was speechless, then asked, "They found out about it?"

"So you have," I answered my own question.

"Out of pure necessity, Guillaume. I needed money fast, and you know they would not employ me anywhere at that time… I could no longer take advantage of you and my friends…"

"I understand, you don't have to explain," I said. Although I was disappointed to hear him confess to the crime, I had to brace myself and tell him the worst part of the news.

"A certain prior was sent to investigate the case and fooled Guy Tabary into thinking he was a criminal looking for a good locksmith. The boy trusted him and that's how they found out he was involved."

"That damn fool," muttered François. "What happened to him?"

"He was taken to the Châtelet and questioned. His loyalty to you must have been strong, as he didn't reveal your name during the first two rounds of torture. It was only when things became unbearable that he began to speak…"

François shook his head in disbelief. "Please tell me he isn't dead."

"He died in the prison soon after the confession. I heard it was a consequence of the injuries he received during the questioning…"

François closed his eyes, digesting the sudden tragic news. "What about Colin?"

"The Benefit of Clergy didn't help him either," I said, startled by the feverish intensity of his gaze. He wanted to know more even though he dreaded it. I had to look away to be able to say, "He was executed at the Gibbet of Montfaucon."

I was silent, letting him deal with the distressing news that he hadn't been prepared for. I knew that nothing would make him feel better at that moment, and that he simply needed to mourn his friends, yet I had to deliver the final blow.

"I want you to know that I was present during both executions, François. I wanted to pray for your friends in their final moments, send them love and courage as they left our world…"

"Both?" he repeated confused. "I thought Tabary died at the Châtelet."

I reached for his hands and squeezed them tightly. My lips were shaking, I was dreading speaking, so I only managed, "Regnier was the first to go."

"Regnier? That's impossible!" He freed his hands from my grasp and stood up in trepidation. "He was not part of that robbery!"

He was unwilling to accept the truth so a part of him hoped I was wrong or lying.

"He was found guilty of murder, François."

"That's preposterous! Regnier would never kill anyone," he argued again, his eyes begging me to deny it all and save him from the inner torment.

"All I know is that he robbed someone and killed him during a fight when he was caught... It was undoubtedly an act of self-defence, but his past criminal charges went against him. Like Colin, he was also pronounced beyond redemption."

François kept shaking his head, unable to react in any other way.

"I know this is all too much for you to digest, François, but it is very important for you to understand that you will face the same fate if you are not careful. They are looking for you now... Robert d'Estouteville warned me while he was still in office that even he would not be able to help you anymore. He has recently been replaced by one Pierre de la Hors, an ex-sergeant who is especially bitter towards students and graduates. Therefore, you must promise me that you will stay here in hiding until we come up with a better plan."

François didn't seem to care, though. "I don't have to hide," he insisted. "They wouldn't recognise me anyway. Just look at me, Guillaume: I look like a sick old man. Please, tell me where they buried my friends."

"Regnier is still at the Gibbet of Montfaucon," I admitted. "The remains have not been taken down yet."

François was livid. "How could they do that to him?"

I lowered my head, knowing that the last time a body had been displayed on the gibbet for so long was decades ago.

"I'm so very sorry for your loss, François. I have been praying for your friends every day since it happened. We have to believe that they found peace in heaven."

I stopped speaking, realising it was pointless. François didn't react. He just stood in the corner of his chamber, pale as a ghost, frozen to the spot. I could tell he wanted to be left alone, so I rose from the chair and said, "You know that I'll always be here for you, François. Please come to me when you are ready to talk about the grief and your next escape... We must save you. I will do anything to provide you with a comfortable living somewhere far away from here."

With a heavy heart, I left him alone in the chamber where only a single flame lit up the all-consuming darkness.

✦

A nightmare woke me up that night. I dreamt of walking through some country cemetery where I found Magdalene planting black roses on someone's grave, shrouded in a thick pre-dawn fog.

"Aren't they the most beautiful flowers you have ever seen?" she marvelled. The ominous silence around us frightened me even more than the gloom.

"Why are we here?" I asked her. Magdalene turned to me, placed her finger on her lips, and continued planting the black roses with a chillingly calm, concentrated expression.

I could not fall asleep again after the strange dream, so I turned to some soothing literature instead. Soon, the church bells struck three and I decided to check on François, as I had been worried about him ever since I told him about the sad lot of his friends. I hoped he would be fast asleep, but to my shock, he was not in his chamber. I anxiously searched every corner of the house for him including the cellar. He was nowhere to be found.

I wondered if he had gone out for a walk deep in the night as he had done in the past. Supposing that was the case, I hoped he would be sane enough to return before sunrise. I was about to return to my chamber when a thought made me stop. Could it be that he went to pay his respects to Regnier? Would he have gone all the way to Montfaucon at such a late hour? I knew he was reckless enough for that, particularly if he had found himself in a desperate state of mind. I didn't want to risk anything, so quickly made preparations for the late-night trip. I grabbed my overcoat, warm shoes and a woollen blanket in case François had gone out unprepared, and stepped out into the cold wind.

I walked at a fast pace, praying intently for François' safety and health, but could not help myself from pondering his fate at the same time. He had triumphed over death thus far. He had been pardoned for a crime others would hang for and had even been miraculously saved from a life of imprisonment. Something or someone powerful must have been on his side. Whether it was fortune, our all-loving heavenly Father, or perhaps the spirit of his own father, he had been blessed with unusual luck. However, I felt that he never really learned from his mistakes. He was unable to tame his wild spirit and change his ways for the better. That's why I was so afraid for him. You can only mess up for so long before it is too late.

No matter how many times I visited the Gibbet of Montfaucon I was always petrified at the sight, and that October night was no different. The stone base that supported the massive wooden construction was shrouded in a pre-dawn mist and surrounded by flocks of shrilling ravens coming to satisfy their hunger. The bodies of the condemned swung in the air, resigned to their grim end, and in the dead of night, the vision was even more harrowing. The moon was growing fuller, so its soft light revealed the pitiful state of the corpses.

Some of them had already had their eyes, brows and hair pecked out while others were still untouched by the birds of prey.

Regnier was the oldest one there. Six years was simply too cruel. His red boots were long gone, probably stolen. Since his bones had found no peace in the subterranean kingdom, I prayed once again for his soul to find salvation in the heavenly paradise.

As I gazed at the fragile bones that had once belonged to a strong, youthful man, a strange noise disturbed me. It sounded like someone digging, but that seemed illogical at such a late hour, so I followed the noise to find out what was going on. I couldn't believe my eyes when I saw François digging a hole in the ground. At first, I didn't understand the madness. It was only when I made out the motionless canine body beside him that I realised he was preparing a grave.

We all knew that Regnier's hound, or Estienne de Montigny II as he liked to call him, remained loyal to his master even after he left our world. He travelled between the gibbet and Regnier's favourite inn until the end. From time to time, I brought him some food, and noticed that two women did so as well. Judging by their attire, I assumed they were Regnier's friends from the brothel. Other than that, nobody cared about the hound. I heard that he always distanced himself during the executions and returned only once it was all over. I supposed he must have died very recently, because I came to pray there at least once a week.

The sight of François burying the hound's body touched and frightened me at the same time. He was not healthy enough for such hard labour and although it was still too early for anyone to show up, he could be spotted on his way home. I quickly hurried to his side.

"François! What are you thinking? It's too risky to be out here!"

He didn't seem surprised to see me and went on with the digging.

"Regnier would have wanted me to bury Estienne de Montigny II," he insisted. "Everybody deserves a decent burial, especially such a loyal hound."

He coughed then continued with his work. I knew he wouldn't listen as he rarely heeded my warnings, therefore the only thing I could do was help him dig faster.

"Where did you even get this?" I asked as I tried to take the spade from him.

"From the graveyard," he muttered, trying to fight me off. "I can manage on my own, Guillaume, just go home."

"I'm not going without you," I insisted. "Let's just bury the animal and be done with it."

François didn't let go of the spade until one of his coughing fits weakened him. I seized the opportunity and took over the digging. It must have been the apprehension or the built-up rage, either way I worked incredibly fast. François was still in shock. The fearful sight of Regnier's remains must have shaken him to the core. Once my conciliatory work was done, I blessed the animal and we lowered him into the grave together. As I poured the mud and gravel on top of the stiff body, François whispered, "I'm sorry I came too late, my friend…"

I wasn't sure whether he was addressing the hound or Regnier, and supposed it didn't matter anymore. The private ceremony was over and I prompted him to follow me home. François didn't react, though. Instead, he looked up at Regnier's swaying remains and I could tell that another mad idea had crossed his mind.

"Come on, son," I prompted him, covering him with the woollen blanket to keep him warm. "Let's go now."

I nudged him ahead of me, but he would not budge.

"Please François," I pleaded with him, "it's not safe for you out here. We can pray for Regnier at home."

François shook his head. "I have done enough praying, Guillaume. Regnier should not hang in the air like bait for the ravens. He deserves the same respect as his hound."

He strode towards the gibbet with firm determination. I looked around, worried that the city guards would show up, but luckily, there was no one there, so I still had time to reason with him.

"François, the remains belong to Regnier's family. They will certainly arrange a proper burial for him as soon as he is taken down."

"When?" he asked. "Once there is nothing but dust left of him? This is not right, Guillaume. He was a good man, no matter what poverty and disgrace made him do, he was still a good man..."

François stopped at the wall that loomed over us and headed for the gate. There, he pulled a wire from his overcoat pocket, and said, "Colin taught me this."

I stared at him in disbelief as he began unlocking the gate.

"Stop it! Someone will see you!"

He wouldn't listen and persistently worked on the heavy locks like a crazed man. At the sight of him behaving like a common thief, I came to a realisation that I had been inwardly struggling with for years: the man who was like a son to me really had turned into a criminal. I hated myself for thinking it but couldn't help it at that moment. I was angry with him and furious with myself, which made me want to fight with him, at least to try and make him physically stop even if I wasn't able to mentally. We hadn't been paying attention to our surroundings while we argued, not until someone's hands separated us.

I froze when I faced the city guards. The two sergeants pushed me aside and held me tight as the other two took hold of François, punishing him when he tried to escape them. The punches and kicks eventually made him obedient. I was stuck in the grip of their strong arms, unable to do anything but beg them to stop. I wasn't sure why they left me behind and took only François away, perhaps because I was fighting him before they caught us or because I wore my clerical cloak. However, as they dragged François away, he finally came to his senses and shouted after me, "I'm sorry! I'm so sorry!"

It was as if he had finally woken up from the insanity and realised what he had done. The desperate sound of his voice reverberated in my mind while I stood there, rooted to the ground like a tree. I believed that would be the end of him.

CHAPTER 17

THE TESTAMENT

I could not hide the truth from Magdalene any longer. I told her about everything that had happened, including the College of Navarre robbery. I had to prepare her for the worst and be strong as it was most likely that François would soon end up at the gibbet next to his friends. The fact that we were unable to help him was unbearable. All we could do was pray and wait for the news to reach us. That time, I mainly prayed for him to be given another miraculous chance.

When we still hadn't heard anything about his ordeal the next day, I began to lose my mind. I pictured him in the torture chamber at the Châtelet and it pained me to such an extent that I could not eat, sleep or even pray. However, when a new day came, fortune surprised me once again. François returned home as though nothing had happened. He was even smiling, which told us that he came with good news. We were elated and sat him down right away, urging him to share what had happened with us.

"The sergeants didn't recognise me," he explained, "and so I reasoned with them. I said that I wasn't going to steal anything, that I was just showing you an old trick I had learned once. 'What would I steal at the gibbet anyway?' I asked them. 'A corpse?' They laughed at the idea and I had no alternative but to join in although I hated mocking my own plan..."

He locked eyes with me. Of course, nobody would believe that he wanted to steal a corpse. Still, I couldn't believe it would be so easy for him to fool such tough men who were used to dealing with all kinds of liars and crooks.

"They didn't find it strange that you were out so early in the morning at such an odd location and with a priest by your side?"

"They did, however, I told them that we are used to waking up very early and going for a walk in the countryside."

I shook my head in disbelief. "And they really didn't recognise you?"

"One of them did," he said, "but God knows how. I look like a shrivelled up scrotum."

"That's nonsense," objected Magdalene, as in her eyes, François was still the handsome boy that all the girls chased after.

"Anyway, the bastard revealed who I was, and I couldn't deny his allegations once he pointed out that François Villon had a scar on his upper lip. He called it the mark of the devil." He smirked at the thought.

"And then what happened?"

"They kept me locked up for two days but compared to the pit in Meung it was luxury. I also had some company there, though most of the men were complaining rather than making conversation."

"Did you plead the Benefit of Clergy?" I inquired again, keen to finally learn what verdict he had left the prison with.

"I did, and was taken to the ecclesiastical court the next day, which was already good news."

I nodded, as had he faced the provost instead, he would have stood little chance.

"The judges confronted me once again about the unfortunate accident with Sermoise and were particularly sneaky about it since they knew I no longer had the protection of Charles VII. Then they started with the College of Navarre robbery."

He checked Magdalene's reaction, then mine, and read in our expressions that I had already told her. He gave her a smile and said, "Don't worry about my soul, dear mother, I will make amends."

"Oh no!" wept Magdalene, but he quickly calmed her down.

"Don't cry. I'm not going to be killed, at least not yet. What I am trying to say is that I have decided to stay here and live a calm life with you two."

"What do you mean... did they just let you off the hook?" she asked, confused.

François nodded. "I managed to convince the judges that it was in their interest to let me live, because only by staying alive would I be able to pay back the sum that I stole. I promised to find myself some decent work and pay back every last sou, even more if God allows."

"Are you serious, François? How could you possibly have persuaded them to believe you?" I asked, unable to wrap my head around it.

He gave me a mysterious smile and I noticed that his eyes were lit up by that rebellious glint again. I could tell that he was back to normal and it soothed my soul. His resilience was simply astonishing. No matter how much he had been through or how he had changed over the six years, those two things remained the same: his immense inner strength and an unbreakable sense of humour.

"Do you remember the first time we met, Guillaume?" he asked, taking me back to the moment that I treasured in my heart.

"Certainly, how could I ever forget?"

"I told them the story about King Alexander the Great and Diomedes the thief. I told them that like Diomedes, I would change my ways if they gave me a chance. I urged them to let me pay back what I had stolen in cash instead of executing me. 'If I join my companions at the Gibbet of Montfaucon,' I said, 'the college won't gain anything. What good did it do anyone that my friends died? The chest at the College of Navarre is still as empty as their pockets.'

"I could tell they were contemplating it, so I reasoned with them some more, philosophising about how my death would bring no solution to my crime. I asserted that God would rather have me live and repent my deeds than let me perish without the ability to become a better man. Why would he have spared my life so many times before had he not had further plans for me? The drama of that statement made them smirk, I could tell that they were going to laugh at me, so I tried to persuade them in another and perhaps more appealing way. I offered them a deal. I told them that if I don't pay up the debt in one year, I'll let them do whatever they like with me."

"And they really gave you another chance?" asked Magdalene, still unable to comprehend how it was possible.

François nodded and exclaimed, "They did, Mother, I'm a free man!" Then he hesitated and added, "Well, at least for a year…"

"That's simply unbelievable!" I laughed, finally feeling all the built-up fear leave me.

"It may be unbelievable, but it's true," said François contently.

Magdalene and I gaped at him in astonishment. We didn't understand how the same law that had condemned all his friends to torture and death could be so lenient in his case. Was it just because he told them an ancient story and philosophised about God's intentions? It sounded like a fairy tale. However, I remembered the many times I had witnessed François' persuasive, charming nature and concluded that God must indeed still favour him, perhaps because it was so entertaining to watch his unpredictable story from the heavens.

"But how will you manage to pay it all off?" asked Magdalene then. "You would have to find a really good job if that's even possible in your condition."

François just threw his hand in the air and went off to fetch us all some wine. "Don't worry about that, Mother, I will probably be dead in a year anyway."

"Don't you dare die before me!" she frowned, so he kissed her cheek and made her smile again.

"No matter when and how we go," he said, handing us our goblets, "let's enjoy the here and now to the fullest!"

He poured us all some burgundy and finished his in one gulp. As I watched that same old recklessness return to his face, I began to doubt if he really meant what he had said before. Seeing him use the third chance he had been given wisely seemed just as impossible as the news itself. Although I believed that he was honest in his intentions to make amends, I couldn't help but foresee that his uncontrollable nature would not let him live peacefully even if he wanted to. He had a great talent for poetry and rhetoric, but unfortunately also for attracting trouble.

✦

Despite the fact that François was once again absolved, I was still haunted by the nightmare I had had before the madness at Montfaucon. I decided not to think about it, though. Having him in the safety of our home, relatively healthy and out of prison was a miracle and I wanted to enjoy his company while I could. True to his word, François did start looking for some decent employment during the day, and in the evenings he retreated to his attic room to work on his new collection of poetry. He was pouring his whole heart into the verses, and I was curious to read them, as I believed that they would be quite different from those he had written before, especially after what he had experienced.

Therefore, one evening, I grabbed a bottle of burgundy and joined him in his attic chamber. François welcomed my company and soon afterwards, he began discussing his work with me like in the olden days.

"It's similar to *The Legacy*, but more compact. I have included some of my older poems as well."

"What do you call it?"

"*The Testament*," he replied, making me smile.

"Again, such a grim prediction?"

"No, this time it's real," he said in all seriousness. "I feel that I'll pass away soon after I finish it. I can't bring myself to write a simple last will, though."

Although the words sent chills down my spine, I hid the uneasiness behind a chuckle.

"Oh François, you have been dying since I have known you!"

He smiled at the comment. "I thought you'd laugh because I have nothing to leave behind…"

"Nonsense, you have plenty to leave behind, you know very well that physical possessions are not the only riches one accumulates during his lifetime."

He thought about it, then silently handed me one of the parchments. I knew what it meant. He was ready to share his work with me. The ink was still damp, so I was careful not to smudge it as I read part of it:

> *Item: I leave to my loving mother*
> *This prayer to our Lady in the skies*
> *For she suffered for me like no other*
> *God knows well of her silent cries*
> *I have no castle or fortress to reside in*
> *Nowhere our bodies or souls could subside*
> *So if bad times should come again upon me*
> *Please spare my mother, the poor lady!*

"You wrote a prayer for your mother?" I gasped in disbelief, touched by the thoughtful gesture.

"I hope she will enjoy that one for she will certainly not like the rest," he grinned and handed me another parchment. I read the beginning quickly:

> *And regarding those atrocious beasts*
> *Who treated me like some watermill*
> *And gave me hard crusts for a meal…*
> *I no longer fear those stinky shits*
> *I'd leave them some farts and belches*
> *But my stomach feels too empty…*

I shook my head, marvelling at his ability to find humour even in such dark memories as his torture. I always appreciated that about his poetry, along with the balance between grace and vulgarity. That was his strength in everything – to merge opposing dualities and turn them into something unique.

"I can't wait to read the whole piece, François," I said earnestly, "I bet it will be your best work yet."

He shrugged and became a bit downhearted at the mention of it. I wondered whether it was making him think about his first poem collection and its bitter backstory.

"What about Katherine? Will you leave her something?"

He shrugged, trying to remain unemotional. "If the muse strikes me, or if she does…"

I smiled, weighing up whether or not to give him my opinion of the situation. I even felt tempted to discreetly mention that she came to Saint Benoit for a confession, however, I knew that he would beg me to disclose more so I quickly abandoned the idea.

"I thought of Katherine while I was away," said François suddenly, rousing me from my contemplation. "In fact, I thought of her a lot."

He checked my reaction, clearly seeking some ray of hope. I opened my mouth, wishing to let him know that he was on her mind as well, but realised that even if I betrayed my clerical duties for him, it would only make things worse. As I knew

François, he would try to win her back, and would end up in another kind of trouble. Noël Jolis had beaten him up once, and that was before Katherine was his wife, so I dared not to imagine what he would do if he pursued her again.

"How is she, Guillaume?"

"I think she is doing well enough..."

"Any children?"

"No, the couple hasn't been blessed yet."

He couldn't contain a bitter smile.

"I should have fought harder for her," he said. "I should have been patient with her, insisted on talking to her once again... But I was as proud as her. She condemned me too mercilessly back then."

I nodded in silence, unable to add anything to that, so he went on, "When I was younger, I didn't want any woman to weigh me down, but in that prison pit, I wished for nothing more than the common life I used to find so boring and limiting."

I patted his back and attempted to console him. "Don't focus on what you have lost, François, rather envision what you may have."

"I should think about the consequences of my actions, though, don't you think? In the past I never did that…"

"Not just in the past. Remember what happened a few days ago," I reminded him.

"That was grief," he said, and the distress caused him to cough. I didn't like how the cough attacks lingered and grew in intensity. He cleared away the itchy feeling from his throat with another gulp of wine and added, "Still, it's about time I changed my ways. I often regretted all the mistakes I had made, especially during my student years. Why didn't I spend my days buried in the library at the Sorbonne without feeling the need to scale its walls and play with fire? I need to start anew."

Despite wholeheartedly agreeing, I decided to leave out the fact that I had been secretly praying for it.

"You are wise to consider that, but please don't do it for me or your mother, do it for yourself."

"But I want to do it for you," he insisted. "That was all I could think of when I landed up back in prison the other day, awaiting the worst verdict possible. You can't imagine how much I hated letting you down because of my reckless behaviour. All the promises I made to myself in Meung were suddenly broken. I hated myself for that. I kept recalling everything I used to take for granted, even details like Mother's warm hands, the wrinkles by her eyes, her rosary… Your impish laughter or your favourite book of philosophy you keep re-reading… You two have always been there for me, you are the two most important people in my life. I never want to see you sad or worried because of me again. I can't let my mistakes ruin your lives. I just want to make you proud."

"I am proud of you, François," I assured him, as I needed him to know that no matter what had happened, he was still a remarkable man in my eyes. "I would never survive what you went through, and I would never write what you have written. You know I have always appreciated you for who you truly are with both your light and dark sides. We all have our weaknesses…"

I gave him a mysterious smile, which made his face light up.

"What are you trying to tell me, Guillaume? Do you have another weakness apart from wine?"

I shrugged. "Well, it's actually connected. Did I ever tell you about the time I was in prison myself?"

"You were in prison?"

I nodded. Although I was embarrassed to confess to my biggest sin, I decided to do so anyway. After all, who could understand it better than François?

"I stole a barrel of wine and was kept in the prison of Notre Dame for a day."

François' grin froze for a moment, but then he burst into laughter.

"And the whole time we were wondering who the bad influence was!"

I couldn't help myself and joined in his laughter.

"No worries, Guillaume, your secret is safe with me."

As I watched him cough and laugh at the same time, I realised that even though he had changed, he was still just a cheeky boy with a crude, dark streak. That was François Villon with all his force of character, but what a character he was.

*

PART FIVE:

FRANÇOIS

Item: My sepulchre should be
At Saint Avoye, nowhere else
So that everyone may see me
Not in flesh but in my broadness
Let someone paint me with fondness
But please don't spend too much money
A tombstone? I don't care about such luxury.
It would just burden the ground.

Item: I wish to have my humble pit
Decorated without much ado
And if you make the letters big
The following poem will do.
Use some charcoal or black chalk
But don't scratch too hard on the rock
To keep my memory alive and strong
If a wild man like me deserves it:

"In his attic he lay to rest
Struck by Cupid's merciless arrow
A poor and useless student

Who as François Villon was known
He never kept a thing in this world
As he gave away all that he owned:
Tables, chairs, bread, baskets, bowls
Upon saying amen, read him this rondeau:

While his body sleeps here in a final rest
His soul shines in an everlasting brightness
He owned nothing, not even a plate
Nor could he afford a sprig of sage
He lost his beard, hair, everything
Until he looked like a potato peel
May he rest in eternity!

Rigour banished him into the country
And whacked his arse with a whip
Even if he called out for mercy
And trust me - that is no small thing
May he rest in eternity!

Extract from *The Testament* (1461-1462, François Villon)

CHAPTER 18

MARGOT

Paris, December 1462

Oh Paris, how I missed being at one with you! So why did you make me feel like a stranger when I found myself back in your embrace? Every nook whispered the secrets of my youth, but you suddenly seemed so distant. Nevertheless, you were the love of my life, the only city with such unique grace. I have always liked your glamour as much as your filth and found your kindness equally as moving as your cruelty. I promised myself that I would enjoy your spirit while I could and so I roamed your streets as often as I was able.

At last, I was free of public shame. I had been given a new chance and was careful not to mess it up again. I became a scribe at a nearby monastery and spent most of my days inside its peaceful walls or at my home at Porte Rouge. Still, I supposed that no matter how much I tried, Saturn had already packed my bundle of destiny. My heart often argued against my mind, claiming that I could change whatever the god of fate had decided yet my reason feared that everything was already sealed.

One afternoon, shortly after work, I sat on the bench by Saint Benoit where I had given Philippe Sermoise his fatal wound and prayed for the peculiar young priest. I hoped his soul truly forgave me for everything as he claimed he had on his deathbed. Recalling the tragedy made me think of my friends who had also lost their lives over the years. I wondered why I was still standing. Was the Duke d'Orleans right when he said I could talk myself out of any kind of trouble? For some reason, it was hard for me to believe Guillaume and Mother, who both thought that I was guided by some higher power. Maybe Margot had nailed it when she said that I was simply a child of fortune.

The thought of her then lured me to the sinful parts of the city where I tainted each ray of hope with a seed of darkness. Although I had promised myself not to spend my time at such taverns anymore, I at least had to meet her, tell her that I had returned. After all, she was the only one of my old friends who was still alive.

On my way, I thought of all the things I longed to share with her and all the questions I needed to ask. However, Saturn was laughing in my face that day, clearly not letting me visit Margot without that familiar guilty conscience. One would think that after all I had been through, I would be prepared for everything, but meeting Katherine caught me completely off guard. Just the sight of her sent me to the dim, spoilt corners of my soul. Even worse was to face the unfortunate fact that neither she nor my feelings had changed during the six years I had been away.

I often fantasised about running into her again, wondered whether she would talk to me and if so, what she would say. I had prepared a few words for her in my mind, just in case it happened, but no matter how spectacular I thought them to be, I knew I would never dare to utter them aloud. Even though I was usually confident with words and women, times had changed. I suddenly felt like a timid young boy in her presence. It was as if she had some kind of spell over me; perhaps it was so because she still owned my heart.

Seeing her after such a long time reminded me of the moment we met after my first escape from Paris. She was so amazing to me then. She proved to be a true friend. She didn't judge or blame me, she even understood the dreadful situation better than I did myself. Back then she saved my soul from drowning. I admired how fearless and genuine she was in those days. She didn't care what others thought of her friendly behaviour towards me. She stood by me in spite of everyone's opinion. That's why it came as such a shock when an insignificant thing like that nasty old poem made her condemn me to the pits of hell. Many years had passed, and I still didn't fully understand it. Guillaume once advised me to look at the situation from her point of view. She was a maiden dreaming of a chivalrous knight to rescue her while I was a libertine who had experience with the female body but not the spirit. Still, I thought she knew me well. How could she not realise that the poem was just an exaggeration? Perhaps I should have fought harder, explained myself more clearly, however, at that time I believed Margot when she said that had Katherine truly loved me, she would have given me another chance.

I couldn't face Katherine's disdain, especially when I was in such a pitiful condition. I was going to turn around and take a detour rather than pass her, but it was too late. Her eyes had found me and become locked with mine in the unmerciful cage of our past. Only once I saw the shocked expression on her face did I understand the contrast between us. She was still the same gracious woman, while I had become a dried-up prune with no juice left to squeeze. Although I never cared much about my looks, I knew I used to be attractive to women before Meung took its toll on me.

Katherine must have been appalled, because she turned away from me and rushed into the narrow streets as if her arse was on fire. It didn't surprise me all that much. I made an excellent scarecrow, and if I were a woman, I would be fleeing at the sight of myself too. Another reason to go to Margot's, I thought. At least she would greet me with dignity and if not, I could always pay her to. I laughed at my foolishness as I strode on with determination. How could I think that we would be able to stop and have a chat about the times gone by? My anger pushed me onwards, encouraging me to go where I was welcome as opposed to where the door was shut in my face.

✦

It felt good to be back in the sordid little tavern. The atmosphere of our rebellious student years filled me with new vivacity after the cold encounter with Katherine. My friends and I had spent some incredible nights there, and I would treasure those memories forever. I knew each and every corner by heart: the open space with its old, stone fireplace, the dilapidated tables and chairs, the creaky wooden stairs, the cherry tint of the chamber doors, the adorable fusion of shabbiness and beauty.

The tavern was empty that early afternoon, which was for the best. It didn't tempt me to drink and make a fool of myself. I sat at our favourite table and only then, the absence of my friends fully dawned on me. I knew that the place would never be the same without my favourite nobleman Regnier, the king of the locksmiths Colin and the young fool Tabary. I had to suppress my tears when I turned to see the man who had quietly entered the room. It was Wolf.

"What in hell's fire are you doing here?" he exclaimed. "Aren't you supposed to be in hiding?"

"Not anymore. I talked the ecclesiastical court judges into letting me go if I paid my debt to the College of Navarre."

"Not possible," he said in disbelief. "How did you manage that?"

"I suppose my tongue is not always useless, but it's mainly fortune, still on my side."

He kept shaking his head as he patted my back. We swiftly embraced and when we pulled away, our eyes locked in nostalgia. We both remembered our mutual friend, Regnier de Montigny. There were times when I used to blame Wolf for Regnier's criminal path, however, that was before I realised that had it not been Wolf it would have been someone else dragging him down. Regnier was born to be a nobleman, not struggle in the streets, and only crime could provide him with that luxury.

"Sit down with me," suggested Wolf. "Let's have some ale and remember the good old days."

"Thank you, Wolf, but I'm trying to change my ways and drinking at places like these is one of the vices I plan on eliminating."

"And you do that by coming here?"

I grinned and explained. "I came to visit my old friends, at least those who are still among us."

He nodded. "I want you to know, Villon, that I did all I could to save Regnier from the noose. As you know, I helped him many times before, but such a high-profile murder? Only someone like you could get away with a serious offence like that."

"I heard about what happened. He did kill the man in self-defence, right?"

Wolf nodded. "It was revenge for Isabeau. He wanted to rob him when the man found him. They started a fight and... Well, you can imagine the rest."

I sighed, as it all suddenly made sense. A part of me knew that Regnier would not let the man get away with what he had done to her.

"Have you gone up to Montfaucon yet?" asked Wolf.

"Certainly. I had to pay my respects…"

"They finally plan to take his remains down. It's been a long time…"

I nodded and when our eyes met again, I thanked him for bringing me back home. "It was the second time you saved my life."

"Well, let's just hope there won't be a third time," he chuckled with that raspy voice of his.

I laughed too, which I should not have done, as it plunged me into another ugly coughing fit. The intensity of it shocked even a hard man like Wolf.

"That's what you get from wandering around in nothing but rags," he said, trying to lighten the mood while he waited until I stopped coughing. "What were you doing on that country road anyway?"

"Escaping prison," I said curtly, unwilling to elaborate, which he understood. "What about you, Wolf? What made you travel so far from Paris?"

"That's a secret," he said mysteriously, "like the big news I received today. Do you want to be the first to know?"

"Why not? You know I can keep a secret."

"I have been promoted. I'm a sergeant at the Châtelet prison now."

"Really? Then you have truly proven to be the king of Parisian criminals."

"I have always had my eye on that job," he said with a crafty look. "How better could I help my men than becoming one of our enemies, huh?"

I don't know how he managed to balance his work for the law and crime so eloquently. The irony made me smile. I began to see him in a better light and finally trusted that he didn't expect anything for saving my life. I wondered why I didn't believe Regnier back in the day. I more than anyone should have known that not all outlaws have dark souls.

With that thought, a familiar female voice cut across the stillness of the tavern.

"I'll be right over, monsieur! I'm sorry for the tardy service, I wasn't expecting customers so early in the day."

I turned around to face the woman who had bewitched my best friend. Isabeau politely nodded a greeting as she descended the stairs, obviously not recognising me.

"One would think you would welcome him with a bit more enthusiasm, Isabeau!" laughed Wolf, enjoying her bafflement. Isabeau stopped a few feet away from us with a frown. I could tell that she was still confused.

"You look even more beautiful than six years ago!" I complimented her, not just to be polite as she truly had aged well, like a good wine. She approached me, still cautious, because even my voice had changed – it had become huskier due to the lingering cough. When Isabeau realised it was me her mouth turned up into a surprised smile.

"Villon!" she beamed.

I gave her a hug, which she returned with a tight embrace. Then she touched my face and I saw tears welling up in her eyes. The way she gazed at me made me turn away. I didn't want pity, especially not from women.

"Excuse me, I am just imagining the horrors you must have been through..." she said with that gentle empathy of hers.

"It's all right." I forced a smile. "And where is Margot? Sleeping late as usual?"

Wolf and Isabeau exchanged a troubled glance.

"What is it?" I asked in alarm. "She is still here, right?"

"Yes, but she is not well," admitted Isabeau.

My heart sank at the idea of Margot falling ill. A woman of her strength should never have to succumb to weakness.

Isabeau sighed. "She has been feeling poorly for a month or so. She says it's her heart, she can feel it growing weaker day by day."

"Maybe Monsieur Villon will make it pump stronger!" laughed Wolf.

"Would you like to see her?"

I nodded and headed straight for the stairs.

Before we reached Margot's chamber, Isabeau warned me, "She might be a bit upset with you at first, you know how she is... She has not been very happy since you left. Sometimes we only realise how we feel about someone when we lose them."

I gave Isabeau a look of sympathy, as we both knew who she was thinking of when she said it. While she was remembering Regnier, I was remembering all the times Margot had hinted at having feelings for me. She was unable to express it, but I sensed it nevertheless. I was never just a lover to her and was definitely more than some random customer. I often wondered why I didn't love her the same way as I did Katherine. Margot was a wonderful friend and a phenomenal lover, but there was something missing. I supposed that my affection for Katherine was simply marked by destiny.

"Go on, knock on her door," she prompted me then. "She should be awake now. I washed and fed her right before you came."

My heart ached even more when she hinted at Margot being so helpless and feeble. I wasn't certain if I was ready to see her that way yet I had to.

"Thank you, Isabeau. She is lucky to have you to take care of her so well."

Isabeau just shrugged then turned around and briskly walked away, leaving me alone at the familiar door that used to lead to paradise, but which had become a sepulchre instead.

✦

It was uncommonly dark inside Margot's chamber. The curtains were drawn, keeping the harsh winter sunshine out. Margot was lying in her bed with her eyes closed and didn't even budge at the sound of the knocking or the floor creaking under my feet. I took a step closer, checking if she was asleep.

"Isabeau?" she whispered tiredly. "Is it you? Could you pour me more water, please?"

I grabbed the empty stoup by her bedside and filled it with more water. When I placed it back, I took in the vision of the new Margot. The face that was so full and round was now emaciated. Her beautiful, chubby cheeks were sunken and her lustrous, golden hair was lank and dishevelled.

She finally opened her eyes and focused on me, the expression in her face caught between incredulity and joy.

"François?" she whispered, calling me by my name for the first time. I was worried, but her next comment put me at ease. "You look awful!"

"I can't say you look any better," I replied, making her laugh along with me.

"I suppose we are not dead yet," she remarked. "We would probably look and feel much better in heaven."

"Who knows?" I grinned. "Maybe we are in hell."

"Could be," she said. "I always thought that hell can't be much worse than this world."

"Perhaps even hell is better than this world."

"Stop now! This is so typical of you. You say something funny and right afterwards something so grim…"

We behaved as if no time had passed until she suddenly turned away in pain. "I feel such discomfort in my chest sometimes…"

"Can I do anything for you? Bring you something?"

She shook her head. "Just stay here with me for a while, would you?"

I nodded. "As long as you want, my lady." I stroked the weak hand that rested in mine.

"Have you been writing? I miss your poetry, sometimes even more than you."

"Actually, I have been scribbling one this morning… I'm not quite sure if it's finished, though."

"Doesn't matter. Recite it for me, before I fall asleep again." She closed her eyes, but her hand squeezed mine with all the strength she had left.

"What is it called?"

"*A Dialogue Between Heart and Mind.*"

"Wonderful. Sounds like something I would enjoy…"

I ached at the sight of her exhausted face so I pulled the scroll of parchment out of my coat pocket, cleared my throat, and began to read:

Who is that I hear? *Just me.* Who? *Your heart.*
Hanging on the thinnest thread
I lose my fluid, patience, strength
When I see you here so alone and torn apart.
Like a beaten hound, crushed too hard

And why? Just for lust, for pleasure?
What is it to you? I suffered my part.
Let me be. *Why?* I need some leisure.
When will we speak again? When I grow up.
I'll say no more then. Good, I'll do fine without it.

What will you do now? Become a decent man.
But you are thirty, that's the age when mules depart.
And you deem yourself a child still? No. *You're mad.*
Foolishness took a hold of you. How? By my collar?
You don't know anything.
I do. *What then?* Flies in the milk.
One is white, one black: they are a pure example
of duality.
Is that all? I suppose I can't say it better, I lack
the quality.
But if it's not clear, I can always start anew.
You are lost. Well, I'll fight until we're through.
I'll say no more then. Good, I'll do fine without it.

Why do you feel so weak? Because of my
weaknesses.
When Saturn packed my tools, he must have put
these in
Along with more of my miseries. *You sound
crazy.*
You speak like his servant, though you are his king.
Remember what Solomon wrote about it:
*"A wise man," he said, "has more power than you
think.*

Even over the planets and their influences."
I refuse to believe that. I am as they made me.
I'll say no more then. Good, I'll do fine without it.

I finished reading and checked her reaction. For a moment, it seemed as though she had fallen asleep, but then she suddenly opened her eyes and said, "Your heart could teach my mind a lesson."

"I don't think so. Your mind is perfect as it is, Margot."

"Perfect. Such an inane word, don't you think?"

Before I could reply, another coughing attack interrupted me. I turned away from her and when I was finally finished, I noticed she was watching me with a frown.

"Gone are the good old days," she said with unfamiliar melancholia. It didn't suit her.

"Nonsense. The wildest days are yet ahead!"

"Then I need to rise on these lazy feet before you go knocking at another chamber."

"You know very well that I have always knocked only on your chamber."

"Ha!" she laughed, "the same old sweet lies…"

We both fell silent, thinking of the heartbreak she had so vainly tried to help me overcome once.

"Have you met her yet?" she asked.

"Actually, right before I came here. She ran away as fast as she could as soon as she saw me."

"No wonder," chuckled Margot. "Every girl should run when you cross her path."

We smiled at each other before she added, "I bet you were pleased to know that her marriage is a disaster."

I was honestly baffled to hear that, which surprised her.

"Didn't you know? Madame Katherine Jolis is known to have taken quite a few lovers since you left Paris. It drives her husband mad. He takes his revenge on her by coming here, crying like a baby while he quenches his lust with my girls. What a pathetic man. If he weren't paying so well, I'd kick him out for what he has done to you."

I thought about it and concluded that it wasn't hard to imagine Katherine becoming so reckless in her love life, as she had been prone to it before. The idea made me happy in some way, as it proved that we were more alike than I thought. Perhaps I was just a reflection of her dark side all along, just like she was of my light side.

"But don't worry about her," said Margot. "Focus on your poetry instead. The poem you wrote today is beautiful. I can see you have grown a lot, and you should keep on growing without worrying about that mule's lifespan..."

I smiled and stroked her golden locks. "I'll take you up on that, dear Margot."

Her face leaned into my open palm and rested there. I could tell she was too weary to keep on talking, so I let her doze off in my arms. We lay there like an old couple burdened by past regrets that weighed us down as much as our heavy hearts. Still, I believed we would rise into little gods one day.

CHAPTER 19

KATHERINE

Seeing Margot so weak broke my heart. I felt that I had to ready myself for the worst: to watch her pass away. I supposed I should be grateful, as I couldn't be there for my other friends during their final hours. I spoke about it to Guillaume, who agreed with my decision to appreciate every moment I had left with her. He also said that if she called for a priest, he would hear her confession. I appreciated his offer, as I knew that unlike many of his colleagues, he didn't usually like to visit that part of the city.

Although Guillaume tried to make me feel better and reminded me that everything had its purpose, it didn't give me much comfort. I had grown bitter after what I had been through in the pit at Meung-sur-Loire. Not even in the privacy of my own mind had I allowed myself to think back. I wanted to erase the memories, but unfortunately, my physical condition kept reminding me of the hell. That's why I was trying to focus all my thoughts on the new collection of poems. Sometimes I felt as if it was the only thing keeping me alive, and in a way I dreaded the idea of finishing it. As I had told Guillaume before, I sensed that I didn't have much time left to live.

The calm solitude of the monastery that employed me suited my peculiar mood. While I was copying the old texts, I often found myself daydreaming about how things would have turned out for me had I lived a calm life after my graduation from the Sorbonne. Perhaps Guillaume was right. Clerical life was the best choice.

I enjoyed philosophising among the walls of ancient books and scrolls. Most holy fathers were sinners and crooks anyway, so I thought I blended in rather easily, though I couldn't imagine myself putting up with the hypocrisy. Guillaume was one of the few decent priests that I could respect. I trusted him when he said that he had never laid his hands on Church property or on a woman. Even though he had stolen some wine back in the day, it didn't change the fact that priesthood was his mission, not just a profession. I knew I lacked such devotion. I was born a misfit and continued to be one despite all that had happened.

After work, I went to the market to pick up some pickled olives, Margot's favourite treat – as bitter as life, she used to say. I also bought some burgundy for Guillaume and a chunk of lavender soap for Mother, and it was there, surrounded by the intoxicating scent of flowers that I met Katherine again. This time she didn't run off. To my bewilderment, she actually walked up to me without hesitation. Her determined look made me nervous. I could have retaliated and been the one to walk away, but it would have been childish. Besides, I was curious to hear what she had to say.

For a moment, we gazed at each other in silence, taking in the familiar features that were once so intimate. How I hated to still adore her petite, pale face with those tiny freckles on her cheeks and the deep worry lines on her forehead. As ever, I was drowning in the sea of her curious, emerald eyes, horrified by the realisation that I had never met a woman before who made me feel so damn good and wretched at the same time. When she had had her fill of my inner torment, she began speaking fast, barely pausing for breath.

"François, I'm sorry for my rude behaviour last time. As you may imagine, seeing you took me by surprise. I didn't know how to react or what to do, so I panicked. It also reminded me of the last time you returned to Paris. I hope you can forgive me."

"To be honest, I was just glad that you recognised me," I said with a sneer, but noticing her genuine look of regret, I became more conciliatory. "There is nothing to forgive, Katherine."

I could tell that my words soothed her and she relaxed a little.

"So where have you been for the past six years?"

I wondered what to tell her. Should I confess to the reason why I left, the crimes I committed and the mixture of bliss and horror I had experienced? It would not be polite to bore her with all the details, I decided.

"Here and there, but as you can see by the look of me, it has not been easy at times."

She watched me with that unfathomable expression on her face. It reminded me of the long looks she used to shower me with. I could not bear to fall into that sweet trap again.

"I don't want to trouble you with my woes and sorrows, Katherine, I'm certain you have better things to do than listen to me."

"Not really," she answered quickly, and I sensed despair in her voice. It was hard to resist, especially since I had often dreamt about reuniting with her. Each time my eyes found hers, it felt as if we had known each other forever. This time was no different.

"Would you take a walk with me?" she asked, but then her eyes nervously searched the busy market.

"What is it? I hope Noël isn't waiting round the corner with a whip." There it was. The words simply rushed out of my mouth before my mind could catch up with them. I checked her reaction, worrying that she would be offended and run off as before, but she actually responded with a smile.

"He leaves his whip at home these days," she said, leaving me with no choice but to answer, "I hope for your pleasure not torture."

She chuckled and fired back like the good old Katherine from before.

"No, he practises self-flagellation."

I had always adored it when she joked around with me. It was more arousing than pure naked beauty. How could she be so cruel and tease me again after all those years, after she had left me for someone else? And how could I laugh at the whip that her husband had chased me with? Perhaps because over time it had become a silly memory and I had lived through much worse since. The thought triggered another violent coughing fit. Although it embarrassed me, I simply couldn't control it. I turned away, unable to allow her to see me in such a weakened state. My chest was on fire when I stopped, so I looked back at her, wheezed, and said, "I don't think the walk would be such a good idea…"

I bowed to her courteously and set off, but she called out, "Wait!"

The quivering, helpless tone in her voice made me spin around.

"Can we please talk?" she asked, nervously.

It would feel good to let her down, give her a taste of her own medicine, but her request was just too tempting, so I took a step back and rasped, "I may not be able to talk right now, Katherine. I get these coughing episodes, particularly in moments like these…"

She tilted her head, though she must have noticed how uneasy I was in her presence.

"Then I'll speak, and you can listen," she suggested, her eyes pleading for me to agree.

"You still don't care about what people think, do you?" I said, because a few curious faces were already staring at us.

She shrugged, and soon we fell into step like old friends, as if no angry words had ever been exchanged, no doors had been shut and no whips used. We walked towards the Seine to avoid the busy streets and to find some privacy. She made small talk at first, but then soon confided in me about her childless and mainly loveless marriage. She hinted that she had married Noël out of spite, but for my sake, she left out the details. I listened, drinking in every word she said, and once my chest had stopped burning, I began to share my side of the story as well.

I didn't shy away from mentioning my participation in the College of Navarre robbery, and explained that I had needed money to pay off all my debts and start a new life. I spoke of Angers and the boredom that drove me to become a street thief and later a court poet at two different palaces. I even mentioned the torments I suffered in Meung and how the long months in prison had resulted in my health problems. I wanted her to know everything about me, perhaps to finally show her who I truly was without any glamour or pretence.

I was testing her, but mainly myself. I needed to know, based on her reaction, whether she would accept me for who I truly was after all these years. I saw no judgment in her face, just a whirl of confusing emotions, which proved that she was listening seriously. I broke into the hacking cough a few times, but she didn't comment on it, just stood next to me, letting me rest until I was ready to continue walking. When I was finished with my story, she took some time thinking about what I had shared, and finally said, "You left out only one thing: women."

"That's because there were none worth mentioning," I said with blunt honesty.

"Really? It's hard to believe that a man like you wouldn't encounter at least a few interesting women." Before I could answer, she added, "Although it took me some time, I admit that I eventually came to understand the verses you wrote for that prostitute. I was young and innocent. I realise now that I had romanticised you, me, us..."

"There is nothing wrong with that," I objected. "I wish you could have let me explain it properly… I should have kept on trying, but once I heard about your engagement, my courage failed me." I paused, still lacking that courage yet trying to fight through it. "To be entirely honest with you, Katherine, the fact that you took the poem so seriously triggered an idea. I took my own revenge on you. I needed money fast before my departure from Paris, and actually did end up pimping Margot and her girls for a time."

I checked her reaction, wondering if this had upset her. Even though I could tell she was cross with me, she swallowed her bitterness. "Was it a successful decision?"

"Not really. It only made me feel worse. Pimping your friend is nothing to be proud of, but I have done worse things…"

We fell silent for a moment, contemplating the past, when suddenly she asked, "Why did you leave Paris so promptly? You could have waited…"

"For what? Do you think I wanted to watch you stroll down the streets as Madame Jolis?"

I stopped walking and looked down at the cobbles beneath our feet, wondering whether I had shared too much. I didn't like to be vulnerable.

"I hated you at that time," she said in a low voice. "But that soon passed… The love I felt was stronger."

I searched her forlorn face, wondering whether I should believe her. Since I didn't know how to respond, she went on, "I was just afraid, François. I imagined you doing all those things you described in the poem... I thought you wanted me to become your property, like the woman in the poem..."

"I would never want anyone to be my property," I assured her, "especially not Margot, she is the toughest woman I know."

I felt my throat tickle again, so I had to turn away to cough. "I know, I'm disgusting," I said, once I was able to catch my breath.

"You are not," she assured me, "and you never could be."

Her words perplexed me as much as the gentle way she delivered them. I wanted to take her in my arms, let her know how much I still cared about her, but I had to hold back. I couldn't handle another heartbreak, so I changed the subject.

"How have you really been all these years, Katherine? You told me about everything and everyone else but your true experiences..."

The look on her face showed appreciation; she was probably not used to people asking her that. It also made her sad in a way, though.

"Unfortunately, I don't have much to say about myself, unless you want me to bore you with a description of all the lace and embroidery pieces I have made or the gossip I have listened to while I was doing it. There have been no adventures, no changes, just the same old tedious routine."

"What about reading? Did you continue learning after I left?"

She gave me a conspiratorial glance and said, "Well, yes. Reading is the only exciting part of my life. I have secretly read every book that Noël owns."

"Ah, nothing of quality then."

The comment made the mood between us colder, so I changed the subject. "And what about those lovers of yours? I heard you still drive Noël mad with jealousy…"

She turned to me, stunned. "I thought you'd take such rumours with a grain of salt, François."

"I'm keen to learn the grain of truth," I challenged, upon which she chuckled.

"You haven't changed a bit, have you?"

"Well, as far as I can see you haven't either."

To let her know it wasn't meant as an offence, I offered her my arm. She accepted it and we fell into step again.

"Even if there was a grain of truth in it, you of all people should not judge me."

"You are right. Still, it makes me wonder… why them and not me?"

"You weren't around," she teased, but I wouldn't let her off the hook that easily.

"Come on, Katherine, confess your sins. Who else could be a better confidant when it comes to such things than a lowlife like me? You know I've done worse than sleep around."

She blushed and her cheeks turned even redder as she tried to brush the question off.

"All right then. I have responded rather warmly to a few eager gentlemen..."

"How warmly?"

"François!" she could not contain her laughter, but when she met my smile, she finally admitted, "There have been a few innocent kisses..." When she noticed that I didn't believe her, she said, "And then there was that one unfortunate mistake..."

I raised my brow, intrigued to learn more. However, instead of saying more, she just gently caressed her belly. I immediately wondered whether she was pregnant. It didn't show, but it could have been too soon to tell, and her gown concealed her waist well enough. Either way, I reckoned she would not tell me the truth. She couldn't have known how vindictively happy it would make me had I learned that she carried a child that was not Jolis'. It would also explain why they still didn't have one.

"He turned out to be married as well," she added after a moment's hesitation. "And he behaved in the most outrageous way in the end... Thank goodness Noël still doesn't know who he is."

"Did he hurt you?"

She shook her head. "Let's not even talk about him, he's not worth it."

"Sounds like he could use a beating," I said, angry at the thought of the man.

"Like you would do that for me!"

"I would," I said in all seriousness. "And I would have done anything for you back then, you just didn't believe me."

She gave me a suspicious frown, then dropped her hand down from her belly and looked away. I could tell she was struggling with something, probably the secret that she wouldn't entrust me with, at least not yet.

"I wish I had not condemned you so prematurely," she said then. "I wish I had never married Noël. I was so foolish to think he was the better man."

Her sincerity touched me, but I sensed there was something more she wished to say.

"I don't want to talk about the past. I want to enjoy this moment, because now that you stand before me again, I realise that what we had, no matter how short-lived, was more real than anything I could ever have with Noël or anybody else. I wish we had escaped these walls together instead of just talking about it..."

I was amazed by her open affection, and that's probably why I surprised us both by saying, "It's not too late, Katherine. We could still do it." The sudden rush of emotion made me grasp her hands in mine. "If you desire it, I promise I will take you on an adventure one day."

Even though I wished for nothing more than to finally stay at home, I would do anything to be with her. I knew that even Guillaume and Mother would understand that. As soon as I paid off the debts for the College of Navarre robbery, I would be a free man, and her love would shore me up, make me stay in this world a bit longer. I wouldn't even mind if she had a child with another man, I would adore her regardless.

"Thank you, François," she said, and planted a kiss on my cheek. I wanted to move and initiate something more, but I could tell that she was not ready for it.

"Don't thank me yet. It might take some time. As usual, my pockets are so empty that even the rats avoid them."

Her eyes became strangely dejected as she said, "There is no hurry, is there? The hope is enough to brighten up my days."

We both looked past the houses that towered above the river, but a sudden cold breeze made us turn away. Perhaps it was the whiff of destiny or a warning, not that it mattered. What mattered was that we were together, united by mutual forgiveness and the hope of a new beginning.

Chapter 20

The Fatal Mistake

That December, I visited Margot often, trying to make her feel better by bringing her all kinds of treats and presents, telling her about my past adventures and sometimes even reading her parts of my new poem collection. No man had ever been as good to her as she deserved, including me, so I gave her as much attention as I could. Isabeau had meanwhile taken over Margot's work at the tavern and brothel, because Margot had beseeched her to keep the establishment in order. It was the only life accomplishment she was truly proud of and she wished to keep it the same the way that it had been for the last fifteen years of her life. She wanted to have a woman she could trust take over her work with Wolf overseeing it as he had always done.

As for Katherine, I had bumped into her a few times, and she always gave me the warmest greeting and smile, but never stopped to chat. I understood why. We had already said everything to each other last time and the rest was up to fortune. Had we met in secrecy and started a love affair, we would only have made things worse for ourselves. It was better to keep our love platonic until I could take her away from the city that, like Katherine, had cast a special spell over me. I praised myself for being patient instead of following my passion as I once would have done. I supposed I was finally growing up at the age of thirty-two.

"She will be the death of you," warned Margot when I told her about our foolish plan.

"Not a bad Grim Reaper," I joked, although the comment filled me with a strange foreboding. Margot knew that I didn't know how to be completely rational, especially when it came to Katherine.

"Whom would you rather see me with?" I asked her.

"Me obviously. I won't lie around in this bed forever," she replied.

I laughed. "I can see you are already feeling better."

"Not well enough to make you forget all about her."

"You could try."

She attempted to strike my shoulder, but I hardly felt the impact; her limbs were growing weaker every day.

"I hate this," she moaned. "I'd rather die than spend the rest of my days so feeble."

"Don't say that, Margot. Just give yourself time to fight this. You are stronger than any illness. You are the Amazon of Paris."

"What's an Amazon?" she asked doubtfully, expecting it to be an insult.

"An ancient female warrior."

"Oh," she exhaled with relief, "were they beautiful?"

"I'm sure they were, though they supposedly had their breasts cut off."

"Men," she sighed, "always making us suffer."

"Who said that men were behind it?"

"Because they always are," she replied with a sigh, and I left her to it. There was never any point in arguing with Margot so instead, I just smiled and kissed her forehead.

"You can do better than that," she complained so I kissed her on the lips. That seemed to pacify her and make her fall asleep again.

✦

Shortly after Christmas, I finally managed to pay off all my debts, and I wanted to celebrate it with Margot. The tavern was empty as was usual at midday, so I grabbed a jar of my favourite burgundy and headed to her chamber. However, when I knocked on her door, Isabeau opened it with her face wet with tears. She fell into my arms and sobbed, clenching me in a tight embrace. Behind her, I saw Margot staring at us as if struck with wonderment. It took me some time to realise why her eyes didn't have their usual spark. They were lifeless, for her spirit had left them.

I kept gazing at her while consoling Isabeau whose howls resonated throughout the house. Her anguish summoned the other girls and women. I watched them earnestly. Some I recognised, some were unfamiliar, but at that moment, we were all united in love and admiration for Margot. Everyone respected her despite her impulsiveness and grit; there was always more to like than to condemn about her.

At last, Wolf came, and everybody stepped aside for him. He was the second most esteemed person in the house and the one in charge from then on. He walked over to her bed, kneeled by her stiff body and ran his palm over her face to close her glassy eyes. He then whispered something barely audible into her ear. I supposed it was a promise or a prayer that was too private to be shared. I was still trapped in the initial shock of finding Margot dead, so the only thing I was able to do was cling to Isabeau as though she was the only rock I could lean on.

After everyone left, Wolf helped Isabeau to her chamber, and I sat on Margot's bed. It was only then that it dawned on me: I would never see her laugh again, I could never again admire the cascades of her golden locks, never hear her silly complaints. I held her hand, desperately wishing for one final slap. My soul wept yet I couldn't force any tears from my eyes. *Margot*, I addressed her in my mind, *you sleeping Venus, how could I awaken you? You shouldn't have left us so soon. You have always had more drive than any woman I know. You are supposed to be healthy and strong. Your soft chubby cheeks were meant to be rosy, not pale. This emaciated body and stern face is not you, dear one, it is no longer you…*

I kissed her hands and closed my eyes in sorrow. The touch of death made me shudder, it took me to the darkest corners of my mind. I felt its whisper tickle my neck. It foretold something I couldn't fully grasp yet it shook me to the core. Then, as if encouraged by some invisible, gentle power, I stroked her face. Although her body was spiritless, I still sensed the essence of her that was left behind, like an aftertaste of wine, or a breath of fresh breeze after rain.

I felt compelled to kiss her goodbye. Her lips were stiff, but her skin still smelled of her, and inhaling it made me burst into tears.

"Forgive me, Margot, I'm braying like an old mule. You would hate that, huh? You always hated my brooding. I promise I'll compose myself." I rested my head beside hers, and listened intently as a passing verse entered my mind:

Woman, your body so dear
How preciously it used to thrive
Why be subjected to such ills?
Why can't we rise to heaven alive?

Extract from *The Testament* (1461-1462, François Villon)

✦

On the day of Margot's death, I couldn't say no to a drink with Wolf. I was unable to return home to Guillaume and Mother, as they would not understand my pain as well as he did. Wolf knew about my special bond with her, he was aware that it was more than just physical pleasure that I sought in her company. She was the most open-minded and affectionate woman I had ever known. Even her flaws were sweet. She was one of a kind, and I hoped that heaven knew how lucky it was to receive her.

Isabeau was completely wretched, so Wolf ordered the other girls to take care of her and let her mourn in peace. For Isabeau, Margot's passing was the worst. To her she was a rock that she could always rely on. Now all she had left were responsibilities, and we all knew she would rather join Margot in the afterlife than replace her on earth. Nobody could be the next Margot, but she had to keep her promise and try.

Only regulars were invited into the tavern that evening, as our plan for that night was clear: to celebrate the unique personality who had started the best tavern and brothel in Paris. We drank to that, because Margot wouldn't have wanted us to sit around weeping and complaining. She would have preferred to be remembered with songs and laughter, so we made sure to do just that. Of course, our laughs were mixed with heavy sighs when we remembered all the stories she had left us with. There were so many cases of women she had saved from the cruelty of the streets, countless tales about her punishing the customers who misbehaved, not caring whether they were lords or scum. I could imagine she was even capable of taking the King by his collar and dragging him out if he made her mad.

Isabeau sat aside the whole time, unable to shed any more tears yet still drowning in her sorrows, so as soon as the band began to play, I asked her to dance with me. I could tell that she needed some human contact besides that of the horny customers.

"Oh François," she exhaled as we listlessly moved to the jolly sounds of the drums and lute. "I can't imagine this place without her. This house is like her body now – empty, useless, spiritless."

"Don't worry, Isabeau, you will keep this house alive. Now it's time for your spirit to infuse these walls."

"But I fear that I'm not as strong, confident or courageous as Margot..."

"She was not just that," I reasoned with her. "Her toughness was balanced with genuine empathy and care that she offered freely. That's something you two have in common. You will learn to become tougher with time, just like she did, and until then, you have Wolf and his men to rely on. I believe you will make this place prosper." I paused and couldn't help but smile. "Margot put you in charge for a reason. Imagine if she had bequeathed the place to me – now that would have been a disaster."

Isabeau smiled through her tears. "She was actually considering it, but reckoned you were better off free…"

"She was the only woman who never judged me for that," I said, and with the thought, looked around my favourite tavern.

It was the place where I could leave the mundane and my responsibilities behind, a place where I could escape the world whenever I found myself in despair… I came here to be unburdened, to have a taste of unruliness, to allow myself to get away from the everyday. However, the main reason for my fascination with the house was that each time I found myself in the embrace of its walls, I felt appreciated for the person I truly was. I was never judged or reprimanded here. I was free to plan grand rebellions with my friends, sing my hackneyed songs or join the boisterous, wild parties of the Coquillards. There was always some adventure to look forward to when I crossed the threshold to Margot's Inn.

"I will try to make myself useful," said Isabeau, waking me from my contemplation. "I was given a second chance after you saved my life all those years ago, so I will try to make it worth living."

She never forgot to mention how much she appreciated me standing between her and Sermoise on that fateful Corpus Christi day, though she knew I never blamed her for it.

"Forget about being useful, Isabeau," I said, "just try to be happy. That's what matters most in the end, doesn't it?"

She shrugged, then slowly leaned closer, resting her head on my shoulder. We danced more slowly than the others, like two old souls weighed by grief.

As I watched the thoroughly raddled habitués and the unfamiliar newcomers, the scene turned into a strange mosaic of the past and present. I imagined Colin, Tabary, and Regnier in the faces of the unfamiliar young men, and envisioned Margot standing there with her hands on her hips, carefully scrutinising the room. For a moment there, I felt her spirit look back at me through the veil of time. She winked and waved at me. I smiled at the apparition, trying to hold back the welling tears, but was overcome by my tickling throat. I turned away from Isabeau and ran over to the window, spitting out the white slime that was choking me. The coughing was painful and lasted for longer than I was used to. At one point, I thought I would never be able to stop it. However, thanks to Isabeau who brought me some water and honey, I managed to soothe my throat and relieve my chest from the burning pain.

✦

I was woken up by Wolf the following day. He shook my shoulder with friendly concern. "Are you all right, Villon?"

I opened my eyes, realising that I was lying beside Margot's lifeless body. The harsh reality dawned on me right away and anxiety crawled back into my heart as I sat up and rubbed my eyes.

"Is it morning yet?"

Wolf let out a short laugh. "You left our table in the morning. It's afternoon again, that's why I came to wake you."

"Afternoon? Oh no… I missed my day at work. I asked Isabeau to wake me sooner."

"We both thought you should rest, because of all the coughing and drinking," explained Wolf while I cursed myself inside, already picturing the disappointed faces: Guillaume, Mother, Katherine.

"I have to go home," I said taking a gulp of water from Margot's stoup.

Wolf watched me as I put on my boots. "Are you sure? Don't you want to join us for a dinner at my friend's house? Robin Dogis and the gang are curious to meet the famous François Villon. They are especially interested to hear all about the Devil's Fart escapade. They admire you for it."

"There's nothing to admire, as you very well know," I reminded him with a frown, because each time I thought of it, flashes of my dying classmates and the echoes of their anguished screams filled my mind. I felt the sting of old guilt and shivered. Wolf crossed his arms and gave me a thoughtful look.

"What is it?" I asked, uncomfortable with the strange tension in the air.

"I have always found it intriguing that Regnier was so grateful to me for saving his life, but you seemed almost disappointed."

I smirked. "I've always had a strange connection to death."

"A positive one, you mean?"

I shrugged. "Just strange. When it draws near, I dread it, and when it tempts me from afar, I am lured by it. I can't really describe why, perhaps because I have felt her presence so many times."

"Her?"

"I imagine death as a woman, don't you?"

Wolf smiled with nostalgia. "Regnier used to call her Lady Death. I supposed he got that from you?"

I shrugged. "Hard to say. Perhaps it was the other way around. We had known each other for so long..."

I turned to look at Margot's body, ruminating on who had come for her upon her last breath, and whether women had a different angel of death than us men. Maybe it was her deceased husband, coming to make up for all his past mistakes.

"How will you bury her?" I asked in a low voice. "Don't tell me you plan on throwing her on the pile of rotting corpses at the Holy Innocents' Cemetery."

He shook his head resolutely. "Of course not. I wouldn't do that to her, and not just because she was my brother's wife. She was a special person and deserves a special burial. I will arrange a secret ceremony and burn her body in a boat on the Seine. You are welcome to join us."

"Tonight?"

He nodded. "If all goes well, we will start on the stroke of midnight."

I thought about whether it even made sense for me to go home if they were about to have the ceremony in just a few hours. Mother would reason with me and Guillaume would probably insist on coming along to support me. I could never let him do that. It was enough that one of us was associated with the Coquillards. I thought about it some more, but finally agreed to come along, unaware that I was making the worst decision I could.

✦

I spent the rest of the afternoon sharing stories of my youth with Wolf and his new friends, probably students that he had recruited into his gang. The Coquillards were still strong in Paris and the youngsters sought adventure like we once did. I felt like an old man in their company, even Wolf, the raddled hermit, was livelier than me.

It was already dark when we left the house of Robin Dogis where we had dined and drank aplenty. Mainly drank. I was slower than the others, and I plodded behind the group. From time to time, my cough stopped me, making my chest burn as I fought its harshness. During one of those moments, I sensed that someone had stopped beside me and was rubbing my back for comfort: It was the elderly street prostitute who went by the nickname, the Crone Armouress. Her touch was gentle but cold and it made me shiver.

"Are you well, Villon?" she inquired with concern.

"Yes, my lady, thank you. How is life treating *you*?" I asked, taking in her fragile figure and lack of appropriate clothing. She responded with a toothless smile and before we could talk more, Wolf's voice disturbed us.

"Hey Villon, who are you talking to?"

I faced him, confused by his question. "Don't you recognise her?"

"Who?" asked Wolf, and noticing his puzzled expression, I turned back to the place where the crone had stood and realised that she was gone. My eyes searched the empty shadows of the timber-framed buildings. I shivered at the chilling thought. Was she a spectre? Did I imagine her as I had my friends back at Margot's, or was I slowly becoming one with the ghosts of Paris?

Wolf gave me a friendly pat on the back and said, "Listen, I have to go now to prepare Margot's funeral, but the boys are heading to the Mule Tavern if you'd care to join them."

I shrugged. "I might do that, just tell us when and where to meet you."

"At midnight by my bailiwick."

I agreed to be there and followed his instructions to meet up with his young friends.

After another jar of claret at the Mule Tavern, I lost track of time. My mind recovered only when we were back outside. The cold, fresh air sobered me up a bit, but I was wobbly and when I swallowed, it felt as if I had gulped a cup of needles so I could tell that I had been coughing roughly back at the tavern. I wasn't sure whether the boys were leading me to the funeral or not because I was focused solely on trying to keep up with my feet.

At one point, I fell into a puddle, and several hands pulled me up and supported me. I fixed my gaze on them.

"Regnier? Colin?" I stared at the familiar faces and felt confused.

"He's completely out of it," said Colin.

"I know, thank goodness he is not that heavy," added Regnier.

Even though the voices didn't match their faces, my mind was too dazed to comprehend why.

"My friends," I mumbled, "are you taking me there already?"

"Where?" asked the strange Colin.

"Montfaucon," I said, but received no answer. I continued, "Do you remember that night when we joined the Coquillards' wild party? We danced and sang with the dead all night long..." I took a deep breath and began singing my old student song:

Whether you play false dice
Whether you sell indulgence
Whether you play wrong or nice
Striving for quick abundance
Where will all your money go?
To the taverns and whores!

"This one is yours?" asked the strange Regnier. I nodded but stumbled, and as they helped me straighten up and we fell into step again, they started to sing along with me:

Rhyme, have fun, play and sing
Join brotherhoods of outcasts
Play a fool, do a theatre, try everything!
As long as your audience lasts
But hear where all your money should go –
To the taverns and whores!

Suddenly, a distant voice called out, "Be quiet!" I turned around to see who was reprimanding us. "It's late, boys, go home!"

Only when the voice bawled a second time did I realise that it was coming from the building behind us. I swivelled around and locked eyes with an elderly man who looked very familiar, but I couldn't put a name to his face. He was about to close the window and let us be when suddenly the strange Colin beside me shouted back at him, "Stop yelling at us, you old stinker!"

I turned to him in shock, wondering why Colin would be so rude to the man, but someone else now stood in his place. It was one of the boys that Wolf had introduced me to earlier. In the confusion, I turned to the man who I thought was Regnier, and realised it was Robin Dogis. I backed away from the two strangers who for some reason were becoming even more aggressive to the familiar elderly man.

"Mind your own business!" shouted Dogis, "and go back to your scribbling!"

"My thoughts exactly!" chimed in the other one. "We can sing and do whatever we like out here! This city doesn't belong to you and neither do we!"

Their voices joined in with my song's finale:

Grab your doublets, shirts, boots, and coats
Until you stand only in your underclothes
And before things get even worse
Take them to the taverns and whores!

With the final words, the man who I'd thought was Colin spat into the open window. The elderly man cursed and slammed the window shutters in his face. It seemed that the dispute was over, so I leaned against the wall for support, trying to regain my focus in order to get to Margot's funeral on time. However, the three fools had started to sing some other song and encouraged me to join in.

"Isn't this one yours as well, Villon?"

I shook my head, though I paid no attention to their singing. The world around me was spinning; I felt dizzy. I tried to walk on, but my legs felt heavy and disobedient. In my confusion, I stumbled into someone. It was the elderly man whom the two boys had offended before.

"Monsieur Villon?" he addressed me in disbelief. I mumbled something back, attempting to ask his name, but failed to express myself clearly. I staggered, and the elderly man caught me before I fell. The younger boys seemed to take that as some kind of attack, though, as they shouted again, "How dare you push our friend, huh?"

The elderly man fired back, "He almost fell, you imbecile! Now leave before you feel my wrath!"

"Are you serious, old man? Wait till you feel ours!"

The elderly man just spat on the ground then turned to me. "I thought you'd be grateful for the new chance you have been given, Villon! What are you doing out here with this vermin? Looking for trouble again?"

I was too stupefied to reply. The elderly man grasped my arm and tried to force me into the building.

"Get away from him!" cried one of the boys.

"Leave him, you murderer!" yelled the other.

"Who do you call murderer?" the elderly man roared back.

I tried to approach the boys and calm them down, only my body wouldn't obey my mind. As soon as the elderly man's hand released my arm, I slid onto the damp cobblestones, landing on my arse. From then on, their voices became unclear as though separated by an unseen wall. They began to push each other and in no time, the quarrel had turned into a fistfight. I stood up with great effort, but all I could do was totter on the spot, trying to keep my balance.

Then daggers were drawn. I saw the blades' sparks pierce the night, and the last thing I remembered was the elderly man's bulging eyes coming closer as he crashed into me, making us both tumble. My head slammed against the stone and then everything went black…

… until I awoke into a grave silence. I found myself lying on the bench by Saint Benoit Church where I had fatally injured Sermoise seven years ago. I sat up and looked around, no longer confused, just alone and dejected. Then Sermoise emerged from the shadows of the church. Alarmed, I searched my overcoat, trying to locate my dagger, but couldn't find it. I was unarmed and my enemy was approaching me in a slow, victorious manner. However, this time he reached for my hand instead of a weapon and pulled me up. Without explanation, he took a step into the dark streets and nodded at me to follow. I felt it was the right thing to do, so I set off after him.

Sermoise led me through a version of Paris that I was used to seeing only in my dreams. This time, everything was unusually still. It felt as if the city was abandoned, but more likely, it was filled with sleeping bodies whose spirits roamed different dreamlands to mine. Sermoise and I walked all the way to one of the city gates. There were no guards, no sergeants, only the two of us. We calmly stepped out and walked along the uneven country road, guided by the bright light of the full moon.

As I marvelled at the starry sky, something tall overshadowed us. I looked up and saw a skeleton moving past. It turned and bore its empty eyes into mine. I stopped, stunned by the strange sight, however, as it motioned onwards, I realised it was just a person on stilts, wearing a skeleton costume. At that moment, I began to hear the jolly music of drums, lyres, and flutes. I wanted to ask Sermoise what was going on and where he was taking me, but to my surprise, he was no longer beside me.

I hurried after the man wearing the skeleton costume, hoping to receive some answers from him, and eventually a terrifying spectacle came into view: I saw a gathering of people on the hill before me. It was the place I dreaded the most – Montfaucon. I hesitated, then decided to keep my distance and watch the scene from afar. Some people were still approaching while others had already reached the colourful celebration.

A group of three young musicians wearing monkey, frog and pig costumes passed me by. They were playing familiar, fanciful music and were heading for the band that was performing beneath the gibbet. Most of the people wore masks and held bright lanterns. The lively atmosphere was in sharp contrast to the grim location. To my astonishment, even the hanged men seemed to dance in the air along with the living, though they resembled puppets rather than human beings.

I recognised Regnier among them from his red boots, and a brown clerical cloak revealed Colin. Tabary was beneath the massive structure. He attended to the newcomers, offering them goblets of wine. Finally, I saw Margot in the crowd. She looked just as I remembered her, only her golden locks were tied with a big red ribbon. She waved at me to join them, but I couldn't. No matter how appealing the celebration seemed I felt that there was something amiss.

As I pondered what to do, the music was disturbed by a loud howl. I was jolted out of my reverie and saw Regnier's hound beside me. I realised I was standing on his grave, but he was alive, wailing at the moon like his wild ancestors. It was a desperate, urgent cry which sounded like a warning. Soon after, I understood why. The music, cheers, and laughter were slowly turning into a rattle of iron chains, screams, and tears. I was coming back to my senses, overwhelmed by an intense headache and uncontrollable shaking. A sudden burst of coughing woke me up completely and I found myself in another nightmare: back in a prison cell.

Chapter 21

The Dance of the Hanged Men

The prison at the Châtelet was not as bad as the one at Meung. At least I had a cot to rest on, fresh water to drink and a small barred window that let in the cool winter sunshine. I was confused as to how I had ended up there and why, as I remembered very little from the previous night and the lingering headache would not allow me to focus.

I stood up from the cot, wrapped myself in the dusty blanket and gazed out of the window. The city was covered with fresh snow and the sun's reflection made the convoluted streets glitter like a crystallised river. I thought of Guillaume and

Mother, hating the fact that they had to start worrying about me again. I loathed myself for being so irresponsible.

The prison guards soon brought me a bowl of soup and some bread. Quite a luxury compared to Meung, I thought, glad to have something warm in my stomach. I asked them what I was doing here. They didn't know but assured me that I'd find out later that day when I was taken to the provost. Robert d'Estouteville was no longer in service, and the new provost was a former sergeant known to hold grudges against students, which gave me little to no chance of being treated fairly.

Once I entered the large room where the provost was seated beside two official examiners and a notary, I came face to face with Ferrebourc, the papal scribe. I had known the man ever since I had come to live with Guillaume. He had never been fond of me, mainly because of my persistent misbehaviour. He used to say I brought only trouble and shame to the Saint Benoit neighbourhood. I knew he was right, so I didn't hold a grudge. On the contrary, I had a great deal of respect for him, mainly because I knew that he was among the group of clergymen who worked on the documents for Jean d'Arc's nullification trial, which King Charles VII encouraged in the final years of his reign.

At the sight of him, I was able to recall the final images before my collapse: A drunken brawl between the young Coquillards and Ferrebourc that resulted in him accidentally throwing me to the ground. I scanned my surroundings, trying to locate the three young men that I had accompanied the previous night, but it seemed that I was there alone. Ferrebourc gave me a scornful look then turned to the jury before us. I did the same. The new provost was a stern, gaunt man and from his expression, I could tell he was in a bad mood. Perhaps he had had to wake too early because of the trial or he had had an argument with his wife. I held on to anything that would allow me to see the man in a good light as he was my judge, my only way to freedom.

"Here present is Monsieur Ferrebourc, the victim, as well as the only witness to the assault that happened yesterday evening between ten and eleven o'clock. He claims to have been working late at his home in Rue Saint-Jacques, when he heard Robin Dogis, Hutin du Moustier, Rogier Pichart and the here present François Villon singing loudly as they passed by his window. He rebuked the young men for their noise, but they didn't listen and instead began to insult him."

As he continued to describe the scene, I was able to recall everything including the unfortunate accident. It all started when I stumbled and almost collapsed. Ferrebourc supported me and attempted to drag me inside his house. Robin Dogis must have thought that he was trying to hurt me, because he shouted at him to let me be and pulled out his dagger. Ferrebourc took out his as well and the brawl ensued. I remembered being completely befuddled when I fell on my head and passed out.

"The accused men viciously attacked Monsieur Ferrebourc, but the here present François Villon, also known as François des Loges and François Montcorbier stabbed Monsieur Ferrebourc with his dagger."

Upon hearing the preposterous lie, I protested, "That's not true! I had no dagger on me and even if I had, why would I attack Monsieur Ferrebourc? I have never had any quarrel with him!"

"Quiet, Villon!" the provost admonished me.

I didn't listen, though, as I deemed the accusation completely groundless. "But somebody else drew the dagger last night! Where are the others? Why am I the only one on trial?"

The provost nodded to the guards who held me in chains, discreetly ordering them to punish me. One of them kicked me in my loins while the other one delivered a blow with his fist to my chest, which resulted in another uncontrollable coughing fit. The sharp pain made me hunch forward, but they wouldn't let me rest. They forced me to stand up straight before the provost and calmly waited until my cough subsided.

"Be obedient, Villon," warned the provost with a cold, detached voice. "I know very well who you are and what you have done."

Fear gripped me when I realised what that meant. He had already formed an opinion about the case without hearing me out first. I wondered why and tried to remember if I had ever offended him. What seemed more likely though, was that he just didn't like anybody.

"Monsieur Ferrebourc, can you confirm that this was the man who assaulted you?"

The provost pointed at me without giving me the courtesy of even mentioning my name or title. Ferrebourc looked at me. I could tell he was confused and wavered before he responded.

"It all happened too fast. I assumed that we all pulled out daggers before the brawl. Villon was the closest to me at the time of the injury. I could tell he was intoxicated as he could hardly stand or speak. He may have not realised what he was doing…"

"That doesn't excuse him from stabbing you, though, does it?" remarked the provost.

"No," replied Ferrebourc firmly, "it certainly does not."

"But I swear I had no dagger on me that night, Monsieur Ferrebourc," I insisted and tried to reason with him some more. "Perhaps you don't remember? Maybe we both had too much to drink that night?"

"How dare you," hissed Ferrebourc. "I was working late, not drinking like you and those nefarious friends of yours!"

I knew I had stepped out of line and rebuked myself. However, I still couldn't understand why he would think that I was the main villain of the group and wondered how I could eloquently explain myself.

"And it's not like you haven't done it before," added Ferrebourc. "Everybody knows that you stabbed Philippe Sermoise in broad daylight and even threw a stone at him as you ran from the scene of the crime."

"That was an act of self-defence," I replied furiously, my voice trembling. "Sermoise himself corroborated it on his deathbed. I was pardoned for the crime by His Majesty Charles VII!"

"I warned you, Villon!" roared the provost, clearly losing his patience with my impulsiveness. "You are way out of line here! Take a look at yourself! You have done plenty to deserve the noose yet you are still alive, roaming the streets of Paris like an untouchable deity. I don't understand how anyone could be a benefactor to you, but those who have been are now gone, whether it was His Majesty King Charles VII or Robert d'Estouteville! All you are left with now is your appalling reputation.

"You are an incorrigible criminal who has taken advantage of everything and everyone, including the institution that raised you and the institution that gave you your bachelor and master's degrees! And how have you shown your gratitude? By robbing it? I don't know how you managed to talk yourself out of that one before the ecclesiastical court, but if I was your judge that day, I would not have agreed to wait a year for you to pay back what you stole!"

I clenched my teeth, fighting the urge to defend myself.

"Lost for words now?" he sneered. I looked up at him, anxious not to test his patience. "Well? Do you have anything to say?"

Though all the odds were against me, I delivered the only fitting words that I could think of. "Necessity makes people vile, just as hunger drives wolves from the wild."

The provost responded with a disdainful laugh. "Oh, please! Spare us your inane babble. I heard that this is your famous tactic! Do you really think that these metaphors will change my mind? Well, think again, Villon. It won't work on me." He leaned forward to properly confront me, disdain in his eyes. "I don't appreciate poetry. I appreciate justice. And your scales have been out of balance for far too long."

I swallowed hard trying to absorb the hatred he spat at me.

"Now, do you have anything to add besides boring us with your useless verses, Villon?"

I drew a deep breath, readying myself to confront him, however, was silenced by another fierce cough.

"Hmm," mused the provost, "the answer is loud and clear to me – sick body, sick mind."

His piercing gaze made me shiver. I recoiled for a moment, but at the sight of the watchful faces of the examiners beside him, I gathered the courage to keep on fighting.

"I plead the Benefit of Clergy," I said softly, trying to suppress the cough.

"What was that?" asked the provost, theatrically leaning forward to make me repeat it.

"B-benefit of Clergy," I stammered, fighting my prickling throat. "I know I have the right to be brought before the ecclesiastical court like last time."

"You plead the Benefit of Clergy? Now what a brilliant idea that is!" he laughed. "It's too late for that, Villon. You have only brought shame to the Church so why should it come to your rescue?"

With a serious nod to the men sitting beside him, he concluded, "You have wasted enough of our time. There is no excuse for such a wretched soul. People like you deserve an appropriate punishment. Whether you were the one who stabbed Monsieur Ferrebourc last night or not, you have committed plenty to have earned the following verdict: For the countless crimes you have committed and the habitual misbehaviour you have demonstrated after repeated pardons, you are to be executed by hanging at the gibbet of Montfaucon."

The words stung like fiery daggers, straight into my heart. It was decided, there was nothing I could say or do to change his mind. The aftertaste of the conviction made me feel sick to my stomach. How could so-called justice be so unjust? How could they blame me when I was nothing but an innocent bystander? I couldn't believe that they dared to bring up my past, the crimes that I had been pardoned for, and condemn me nevertheless. In my despair, I called out to Monsieur Ferrebourc, who was my last hope.

"Monsieur Ferrebourc! I didn't attack you, I swear! You must know that I would never hurt you! I have nothing but respect for you!"

Ferrebourc averted my gaze. However, I could tell he seemed ashamed, even sentimental. He probably remembered the days when I used to play at Saint Benoit along with the other children. Perhaps he even thought of Guillaume and how much pain he would cause him by incriminating me. Either way, he humbly addressed the provost.

"The truth is that it may not have been Villon who stabbed me. I'm not certain who did it. The others left him there, so I assumed it was him because of what he had done previously. Why else would they abandon a friend in trouble?"

"Because they are not my friends," I answered bitterly, impatient to hear the provost's answer.

"Like I said, it does not matter whether this man assaulted you or not, Monsieur Ferrebourc. He is a recidivist who has been pardoned for inexcusable crimes. Somebody has to put an end to his arrogant behaviour. This is the final straw." With those words, he looked me straight in the eye and smirked. "Enjoy your last day in prison, Villon."

He beckoned to the guards and looked away.

"Wait!" I yelped hoarsely, still not giving up. "I have the right to write a plea to the Court of Parliament!"

The provost flashed me an irritated glance. "As you know, the Court of Parliament usually confirms the provost's sentences. It would be futile."

"But I have the right!"

I kept turning after Ferrebourc as the guards dragged me away, beseeching him to have mercy. "Please, Monsieur Ferrebourc! You are a just man! You know I have the right to appeal to parliament! Just let me send them a letter!"

I begged him as long as I could hold back the cough that was building up, but it eventually overpowered me. Did I catch pity in Ferrebourc's face? I supposed that even if I had, it was too late.

✦

Pacing the floor of my prison cell didn't help me calm down, neither did resting on the cot or staring out of the window. Stillness and apathy were all around me, just not within me. I couldn't believe that I was back there, reliving the emotions I had experienced down in the pit at Meung. The vision of the gallows drove me mad. At least back in the cold dungeon that had bathed my soul in infernal flames, I had a slim chance that one day I could be rescued, and in the end, I truly was. However, after the verdict I received that day, I felt as if I had finally reached the edge. The new provost was merciless. He wouldn't even respect my rightful request of appeal to the higher court.

I couldn't chase away the thought of Montfaucon, the monstrous structure where my best friend had been swaying for years, not allowed to become one with the earth from which he rose. Perhaps he was in the same cell in his final days, waiting for some tiny ray of hope to light up his dimming mind. Was I foolish to still cling to that beacon? Was it pointless to pray to God for mercy? I had already sinned plenty and had been helped too many times. It seemed impossible that I would be that lucky again.

I tried to imagine my last walk through Paris. Would my dear mother survive it? Would Guillaume pray for my soul? Would Katherine come to see me one last time? I imagined their faces filled with the disappointment and pain I had caused them all. I wondered whether I would be brave enough to walk with my head high, whether I would have the chance to apologise to them one last time. What would I say? What words could encompass everything that I felt?

I turned to the window. The heavens were now covered in a haze of clouds which revealed only an island of blue. There was a strange tension in the air. I reckoned it would snow soon. The tranquil gloom made me look away and study the coarse walls of my cell instead. I pitied the stones, for while we, the prisoners, came and went they had to remain here, leaning against each other for support, soaking up the human sorrow. I hoped that perhaps a demolition would break those walls apart one day and move the stones to a better place.

Then, I noticed someone's name inscribed in one of the blocks. It intrigued me, made me feel less lonely, so I looked at the walls more closely. I counted about twelve engraved names and messages. The prisoners wanted to leave something behind, whether it was just a symbol, their name or a prayer. I was tempted to contribute something, add a touch of levity to the dispiriting wall.

My eyes landed on a rusty nail on the windowsill, the perfect prison quill left behind for newcomers. I grinned to myself, and as I picked it up, the verses came rushing in:

I'm François, which gives me no hope
Born near Paris by Pontoise

My neck will soon hang from the rope
And learn the weight of my arse

Soon after I finished carving the message, I heard rapid footsteps and the jangling of keys. Someone was approaching my cell so I stood up, partly in excitement, partly in fear. Whatever was to come was either my end or my victory. To my surprise, Wolf appeared at the bars. I remembered him telling me that he had been hired at the Châtelet and could therefore start helping out his fellow Coquillards. I was never a part of the gang, though. I was the only one of my friends who refused to join, and I would not change my mind even then. I always valued my freedom above everything else.

"I brought my colleagues some ale, so they have allowed me to see you for a moment," he explained quickly as he unlocked the grille that separated us and walked into my cell. "The boys and I feel awful about the harsh verdict you have received, Villon."

I couldn't contain my anger. "So how come they are not here with me?"

"They are. Robert Dogis was brought before the provost right after you. He confessed, but was pardoned for the assault, and so were the others."

I laughed in misery. "Good for them."

"They told the provost you are not to be blamed, that you were just a witness."

I dropped down on the cot. "It doesn't matter though, huh? The provost had already decided I'm a burden to Paris."

"I know it's unfair," said Wolf, "but that's how it goes. The old dogs like us usually take the blame. The young pups are excused and grow even more insolent and careless... I see the same cycle repeating itself all the time."

"I know. I was once one of those pups."

Wolf gave me a smile and handed me the wineskin he had brought. "Here. I know you like burgundy."

I accepted the gift with a grateful nod. "Thank you, Wolf. It's nice of you to remember."

I took a few sips right away, as I had a keen thirst for numbness. Wolf meanwhile paced my cell and noticed the engraved verses. He read the lines and shook his head with a smile. "How can a situation like this be inspiring to you?"

I shrugged and took another swig of the wine. "I thought it might amuse someone who came here after me."

"It certainly will," agreed Wolf and read it once again.

"I appreciate you coming here, Wolf," I said, "but I wonder why?"

"Always expecting the worst from me, huh?"

I didn't have an answer for him, so he explained. "Don't worry. I came to deliver good news. After Robin Dogis confessed, Ferrebourc reasoned with the provost who in the end agreed to let you write an appeal to the Court of Parliament."

"Really?" I stood up excitedly, swallowing the cough that was tickling my chest.

"I don't want to give you false hope. You know very well that most appeals are useless. The Court of Parliament usually confirms the verdict of the provost. However, you are allowed to try. You may not be as lucky as someone without a criminal past, but what matters is that you are given the chance to use your greatest gift: your mind."

I felt a new verve rushing in so I promised, "I will try my best to use it well."

Wolf patted my back and said, "I paid the guards and ordered them to bring you some ink, a quill and a set of parchments."

Although I was relieved, I had to remain alert. I wondered why he was helping me. I was useless to him in my present state and he didn't strike me as a sentimental man either. I wondered if it was because of Margot. Perhaps he didn't want to disappoint her, especially not now that she was dead. Knowing her stubborn spirit, she could easily come back to haunt him.

"How was the funeral?" I asked. I regretted having missed it.

"Like any other," he replied. "Don't worry about not being there. I'm sure Margot would understand."

Our eyes met. I could tell he missed her too, though he wouldn't admit it. The mysterious scars on his face spoke for themselves; he was a private man with a tough past and a thick armour around his heart.

"I should go," he said after a moment. "Give me the wineskin back. I can't leave it here. The guards could find it and make a fuss, but I'll try to smuggle in some more later."

I slurped the last drop of burgundy to soothe my throat and nerves. The taste reminded me of my evening conversations with Guillaume.

"If the appeal won't be heard, could I beg one last favour from you, Wolf?" I asked. He nodded, prompting me to tell him.

"Could I have a confessor visit me?"

He smiled and guessed. "Guillaume Villon? Of course, but let's hope it won't come to that."

After Wolf locked the door, he paused with his back to me then turned around with all the earnestness he could muster. "Good luck, Villon."

Then he briskly set off into the dark corridor where the only source of light was a simple torch. The good news he had left me with lit up that familiar spark within me. I would not give up, not until I drew my last breath.

✦

Just as Wolf promised, one of the guards brought me a simple meal and all the writing equipment I could need. It cheered me up, and I couldn't help but marvel at it. "You make me feel like a king!"

The guard just grimaced at me and replied, "Save the jokes for the judges."

I grinned and sat down on my cot, preparing to write. "I suppose the provost changed his mind about my poetry."

"Don't flatter yourself," scoffed the guard. "And it better be ready in the morning. Every day you are here costs the prison more money."

"I understand," I said with a nod. "I'll try not to use this inn for too long."

"Better shut up or the inn won't provide any breakfast."

After he left, I realised that the guard had answered the question I had been contemplating while composing *The Testament*: would I have been better off in this world had I simply learned to shut up? It was my uncensored use of words that had brought about most of my trouble, whether it was the silly poem for Widow Bruyer, which caused the problem between her and Regnier and resulted in the bloody street battle, or my verbal mockery of Philippe Sermoise that brought about his death.

However, it had also managed to save me many times. Our student crimes had been pardoned by the previous provost Robert d'Estouteville who liked my ballads, and the mercy I received from King Charles VII was down to the poem I recited for him back at the Sorbonne. Even in Orleans, I had managed to save my butt thanks to some random verses I put together on my way to the Duke's palace.

The only time my wits didn't pay off was at Meung. Not in vain do they say that the devil has no sense of humour. Canon Aussigny surely stayed true to those words. Thinking of him increased my fervour. I could imagine the grin of satisfaction on his face when he learned that I had been executed. I could not give him the pleasure. I had to survive, like I always had before, despite everything that stood in my way. After all, I still had something to live for: Guillaume and Mother still cared for me, and Katherine's affection had ignited me with the hope of a new beginning.

Words were my greatest gift as well as my biggest curse, so I had to use them wisely. I thought about where to start and how; what would be the best way to address the judges of the Parisian parliament. I thought about Guillaume, asking myself what advice he would give me had he been there, and the answer came soon enough: *It's easy, my boy,* he would say, *just be yourself,* and so I tried:

All of my senses: my nose, ears, eyes
And mouth so sensitive to touch

Including the most sinful parts
Each in their right place cry out:
"Oh Court, thanks to you we are safe
As you judge us so rightfully
And since my tongue by itself
Can no longer speak as adequately
I let the rest of me implore our Lord's daughter:
Mother of goodness, our angelic sister.

Break my heart if you must or pierce it
But I beg you to not be much harder
Than the grey stone pots so sharp and arid
From which the Jewish people drank water
With a sigh of my heart's hushing fire
I let my tears fall in my prison corner
Praise the court! Praise the holy empire!
Joy of the French as well as the foreigners
Created in the kingdom of the sky's glister
Mother of goodness, our angelic sister.

✦

Until the last moment, I kept on perfecting the poetic appeal, though I still had my doubts whether it would be enough to win the case. I supposed it was the best I could do under the circumstances. The following night and day, I found it hard to rest, partly because of the frequent and aggressive coughing fits triggered by the cold prison environment, but mainly due to that all-consuming fear.

I lay on the hard cot, contemplating my future and where it would take me from then on. Would I be given another chance or have I wasted too many of them already? Would I have to face death by hanging? I called to Regnier and Colin in my mind, asking them how it felt, if it was over quickly. The silence that followed chilled me to the bone. Everything felt empty and dead, as if I were already lying in a grave.

Even though I may not have acted like one at times and still had my doubts, I had always considered myself a believer. However, after the pain and struggle that I had seen and experienced, I had conducted an inner quarrel with God. There were some things that I considered incomprehensibly unfair: the aftermath of war, the deadly sickness and famine I had witnessed during my childhood, the many people tortured and executed at the Gibbet of Montfaucon or Place de Grève and the way I was treated in Meung. That place still had its claws in me. It not only darkened my soul, but also wracked my health. After the few days in prison, my chest ached with each breath I took, and I could tell it was not going to get better, especially not in the cold prison conditions.

In such difficult moments, I often thought back to the conversation I once had with Guillaume. It was shortly after the street battle with the sergeants. I had felt the waterfall of injustice pour down on me, and blamed God for the bloodbath my classmates died in. We were sitting by the fireplace in his chamber, drinking burgundy for comfort, pondering God's love and cruelty. Guillaume listened to my woes in patience, and then spoke his mind.

"I understand your feelings, François, but try to look at it this way. Would you rather give up your free will and have God play us like puppets? Have us take on roles that he has decided for us? Let us perform a heavenly, beatific play where only love and peace is permitted? Or would you rather have the freedom to decide how your story goes?"

Like usual, Guillaume made more sense than any other priest. It was because he preferred philosophy to dogma. He conveyed his soul's wisdom through every word he uttered whether it was at church, in the confessional or in the privacy of his home.

"To me, free will is the greatest gift," he elaborated. "I prefer a parent who lets me experience life as I like it instead of a tyrant who keeps me in his trap. That's not true love, is it? Of course, it hurts to see your children make mistakes, sometimes repeatedly, but if you let them, they are more likely to love and appreciate you."

I didn't reply to him straight away, as I could sense he was not finished speaking.

"What if we separate from God to go after an adventurous riddle, and once we put all the pieces together, we return home. That's why, whenever I start to blame God for something, I firstly look within myself, for although he lets us make mistakes, he knows that we will return home one day. Everyone turns back to light when the road through darkness has been too long..."

"And what about those who have never made a mistake and still suffer?"

"I often ask myself that too, François. I suppose we just don't have all the pieces of the riddle yet. However, I believe that someday, when we see the greater picture, everything will make sense to us. Life is like a mosaic: it may not make sense up close, but from a distance it creates a beautiful picture."

"I like your perspective, Guillaume," I told him, "but what should I take from it? Should I simply repent my sins, try to be a better man?"

"I suppose it's more complicated than that. I believe that we are part of a chain of events. Your free will ties in with the free will of others and these wills often interweave. It's the forest and tree philosophy."

"Forest and tree?"

"Yes. It's like with the mosaic. You may decide to focus on individual trees, mushrooms, moss, plants, but that doesn't change the fact that together, they create a forest."

That evening in my prison cell, I once again thought about Guillaume's mosaic and forest metaphor. Whether it referred to my situation or not, I reckoned that the God who created me had humour for his art. Perhaps he still enjoyed the tragicomedy I performed for him or he was already fed up with its repetitiveness. Either way, I supposed I would find out quite soon.

The thought again brought me to the idea of my death. I suddenly recalled the dream I had had before I was taken to the Châtelet, in which Sermoise led me to the peculiar carnival of the dead. Its mood enveloped me in its colourfully morbid atmosphere. It felt as if the deceased were calling me, summoning me to the wild celebration in the afterlife. I imagined myself as one of the dancing hanged man, swaying right between Colin and Regnier. My throat tightened at the idea.

In order to keep myself sane, I focused on my poetry. That was what had saved me in the past and what saved me then. Even in the darkest times, I used to construct and memorise verses, and that night in the cell was no different. I still had the parchments, quill and ink, and so I began writing a poem in honour of my friends. I called it *The Ballad of the Hanged Men:*

Human brothers who live after us
Don't let your hearts harden against us
Please try to take a pity on our shame
And God shall reward you with grace

Look as we hang here, five, six bodies
The flesh that we so overly nurtured
Now rotting away, a feast for vultures
Our bones shall turn into dust and ashes
But please let no one make fun of our fall
Rather pray that God absolves us all!

Brothers, we beseech you, have some mercy
Although punished by common justice
We were still murdered, so don't show us disdain
You know well that not all men are born sane
Forgive us as we shiver and ache
Before the holy son of Mother Mary
May he demonstrate his divine glory
And keep us away from the infernal gate
We are dead but don't yet hear hell call
So please pray that God absolves us all!

Rain stained and washed us
Sun dried and darkened us
Our eyes were plucked out by magpies and crows
They tore off our beards, eyelashes, and eyebrows
We never rest and never seem to be heard:
Swinging back and forth as the wind pleases
Tossed around whether it's warm or it freezes
Birds surround us in their merciless herd
So avoid our brotherhood and its evil thrall
And instead pray that God absolve us all!
Prince Jesus, show us your immense power
Don't lead us astray upon our final hour
We are pitifully tattered
This is no laughing matter
Please pray that God absolves us all!

Extract from *The Testament* (1461-1462, François Villon)

CHAPTER 22

THE PROMISE

After another sleepless night, I found myself pacing the prison cell like an animal anxious to return to the wild. I could not rest, could not think, I just needed to know the verdict. When the guards finally came, a wave of apprehension crashed over me. Despite my high hopes, I still expected the worst. The choking anxiety made me feel sick and I almost returned my evening meal to them before one of them exclaimed, "Someone must be looking out for you up there, Villon!"

My heart began racing at the thought, but I knew there was still a chance they were toying with me to satisfy their natural thirst for cruelty. I quickly grabbed the letter from the guard's hand, tore the seal open and began to read:

Regarding the matter of the trial led by the Parisian provost or its deputy against Monsieur François Montcorbier, alias Villon, during which the condemned was sentenced to death by hanging: The court had concluded that the verdict shall be denied. The accused, François Villon, is therefore absolved from the death penalty and all criminal charges. However, due to the accused's repeated misconducts, he is to be banished from the city and the vicinity of Paris for ten years.

It seemed impossible, but it was true – I was free! Once again, someone or something mighty was on my side. No matter whose mercy it was, I thanked God for giving me yet another chance as I pressed the letter to my heart. The guard didn't share my enthusiasm. He was probably looking forward to seeing me hang.

"Now hurry up," he ordered grumpily. "We have no time to spare. There's high demand for this private cell. If Wolf had not intervened, you would be in the larger cell with the other prisoners."

Only when his strong hands seized me did I realise that I was not absolved completely. I had to leave Paris and head into exile, this time for real.

"When do I have to leave the city?" I asked.

The guard let out a malicious chortle. "Right away, of course."

"But I don't have any proper clothing with me and no money… Can I first stop by my home at Porte Rouge?"

"No detours," hissed the guard. "You can beg on the way out of Paris, perhaps someone will throw you a few sous or some warmer clothing."

I could not believe how quickly my relief could turn into a state of panic. How could I leave without saying goodbye to my mother and Guillaume, and without kidnapping Katherine like I had promised? I couldn't disappear without any explanation and disappoint her all over again. No, I had to keep on fighting otherwise I would never forgive myself.

"I have to write another appeal!"

The guard stared at me in disbelief. "Are you serious? Is this some kind of a joke?"

I grinned and hurried over to the pile of parchments. "I know I have the right to appeal again so I will."

I looked up at the guard, wondering whether he would let me do it in peace. He was totally perplexed as well as intrigued. I supposed that like me he was curious as to whether the court would actually hear me out or change the verdict back to the worst option just to stop my complaining. Perhaps that was why he let me write the second appeal. He would rather see my rude tongue twirl in agony than smack in joy.

Therefore, I was able to write the sequel to the previous poem, completing my final appeal to the court:

...And you, my feeble teeth, don't fall out just yet
Stay strong and let me cry glory
As loud as the heavenly choir, organ, and trumpet
Don't worry about chattering
It could have been worse than this
Liver, lungs, spleen, you are still alive and fitting
To accompany my vile, sinful body
Filthy as that of a beast who sleeps in his droppings
And applaud the court for its mercy
Mother of goodness, our angelic sister.

Prince, would you grand me three days
To ready myself for the journey?
I need to raise some money before I stray
Triumphant court, please hear my plea:
Mother of goodness, our angelic sister.

When I read it aloud, the guard laughed at me.
"You're a fool, Villon!"

He continued laughing on his way out too, but to my utter relief, his laughter ended when the second appeal was heard as well. I was granted three final days in Paris before my departure, and I was going to make most of it.

✦

The next day, I returned home into the arms of my mother and Guillaume. We all wept tears of joy, celebrating the moment of our reunion. The situation was not perfect, but at least we had those three full days left together, during which we could strengthen the divine ties that would never let us part completely.

"I really thought this would be my end," I admitted to them both as we sat by the blazing fire.

"The Lord spared you again," beamed my mother. "How could it not be so if I was praying for you day and night?"

I hated the idea of her constant worry for me.

"Oh Mother, all I ever gave you was hard skin on your knees…"

She just threw her hands in the air, though.

"That's the fate of every mother, François, we gladly pray for our children."

I planted a kiss on her gentle hands then turned to Guillaume who was unusually quiet and distant.

"What's troubling you, Guillaume? Is it my banishment? Don't worry about it, maybe I was wrong when I said I would not last longer than a year. After surviving death so many times, I'm starting to feel invincible. Ten years will fly by fast and in no time, I'll be back here drinking your wine and eating your food."

I wrapped my arm around his shoulder, trying to cheer us up a bit, but it seemed to only make him gloomier.

"I'm concerned about your cough, François. I don't like the idea of you wandering through the countryside in such inhospitable weather…"

"I have survived worse," I said, not willing to let him see that I was also concerned about that. "It's my body. I am in control of it and I won't let it fade away just yet."

Fortune must have delivered one of her slaps to punish my arrogance, as I was suddenly overcome by the sharpest and most painful coughing yet. I smiled in pain, inwardly laughing at the irony, but mainly trying to calm the two worried faces before me.

"It's just a cough, nothing else," I kept assuring them, yet that gave them little solace.

"We can't take this lightly, François. We all know that it's worsening so we need to make a plan. I was thinking of arranging a carriage for you. It could pick you up at the crossroads beyond the nearest city gate, the one behind the old oak tree."

"But where would I go?" I asked, dispirited at the idea of heading into the unknown alone. I wondered if I could persuade Katherine to come along, despite my empty pockets. Maybe she would do it for me, for the idea of the two of us finally having the chance to be together.

"We could have you transported to Angers. Your uncle would surely take care of you," explained Mother.

I couldn't help but laugh at that option. "Uncle would not welcome me in his house again, trust me. I was too much of a burden last time and he didn't shy away from letting me know. Anyway, I don't want to fool myself or anyone else anymore. Who knows if I am even capable of being a better man. You must have noticed the pattern. Whenever I do wrong or try to mend my ways, something always prevents me from living a normal life."

"You will live a normal life from now on," insisted Mother, "and your uncle will help you out again. If not for you or me, he will do it for your father's memory. I will write him a letter tonight and have it delivered first thing in the morning."

"Thank you both," I nodded to Guillaume and my mother earnestly, "but let's plan it all later. I triumphed over death today so wish for nothing else than to imbibe the peace of this house and fill my belly with some wine!"

I went on to pour us all some burgundy. Guillaume forced a smile and my mother too, but I was the only one to raise my goblet in the air and down it.

✦

After Guillaume and Mother went to bed, I retreated to my attic room to resume my work on *The Testament*. After a few busy hours, my inspiration ran dry along with my goblet, and I fell asleep over my favourite, *Romance of the Rose*. However, the strong moonlight permeating through from my window eventually woke me up. It was a full moon that night, like in the strange dream I had before my imprisonment. I reimagined Regnier's hound howling to the heavens and suddenly wondered if it was actually a cry of welcome, whether he was summoning me to join the Dance of the Dead. I sincerely hoped not as I didn't want to join that party just yet.

To escape the thought, I looked out of the window, admiring the various shades of blue and amber in the sea of roofs. I tried to find the one that belonged to Jolis, as it would make me feel closer to Katherine. I yearned to pay her a night visit like I used to. Not that I would expect to fool around, my loins had been useless since I returned from Meung, though I still hoped for a turn of fate in that department. I wanted to go to her because back at the Châtelet, I promised myself that if I were to be released, I would hold her in my arms and let her know how much she meant to me.

I decided to follow my heart. I didn't have much time to spare, and I no longer cared about Jolis, her family or what people thought – it would be pitiful to waste my last days in Paris in some cowardly hesitation. She had to know that despite the years of understandable doubts, I had become certain that she was the only woman that I had ever longed for. Therefore, I gathered my courage, threw on some decent clothes and headed for the stairs. On my way, I eavesdropped on Guillaume's chamber. Hearing him snore calmed me down because it meant I wouldn't have to argue with him about leaving so late at night.

I snuck out of the house and hurried into the night, heading for the Right Bank, the wealthier district, which was lit by torches. The church bells chimed eleven as I paced the cobblestones, and the tolling of the bells kept time with my heartbeat. I felt like a young boy again, anxious to see the girl who filled me with sweet anticipation.

Just like in the olden days, I picked up a stone and threw it at one of the windows. Of course, I had no idea where her bedchamber was and risked waking Jolis or their servants, but I was ready for anything. I believed we would overcome whatever stood in our way. I threw about five stones at the window and when I noticed movement behind the mullioned glass, I hid under the arches of the opposite building.

I peeked from behind the pillar, and saw Katherine's face looking out, searching the street. Her raven black hair blended in with the sky but her white nightgown shone in the darkness. She resembled an angel hovering above, benevolently inclining towards the sinner below. I stepped out of the shadows and waved at her. She froze upon seeing me and then, after a moment of hesitation, she closed the window and disappeared.

All that was left for me to do was wait. Wait to see whether she was willing to give me another chance or give up on me for good. She must have heard about what had happened and that I almost ended up on the gallows again. I bet Jolis would have enjoyed watching my final public humiliation and would sneer at me one last time before I took that fatal swing through the air. I clenched my fists at the thought of him, not only because of my jealousy, but also because of how spitefully he used to behave towards me. I had always imagined that he was not as decent as he pretended, and he managed to prove it when he whipped me through the streets of Paris.

To my relief, Katherine soon ran out of the house, wrapped in a long velvet cape. She joined me under the arches and as soon as she was within reach, I grabbed her hand and pulled her closer. There, under the dim light of the street torches, I cupped her lovely face and lost myself in those dear curves, wrinkles, and freckles. She was as beautiful as ever, shining through the night like a bright star that I was meant to follow.

"Thank God you are safe," she exhaled in relief. "I was so scared when I heard…"

She stopped the tears welling up in her eyes and buried her head in my chest. It was hard to believe that she could still be attracted to me. I was just an old, dried up potato rotting away beneath her blossoming beauty. Suddenly, it felt as though the past years had never happened. I returned to that moment before our first kiss when I was still filled with so much confidence and vigour. As I reawakened to the present, I dared to press my lips to hers again, forgetting all about the pain we had caused each other. We surpassed everything with that kiss, and as I felt her warm body lean against mine, I could tell that even my lower regions would awaken in her fire.

Our lips separated and we took a breath of the frosty air; she caressed my cheek and said, "When I heard that you were pardoned again, I knew it was a clear sign from above. I have to be with you, François, I can no longer live in this pretence. No matter what you have done or will do, you are the most exceptional man I have ever known."

I grinned, because in her eyes I was always more than just a misfortunate crook. That's why the encounter with my dark side had broken her heart years ago. Yet, despite it all, she still believed in me.

"I have not been pardoned," I explained quickly. "My death sentence was changed to ten years in exile."

The news silenced her. "How many days do we have left?"

"Three," I said, but then corrected myself. "Well, actually now it's just two."

She sighed and softly brushed her lips against my scar.

"What should we do?"

"What we've always wanted? Although I haven't managed to save any money for our trip, I believe I will manage. Your love will make me stronger."

She looked at Jolis' house, struggling with herself. I knew she wanted to say yes, however, her old life still held her back.

"This is our chance, Katherine, our paths are finally coming together."

She frowned, obviously burdened with something. I felt her shiver, so I rubbed her arms for warmth, but found out she was actually shaking with unease.

"You won't want me when you learn the truth," she said.

"What truth?"

Katherine moved her hands to her belly and gazed down, ashamed. Her expression spoke for itself, as did the rounded stomach bulging beneath her nightgown.

"It's not Noël's. It can't be. I haven't allowed him to touch me for more than a year. I have managed to hide it thus far, but it's more difficult now that... Well, you can see for yourself."

I had sensed she was with child the last time we spoke, yet the confirmation shook me a little. It didn't change anything, though. I wanted her nevertheless.

"Another reason to run away with me," I said. "I don't care whose child you are carrying or how many men you have bedded as long as you bed me." I paused and added, "At least once."

She laughed in tears. "Do you mean it?"

"With all my heart," I insisted, stroking her back for comfort. "I have never been as certain that we are meant to be. Paris is already the past to me, you are the future."

We smiled at each other. I could feel that we were both ready to pick up the broken pieces of our love and restore them to their original beauty.

"All right then," she finally said, her voice trembling with the thrill of the brave decision she was about to make. "When do I meet you and where?"

"At dawn, two days from now, by our tree."

"Our tree?" she repeated, touched by the idea. "You mean the oak where we met for the second time?"

I nodded and sealed the deal with a long kiss that left us both hungry for more. It was hard for us to separate, but we had to. I did not feel heavyhearted when I walked away from her that night, though, because I was leaving with a vision of our reunion.

On my way back home, I began to plan our journey. Guillaume was right. We should arrange a carriage and go to my uncle's. I was certain that no matter how awkwardly we parted years ago he would provide us with some hospitality before I found myself proper employment and a private abode. I was hoping that he would be understanding, particularly if we had a child on the way. Nobody had to know that it was not mine. We could both change our names and pretend to be married.

I counted my savings and knew that we could survive if we lived humbly at the beginning. Everything was clear and perfect in my mind, and my heart had never felt as calm before, despite the coughing fits that kept me up for the rest of the night. I could still feel Katherine's closeness, and that overpowered any physical discomfort and pain. I once believed that I would perish upon finishing *The Testament*, but after the promise Katherine and I had made to each other, I began to think that perhaps it was the old me that had to die in order to let the new me be born.

CHAPTER 23

MY LAST WALK THROUGH PARIS

After Katherine and I decided to run away together, I no longer felt anxious about leaving my beloved Paris. I envisioned the tree where we were to meet, compelled by its magical allure. That majestic oak had witnessed many stories during its lifetime, including those of the children who liked to climb its generous branches.

Katherine and I met there shortly after our first encounter during which I had managed to steal her favourite toy. I had been biding my time at its foot, waiting for Regnier, but instead saw her coming towards me. I recognised her instantly: that unruly, raven black hair and those bright green eyes, her physique almost too fragile for the tough world we were born into. She was like a spirit from a different world, like a nymph from the ancient Greek tales that Guillaume and I liked to read. I couldn't understand why I felt so drawn to her because at that age I had no thoughts of girls, yet I was curious to find out more. I could feel the child within me rise up as I relived the moment in my mind. Soon we would be standing there again, without all the awkwardness and insecurities of our younger selves, finally ready to explore our unique attraction.

To close the old chapter of my life, I headed to Margot's, ready to say goodbye to the place and thank Wolf for the kindness he had shown me at the Châtelet. As I crossed the street to the shady district where I had once found a haven, I sighed over the memory of Colin, Regnier, Tabary, and Margot. How I wished to meet them all and celebrate my departure with them like I once would have.

As soon as I entered, Isabeau ran over to me, not minding the busy tavern.

"Wolf told us the good news this morning!" she exclaimed and greeted me with a short but tight embrace. Then she looked me over and shook her head. "I still don't understand how you manage to go on despite everything that you have been through, Villon…"

I replied fittingly – with a cough.

"As you can see, hardly," I rasped when it was finished.

She patted my cheek and moved across the room to grab me some ale. I could tell that she had no reason to be afraid anymore. She had already become the new, powerful mistress of the establishment, Margot's proud successor.

"I came to say goodbye," I announced, as I sat at my favourite table. Isabeau waved at the girls to serve the incoming customers and hurried to join me.

"Again?" she asked, confused.

"This time I have no choice. They gave me ten years in exile instead of the gallows."

"Well, at least you have experience with that already, huh?" She was trying to cheer me up, not knowing that I didn't really need it. I couldn't contain the joy that filled my heart, so I smiled to myself.

"You have some wicked plan, don't you?"

I grinned even more, which made her laugh. "Oh, Villon! You never change!"

She moved her chair closer to mine, her eyes sparkling with excitement. "Tell me about it. Light up my boring life."

"I'll tell you only if you swear to secrecy," I said in all seriousness.

"But of course," she promised, almost offended. "As if I have ever revealed any of your secrets! You boys have already tested my loyalty many times."

She was right. Whether it was out of sympathy or the soft spot she had for Regnier, Isabeau had always helped us, ever since our student years. Therefore, I leaned closed to her and whispered, "I will not be going alone."

"Really? Who will join you?"

"Try to guess."

"Father Guillaume?"

I shook my head. "I wouldn't leave my mother alone here…"

She tried to guess again. "Is it one of the young Coquillards then?"

When I shook my head the second time, she threw her hands in the air and said, "Then it must be a woman."

I nodded and she covered her mouth in surprise. "Is it one of our girls?"

"No, it's someone from my past."

"Katherine Jolis?" she whispered in disbelief. My impish look answered her question.

She pulled away, staggered. "I didn't know that you still cared for her."

"Do you deem it foolish? It might be, I just can't let her go, Isabeau. I thought I could once, however, as the years have gone by, I realise I would never feel the same way about anybody else… It's the right thing to do. She's not happy with Jolis, she never was, and she wants it just as much as I do.

"The cold, cruel queen that sent me packing last time is gone, the good old Katherine I once knew melted her heart in the end. Back then we were not ready for it, but this time it's more than just puppy love, we have both matured, and I have planned everything well. Once we finally escape the restrictions of society, we will be truly free."

"François," her usually calm voice was tinged with urgency. I stopped talking and watched her trembling lips as they struggled with the words that were about to come out. "There was a commotion by Jolis' house this morning..."

"What do you mean?"

"I don't know what had happened, but when I went to the market earlier, I saw people gathering there, speaking about Katherine's screams reverberating through the streets. Someone saw a midwife rushing in... I didn't know she was with child..."

Anxiety spilled over me. I had to go to her straight away. Isabeau called after me, but I no longer listened. I had to see Katherine, make sure she was all right. I met with Guillaume on the way, and from the look on his face, I could tell that something awful had happened. He vainly tried to take me home. I didn't listen to him either. His comforting phrases were like buzzing flies that I kept chasing away. I was focused on only one goal: my love, needing me by her side.

Large groups of people surrounded Jolis' house. Among the faces, I saw Katherine's father, Denise, some other servants and Jolis himself. Then I saw two men carrying out a female body wrapped in a white sheet. In my distress, the idea that it could be Katherine herself didn't even cross my mind. It was only when I heard someone say, "Poor Monsieur Jolis... poor Monsieur de Vaucelles... neither her nor the baby made it alive."

The words stung like arrows. I could not absorb the information. My crazed mind tried to come up with another explanation. I wondered whether it was all just a stage show that Katherine had constructed to be able to escape home unnoticed. Oh, but when I came closer and saw her father uncover the sheet to reveal her stiff, pale face staring up at the skies, I felt my heart stop. It didn't want to beat without hers.

I could not bear seeing her that way, not her. My knees became weak under the sudden weight of anguish, and I collapsed to the cold, damp ground. I was unable to budge, hoping to be awoken from the impossible nightmare. I silently cried out her name, but the only response was silence. It gripped me in its merciless claws. I knew it then – it was over. Everything was coming to an end.

My gaze shifted to Jolis. He stood there by the front door, searching the faces around him as if seeking a way out of the misery. I wanted to confront him and demand to know what had really happened when all of a sudden his eyes fixed me to the spot. The strength of his passion matched mine. It was the first and last time we had some kind of connection. I knew that we would both do anything to take her place. There was no need for words, nothing left to say. The cool air swished around me. I realised then I had been holding my breath, and when I finally inhaled, my chest tightened in the sharpest pain. I bent double in agony and coughed up blood.

✦

Had Guillaume not been there, I would have probably headed straight to Margot's to drown the intense sorrow in wine, or made for the river Seine to drown myself. I wanted nothing else than to forget about the horrendous tragedy that had snatched my love away. Guillaume would not let me go anywhere, though. He dragged me home, trying his best to comfort me, not realising that there was no solace, no way out. I was trapped. I didn't know what to do with myself. Her death seemed so unreal, impossible to be true.

My mother was at church, so she didn't have to bear witness to all the cursing, crying and the blood I was coughing out. After a fourth goblet of wine, I told Guillaume the truth. Katherine and I still cared about each other, and she was willing to leave everything behind and go into exile with me. I even admitted that I knew about the pregnancy and I couldn't care less. Katherine wanted me, the whole me with all my sins and shame, nothing else mattered.

"Her love filled my life with a new purpose," I said, gulping more wine, but it still wasn't enough to stop my mind from driving me mad.

"When I realised that what we had was real, I wanted nothing more than to start living it. I believed that I could overcome all that had happened, even this dreadful illness. I ignored all the ominous premonitions and focused only on the light, yet I have been dragged back into familiar darkness. It seems that light is simply not meant for me…"

"That's utter nonsense," disagreed Guillaume. "You deserve all the light in this world."

I shook my head. "I hate this world."

"You don't mean that, François. I know you don't."

"I do. I hate it and it hates me back. It has killed all my friends, the love of my life, and it's slowly killing me as well… I don't belong here and I don't even want to be here anymore."

"So where do you belong?"

I shrugged. "I hope somewhere. Right now, I can't picture myself anywhere other than in her arms."

I looked into his eyes. I could tell that he empathised with me, he always understood me, even when I spoke of things he had no personal experience of.

"Aren't I or your mother a bright enough beacon for you?"

I squeezed his hand. "You two are more than enough, more than I deserve, but can't you see? I won't make it back home, Guillaume, let's not fool one another anymore. Even if I did, my life is nothing but a shadow of what it used to be. I'm a stranger in my own land…"

Guillaume let out a deep sigh. "Oh, but we all are, François, we all feel that way sometimes. That's why I pray that we return to our true home someday, and that it will be the place where we will never experience loss and pain again."

The sixth goblet of wine finally numbed me a bit, so after Guillaume left my chamber, I lay down on my bed and succumbed to emotional paralysis. I hoped to fall asleep and never wake up again, however, as so often happened, my mind would not let me drift off… The words of deep anger and grief emerged from the depths of my soul and cried out to be heard. The set of parchments on my desk beckoned to me. I knew then that *The Testament* was not complete. There was one page missing, one that should not be the last, but rather immortalise the final blow to my fortunes:

> *Death, I appeal your rigour*
> *Why snatch my love away*
> *And drag me even lower*
> *Cruelly waiting for me to fade*
> *Rob me of all joy, all vigour*
> *Why show her so much hate?*
> *Death!*
>
> *We were two, but one heart we shared*
> *Since hers stopped, mine should follow soon*
> *Or walk a lifeless journey, hope for the end*
> *Like a phantom trapped in an endless gloom?*
> *Death!*

✦

The next day I woke up with a fever. My chest and throat hurt so badly that I could hardly speak, which did not matter, as I had nothing to talk about anymore. I buried myself under the blankets, blankly listening to the distant discussions between Guillaume and Mother. They worried for my health and my spirit, not realising that it was useless. A part of me was already gone; I was just waiting for the other half to catch up.

To escape the physical discomfort, I tried to recall Katherine. I could still picture every detail of her face, the way she moved, felt, smelled... and was more obsessed with her than ever before. I spent my last day in Paris with her ghost.

I had no desire to go on living, and suspected that my health wouldn't let me anyway. I tried to remain strong while I remained at home, for the sake of Mother and Guillaume, but even when I dined with them and listened to their encouragements, my energy faded with each breath I took.

On the morning of my departure, I let Mother dress me like a child, drank her stinky onion stew to make her happy, and allowed her to comfort me all she liked. I played the role gladly, enjoying the warmth of the woman whose blessed heart loved me no matter what. She deserved a better son, yet I knew she would never replace me for any other.

When someone finally pulled on the bell outside and announced the beginning of my journey into the unknown, Guillaume pressed a leather pouch with a hundred sous into my overcoat pocket and said, "Keep it safe, there might be thieves on the way."

I nodded and wheezed a barely audible thank you.

Mother gave me a scarf bag with some pastries and a wineskin of burgundy. They hugged me tightly and reminded me to wait for the carriage at the crossroads, which was further down the road from the majestic oak – the place where I was to meet Katherine.

I nodded, though I felt that the driver would probably just end up loading my corpse, steal all I had on me, and drop me off in some faraway forest. I had no hope of surviving my last walk through Paris. I was a wretch tormented by a trinity of physical, mental, and emotional affliction. However, I could not tell these two precious souls that because they still desperately clung to the hope of my return although deep inside we all knew that it was the last time we would see each other alive. We sensed that we would only reunite in our original home, as Guillaume called it.

Before I opened the door to leave my beloved Porte Rouge, I suppressed the pain and whispered to them, "Thank you both for everything. I love you."

Then I stepped out to face the two sergeants, my guides for the day. One of them was unfamiliar to me, but the other one was Wolf. I suspected he would be there, so it didn't surprise me that much. We nodded to each other and set off into the fresh snow. I turned to take one last look at the house, Mother and Guillaume standing in the deep red doorway. My view was interrupted by snowflakes, the heavenly heralds that covered the space between us with their frosty veil. The whiteness suited my mood: the colour of endings and beginnings, whatever they were or would be, the moment uniting them in its simple stillness.

Wolf noticed that I could hardly walk so he supported me, but I gestured to him to let me be. I wanted to take that final walk by myself. I supposed it was odd for him to see such a big talker like me unable to speak. I could tell that he understood, though, and gave me the space to leave my hometown peacefully, at a calm and steady pace. In the chill of the wintry morning, I didn't feel the fever as much, only the ache in my chest. I tried to enjoy my last moments in Paris, the belle of my country.

In my mind, I said goodbye to familiar places: the cloister of Saint Benoit where I found my home, the bench by the Saint Benoit Church where I fought Philippe Sermoise, the streets where I used to play with Regnier as a little boy. We also passed the bridge where the battle between my fellow students and sergeants took place, the towers of Notre Dame, the river banks of the Seine, and finally, the distant roof of Katherine's house. *I'm coming to you, my love,* I promised her in my mind, as with or without her, I was still heading for that oak beyond the city.

Death laughed me in the face as we passed the Holy Innocents' Cemetery. The wind howled, swishing through the old cracks in the walls. *I'm coming to you, death*, I whispered, leaving all the bitterness behind. Who would have thought that I would welcome her with open arms? Defeat overwhelmed me and plunged me into another coughing fit. Blood splattered on the snow. Wolf's hands supported me, his voice motivating me to be brave and strong, to face my ordeal with dignity. I wanted to, though it was hard. I was worn out, done in, yet I had to keep on walking, still catching glimpses of the familiar streets, windows, house signs...

And in the whirl of it all, I began to see the figures of those who had left before me. It was as if they had come alive to see Villon walk the streets of Paris one last time. I saw Sermoise standing under the nearby arches. He had an unusually cordial expression in his eyes. Did he pity me or welcome me on the other side? I supposed I would soon find out. I also caught a glimpse of the Crone Armouress, the oldest lady of the night, now young again. In the distance, I saw the students who had died in the bridge battle years ago. Tabary was among them, the fool I cared about so dearly. He had that typical, excited expression on his face. I could tell he was still up for some mischief. Beside him was Colin. He paid no attention to me, too busy trying to charm a group of women, but he was invisible to them, like he had always been.

Then Margot emerged from around the corner. She was as pretty as I remembered her. Her rosy cheeks blossomed against the snow and her golden locks chased away the darkness in my soul. She blew me a kiss and waved at me to go on. She was rushing me out, glad to be finally rid of me. At last, I saw Regnier leaning against a nearby wall, proudly wearing his smart clothes and red boots again. He straightened up upon seeing me then contently patted the loyal hound by his side. We exchanged a smile and then as the thinning worlds merged, he vanished and Isabeau appeared in his place. She came to say goodbye, at least from afar. I nodded to her and she nodded back before Wolf interrupted us. He pointed to the city gate that rose up before me. I knew that from there on, I would have to walk on my own.

Standing on the threshold between my old life and that which was yet unseen, I turned around to say goodbye to the ghosts of my past. *Thank you, friends*, I addressed them inside, *I am ready now*. I nodded to Wolf who beckoned to his colleague at the gate and announced, "We bring Monsieur François Villon! He is banished from the city for the next ten years."

I couldn't help but grin at the reference, as the timeframe of my exile was rather futile given the state I was in. I wondered whether that was why they hadn't wasted the space at Montfaucon for me: they knew I was on the edge of my strength. I looked at Wolf and said, "Take care of Paris for me, won't you?"

He smiled and gave me a friendly pat on the back. With a heavy sigh, I bravely stepped ahead. I was leaving the first love of my life and setting out on the road to meet the last. The road was long and quiet. I heard only the wind's howl as it blew more snow in my face. Yet I kept walking the frozen ground in determination and eventually made out the tall oak through the white haze. I heard the voices of my two familiar advisors.

Continue on this path to reach the crossroad in time, encouraged my mind. *You should go and wait for the carriage to arrive.*

The compelling voice of my heart argued back, *You know very well that you won't survive the trip. Better to wait it out by the oak, the tree of all endings and beginnings.*

I wavered over whether to trust reason or follow my heart. Reason seemed too naïve and my heart was completely foolish, but both clung to Katherine. Of all the ghosts that came to say goodbye, she had not shown up yet. Was she upset with me or was she waiting for me to make the right choice? I felt compelled to fulfil my promise, and stopped by the oak. As I took in its wide, welcoming arms and the strong, still trunk, I felt the desire to rest on top of its roots. The path ahead was long, pointless. My body needed rest and my soul longed to be free. Therefore, I sat down beneath the swaying branches and let its ancient spirit embrace me in its soothing song.

After a moment of sitting there, the fever and pain subsided. I began to feel more like myself again, like the man I used to be before fortune had broken me. I felt as if my body had connected with that old tree, rooting deep into the ground, spreading between Paris and the lands beyond. I absorbed the essence of the place and sent it mine in a harmonious exchange. Its subterranean veins filled me with new vitality, reanimating me in some strangely familiar way. Could death give the kiss of life?

Perhaps I should go to the crossroads without Katherine, I thought to myself again, maybe I was not ready to leave the world just yet. I vainly searched the blizzard of icy stars for answers.

Give me a sign, I pleaded my mind and heart.

Why are you always in such a hurry? I heard my heart say. *Just wait. She will come when you are ready.*

You are incorrigible, my mind reasoned with me. *You know that she has always been unattainable.*

I'm so tired of your protests, my heart sighed then. *At least for once, you could let me rest.*

Rest if you must, my mind replied, *you always break one's trust.*

This won't work, leave me alone, I ordered them both. *I can manage on my own.*

On your own, you say? Since when have you known yourself? They both laughed at me.

I smiled at the question and admitted, *You are right. I still know everything but myself.*

With those words, I saw a silhouette forming in the white blur ahead of me. I gasped when I recognised the graceful figure. She had truly kept her promise. I smiled like a fool in love, not caring whether she was my angel or the Grim Reaper. I wanted nothing more than to follow her.

And thus concludes The Testament
With the end of poor Villon
You are welcome at his interment
But be sure to wear vermilion
When you hear the church bells clang
For he died a martyr of love's torment
And this he swore to his faithful balls
As he made his way out to the heavenly halls.

Trust that this was not all just a whim
He was chased as a scullion
For his ardour and unforgivable sin
From Paris to Roussillon
There's not one shrub that didn't scar him
Not one wheel that wouldn't spin him
In the highest leaps and lowest falls
As he made his way out to the heavenly halls.

It is pure fact and no exaggeration
That he died in nothing but rags
Even worse, though, as he lay in exhaustion
Love pricked him once again
Sharper than the words uttered in vexation
And with that painful yet sweet sensation
He finally set off from the city walls
To make his way out to the heavenly halls.

Extract from *The Testament* (1461-1462, François Villon)